'The astonishingly diverse stories in SJ Naudé's remarkable collection *The Alphabet of Birds* count as among the best in Afrikaans, built on recurring motifs and elements such as music; departure and travel; fairy tales and myths; illness, dissolution, dying and death; cities; a search for provenance and origins; forgetting and remembering; instinct and reason; that which is said or described versus that which remains unsaid or incapable of description forever; and the places and shapes of love in human relationships. For any reader who would like to keep up with what is happening at the forefront of Afrikaans literature, this collection is truly unmissable.'

André Brink

'Naudé's beautifully shaped and often heartbreaking stories take the idea of home and tear it apart, fling it upside down, and refashion it into a thing more mobile and less anchored. This is a world in which home increasingly exists as idea rather than place, where people trying to find their way back to a sense of belonging discover, almost too late, how transient their lives have become. At once unsettling and deeply moving, this collection announces the arrival of a writer of great humanity and style.'

Patrick Flanery

THE ALPHABET
OF BIRDS

SJ Naudé

Translated by the author

LONDON · NEW YORK

First published in English translation in 2015 by
And Other Stories
London – New York

www.andotherstories.org

Copyright © SJ Naudé, 2011
English-language translation copyright © SJ Naudé, 2015

First published as *Alfabet van die voëls* in 2011 by Umuzi, an imprint of
Random House Struik, Cape Town, South Africa

The poem 'Hemelkewertjie' on page 226 is by Esta Steyn and is reprinted
from DJ Opperman's *Kleuterverseboek* with the permission of Tafelberg
Publishers.

'War, Blossoms' was first published in *A Public Space*.

An excerpt of 'Van' was first published in *Granta*.

ISBN 9781908276445
Ebook ISBN 9781908276452

A catalogue record for this book is available from the British Library.

CONTENTS

For SM Naudé
(1939–2010)

INTRODUCTION

When I was growing up in white South Africa, 'The Border' was a phrase that everybody knew, denoting both a physical and a mythical place. Physically it meant the northernmost edge of South-West Africa (as Namibia was then known), which South Africa was desperately trying to hold on to. In a more interior, psychological sense, it was the space that separated us from the rest of the world. Out there was the Communist enemy, but also every other way of thinking that was different and threatening. 'We' were not them; 'they' were not us. Inside the border, history hung heavily.

Now that the border, psychologically at least, is no longer with us, white South Africans have had to learn that 'they' are not so very different after all. Nor is the outside world so very remote. These lessons are on full display in the writing of SJ Naudé, whose stories inhabit what he refers to as the 'borderless world'. His characters – 'lapsed South Africans' – move as easily between London and Dubai as they do between Johannesburg and Bloemfontein. Mostly unanchored, drifting, they rub up against other drifters from far-flung places. In the same loose way, characters and images recur in different narratives; sexual identities are fluid; relationships form and dissolve like smoke; drugs are frequently imbibed.

All of this gives a cosmopolitan gloss to some of these stories. But, more powerfully, it also gives them a surreal edge, which is enhanced by the visions that come to their protagonists. One of them, for example, 'dreams he is doing ballet with a Japanese man at the Voortrekker Monument.' Or as another puts it: 'isn't it strange where ex-South Africans pop up these days and which subjects and worlds they join together?' Yes, it is very strange.

Typically, at the heart of these stories, a man or a woman has left South Africa but, after years of absence, is drawn back by something personal. It could be a sick parent; it could be a search for some abstract truth that's buried in the past. As one of them says, 'Perhaps I'm grasping towards a core . . . an origin.' If history is present at all, it's in a form that is almost metaphysical. One character reminds herself 'that she was unable to endure anything other than skimming over the surface of this country; that this was the reason for her original departure.' South Africa is not an historical place (the word 'apartheid' crops up only once) so much as a condition to be escaped from – or come back to.

But then again, 'return isn't possible'. The past has a strong gravity, but it's also paradoxically out of reach. There is a painful longing running through this book, made more poignant by having no object. Something is wanted, but what it is exactly, and what solutions it will provide, is unclear. Instead, the yearning for what is lost is more likely to lead only to further loss. In a disturbing sequence, a woman lives in the empty room of an abandoned garden flat, listening to other rooms being plundered around her nightly. Entropy is felt as a purification, as if cumbersome layers are being stripped away. But towards what?

Only one story is set entirely inside South Africa, with no connection to the outside world, and it's perhaps no accident that it's also the narrative in which all sorts of social issues crowd in. HIV/AIDS, the new racial hierarchy, the problems of poverty and government corruption: Naudé shows that he's alert and alive to the new South Africa's ills. But even here they take on an existential cast, like forces besetting the main character, a woman dying of cancer, in a kind of spiritual onslaught.

In this peeling away towards some essential core, language is one more veil to be shed. It's ironic that a writer like Naudé, who uses words with elegant exactness, should find them so obstructive, but he does. 'You've talked enough,' one character is told. 'Talking is over.' What will replace speech, in this instance, is violence, but in other stories the implications are gentler: 'You should learn to do without words,' a character says. 'There are better things.' He means dance, which is another sort of language. Or maybe music will lead to the truth. And if that doesn't work, even harmony can be broken down: a noise machine, which speaks with hisses and roars and bangs – maybe that will do the trick.

But how can there be an answer, if we don't even know the question? Like their central characters, the stories seem to begin and end in mid-air. Who will finish writing them for us? The birds, Naudé tells us. A bird trapped in a house eventually flies out, leaving shit 'on the interior walls, like crooked letters. Like Eastern calligraphy. Maybe that is an ending.'

Maybe it is. But in order to understand, you would have to speak in impossible symbols. It is this missing resolution, cryptic letters written in bird-shit, that embodies the mystery at the heart of these narratives. Cool and intelligent, unsettling and deeply felt, Naudé's voice is something new in South African writing.

Damon Galgut

THE ALPHABET
OF BIRDS

THE NOISE MACHINE

The two men arrive simultaneously from opposite directions. Their taxis disappear down the street. They stand in silence in front of a steel door set in a long wall.

The drive from his hotel on the other side of the city to these streets, with their warehouses and grey industrial yards, has left Chris dizzy. He gauges the other man's accent when he speaks into the intercom. The vowels between his American 'r's are flat enough to be South African (Afrikaans?). The American South African (or South African American) is impatient, his shoulders pushing against the steel before the bolt retracts electronically. Behind the door is a concrete yard and a row of trucks. In the fading light, the man walks purposefully to a second steel door. Another intercom: the shoulder wedged in again, legs like levers.

Chris is unprepared for the scene behind the second wall: a villa, 1920s or '30s, in a large, treed garden, torches on the lawn. Light falls over them from the open windows. In the tall front door, Chris's friend Frederike appears. Her shadow shrinks when she walks out to him, cheeks lit by torch flames, arms stretched out.

'You've managed to find our estate!' She puckers her

lips in a pseudo-posh manner. 'Here in the *provincias* different spatial rules apply, you know.'

Her breath is all cigarette when she kisses Chris's cheeks. He stoops over her, pressing her close. He has missed her, this Friesian woman, once a fellow student in London. He turns around, but the American has already been pulled into a small group of guests on the lawn. She takes Chris by the arm, leading him inside.

'Come and meet Tita,' she says. Her neck flushes.

'It feels as if I know her like my own sister, Fred,' Chris says. 'Remember the descriptions in your letters?'

Once inside, he needs to raise his voice. The vaulted ceilings of the reception rooms echo with the chatter and laughter of guests in summer outfits. There are tables with cold meats, cheeses, breads, yellow butter.

'It is such a joy,' Fred shouts up at him, 'to be living with her in this place! Like contadini, like peasants, but in the heart of Milan, and in a huge villa, and to be surrounded by so many friends. Oh, here you are!'

She grips the arm of a statuesque woman, drags her away from a posse of guests. Over her shoulder Tita gestures helplessly to her conversation partners. She turns to Chris.

Fred introduces them. An incongruous couple, Chris thinks. Fred is now bent over a cigarette paper, wetting it with her tongue before rolling the tobacco, her eyes behind a dark, oily fringe. And next to her, blonde Tita: a living Giacometti, bones as thin as branches. They are both looking at him, their gazes devoid of expectation or demand. Rarely has he struck up a friendship as effortlessly as with Fred, and he recognises something

16

of Fred's benevolence in Tita's eyes too, the same openness and joy.

'Tita's a concert pianist,' Fred says, lifting Tita's fingers with her cigarette-free hand. I know, he could say, you've been devoting paragraphs of your letters to her talent, but he only smiles and touches Tita's fingers, which are hanging between them as if belonging to no one.

Fred raises her nose as if smelling something that is burning. She drops Tita's hand. She takes a drag on the cigarette and exposes a mouth full of sharp little teeth before scurrying away towards the kitchen.

Tita stands closer to him. 'Fred has told me a lot about you.'

'Likewise,' he says.

They smile broadly at each other. The room is glowing.

'What a wonderful house. Remind me, when did you move in?'

'Fred moved in about a year ago and started fixing the place up. I've only been here a few months. We're very happy,' Tita says. 'It's unimaginable, of course, this place: a country villa amidst the industrial grit, two penniless girls in such a rambling old pile, a structure that Mussolini would have been proud of. But here it is!'

She holds up her pianist's hands in an improbable gesture, as if to support the entire building. 'At night it looks more idyllic than it is – you should have a wander in the garden later, we're on the canal – but during the day it's a different story: shutters closed against the lorries and the factories, dust and ash settling on the garden . . . ' She leans in slightly towards him, the scent of lemon rising from her skin. Her Italian cadences relax him.

Behind her, Fred passes by with a pot of soup, her head in the steam. Against the vapour and the glowing light, Chris looks at Tita's bone structure with astonishment: angular, like something from a Futurist painting.

Fred rejoins them.

'Tita was just telling me about the joys of your monumental house.'

'A nest rather than a monument,' she says. 'A lesbian nest among the machines.' She pouts grandly. 'A crumbling barricade against the merciless march of production.' The sharp little teeth shimmer as she laughs. 'Like a warship that ran aground in the thirties, here at the edge of the canal . . . Oh, Chris,' she says, taking his hand, 'I have to introduce you to someone. There's another South African here tonight – or, like you, a lapsed South African,' she quickly corrects herself.

'Tom,' he says without hesitating. 'It's Tom, isn't it?'

She is taken aback. 'Do you know him, then?'

But he has surprised himself. He does not, in fact, know Tom.

'Well, strange as it may sound, no, but he arrived with me, if I'm not mistaken. Don't you remember?'

The name has come from nowhere. He has no idea how he has attached it to the man – the Afrikaans American, or American Afrikaner.

Fred is searching his face with a frown. Tita keeps smiling as if the entire universe's contradictions are to be reconciled. Her fingers keep moving.

Fred stops trying to figure out Chris's response, but remains anxious. She slips her fingers through Tita's.

'Come, you have to play for the guests,' she says.

She leads Tita to the piano, climbs onto a side table and holds her short arms aloft. On the chair behind the shabby grand piano, Tita suddenly looks defeated. Hungry, thinks Chris; she is looking ravenously hungry. Gradually the guests quieten down.

Everyone is waiting for Tita. Her hair ends are trembling slightly. She resembles porcelain in the moment before it breaks. She has completely frozen, arms by her sides, the keys untouched. No note will flow from her fingers tonight. Chris has to suppress his urge to go to her rescue.

His eyes settle on the figure right behind Tita: a bony Northern European. He looks deeply uncomfortable. He has the kind of body, Chris thinks – his attention now divided between the man and Tita – that will never be able to give and receive unbridled love. At the edge of the silence, he notices someone else move from the corner of his eye. The figure slips out of the front door. Chris hesitates for a moment, then decides to leave the rescue action to Fred. He follows.

It is quiet in the garden. He pursues the shadow around the corner and along the side of the house. At the base, the walls widen, like the pedestal of a neoclassical monument. He keeps his left shoulder against the granite. He opens his palm against the wall, looks up. This side of the house is almost windowless, amplifying the scale. Towards the garden wall some distance to his right, plants are weighed down by weeds. The man in front walks to the edge of the lawn, where it drops abruptly to the canal. The house, Chris notices, is built right to the edge too. The rush of water is audible.

Chris keeps his distance, waiting. The glow of a lawn torch somewhere behind them illuminates the man's back.

He is standing on the lawn between the corner of the house and a birch tree growing over the canal, steadying himself against the tree with one hand and the house with the other. He leans forward and disappears.

Chris freezes. He quickly looks over his shoulder, half-expecting to see the bony Northern European in the glow of a torch behind him. But no one has followed them.

Then he rushes forward. A few metres below him is the black water. The current is stronger than he imagined. It is too dark to see very far down the canal. His eyes search along the base of the house where it rises straight up out of the water. A movement against the wall, above the base, catches his eye. It takes a while before he realises it is the man, moving along a narrow ledge, body flattened against the granite. Further along, he can make out the profile of a balcony.

Chris looks down at the water, tests the ledge with one foot. He takes off his shoes, puts them neatly together by the tree trunk and follows – toes on the ledge, fingers in a groove. Below him, water glides against stone as smoothly as oil.

By the time he has reached the balcony, where the man is now awaiting him, his fingers have cramps. He is helped over the balustrade like someone rescued from drowning.

'That was a rather foolish exercise,' the man says laconically, the accent unstable.

'Ditto,' Chris says.

The man shrugs his shoulders. 'Second nature.'

'What, foolishness?'

Chris has now switched to Afrikaans. He can hear his own voice carrying across the canal. On the opposite side are bright lights against steel towers. Atop the towers, the megaphones of factory sirens glint. Half-light reflects off the water.

The man smiles a sly smile against the reflections, as if saying: No, recklessness.

'You are Tom,' Chris says.

'I am Tom.' It sounds as if his tone is coupled with the raising of an eyebrow, but he has stepped back, into the deeper shadows, his face now a void.

'Fred mentioned you.' Chris leans forward onto the balustrade. The balcony hangs out over the water; it is made entirely of wood. Behind them, louvred shutters cover a door to the house. With Tom, he immediately senses, there is no room for the wearisome kind of questions and tales with which exiled South Africans sometimes approach each other when they meet in foreign parts. He detects no anxiousness on Tom's side to share a history or feelings of alienation. He is nevertheless listening carefully to Tom's dangerous voice, his abrupt utterances, to work out where they might have met before.

Tom lights a cigarette without asking whether it would bother Chris or offering him one. 'So, what just happened in there?'

'Hard to say. Fred told me in a letter that Tita has recently been working through many nights on her PhD thesis. Perhaps she's tired or stressed, maybe a little rusty when it comes to performing, rather than writing about, music. Or perhaps it's the weight' – Chris gestures vaguely to the ramshackle house above their heads – 'that's forcing the air from her lungs . . . ' He is not sure himself what he is trying to say.

'What was she going to play?'

'No idea. Perhaps nothing, perhaps what we saw *was* the performance. She has all kinds of ideas about the boundaries of performance.'

Tom takes his time inhaling the smoke of his cigarette, turns towards the shutters as if wanting to hear what is going on inside.

'What's she researching?'

'History of music. The composer Luigi Russolo, apparently, and his influence on twentieth-century music. The title is something like *From Russolo to Lachenmann*, with a subtitle that I forget.'

'Hmm,' Tom says, and turns towards Chris, his tall body posing a challenge in the dark. He does not say anything. He seems to be taking delight in his own leanness.

'I like Milan,' Chris says after a while to break the silence. 'I prefer it to the threadbare romanticism of Rome; I like the fact that the industrial decay here can't be eclipsed by the glitz of the fashion houses. Milan symbolises the idea of modern Italy better –'

'I don't know either Rome,' Tom says, 'or Milan. This is my first visit.' Chris feels the cold seeping into his feet. Below his soles, the wood is brittle and dry.

After a while Tom turns back to the water. 'During the war between Ethiopia and Eritrea,' he says, 'I was based in Asmara. As a photographer for an American paper. That, I thought back then, is how Italy looks. All those buildings from the thirties, the ice-cream-parlour colours.'

'Yes, *that* I like,' Chris says, excited about the direction the conversation is taking. 'The European landscape through the lens of the colonial city, the idea that the former looks like the latter rather than the other way round. I'd love to visit Asmara. Mussolini's architects apparently built it almost overnight. The old locomotives of the Eritrean railways, I've read, still carry the years of their construction according to the Fascist calendar. I also like the fact that the city's modernist lines are disrupted by the life of an African city, by dark bodies, the chaos of war . . . '

Tom blows slow smoke towards the water, drops the butt. The smoke drifts up, unfurls around them. For a few seconds their heads are out of focus. He is weighing me up, Chris thinks, and finding me too light.

Drily Tom remarks: 'The city is in fact almost untouched by the war. And it is clean and functional. Poor, though – the Brits stripped it of infrastructure when they took over. Asmara doesn't in fact feel like Africa: at dusk people wander the streets with double-breasted suits and fedoras. Odd place.'

Chris cannot get a grip on the character next to him. If it were light, he would be able to read something in the movements of his facial muscles. Nevertheless, Tom's assuredness with his own body, the way in which he stylises even small movements, is starting to unravel a dim memory.

'I presume you live in the US?'

Tom nods, keeps looking at the water's muscular black currents. (Is it starting to rise?)

It takes a while before Tom speaks again. 'I wonder whether these canals ever freeze over. Once I had to take photos for a local paper in Pennsylvania of a child who had drowned in a canal.'

Now it is Chris who is turning to Tom.

'It was mid-winter, in a small industrial town. She had been missing for a week. Children who had gone skating that morning, the surface strong enough for the first time, discovered her. She was lying in her red snow jacket under the ice, looking up. The children and I stood there with our heads together, looking down.'

Chris turns towards the water. They are leaning forward, elbows on the balustrade, shoulders and hips touching. Tom's face is moving into and out of the deeper shadows, unnerving Chris. Tom lifts his head and smiles an unpredictable smile against the glow, testing the wood with his foot.

'I hope this contraption won't collapse beneath us.' And, as he is saying it, he inserts a hand under Chris's shirt. With the lazy, indifferent insistence of a child stirring in its sleep, Tom's fingers work their way up Chris's spine to his neck.

'Christiaan,' Tom says, whispering heavily, 'little Christiaan.'

In the moment before Tom says his name (his vertebrae a string of coals), Chris knows exactly who it is: Tommie. Yes, Tommie from his school days.

From his spine, his bones heat up. Above the water he is hanging from a skeleton of fire.

Early evening. Christiaan and Tommie are cycling up the hill behind their neighbourhood. They are thirteen, perhaps fourteen.

Tommie lives further down the street with his mother, in a far smaller house than Christiaan's. His absent father, so he insists, is fighting terrorists in the war on the border. Tommie's reckless aura has the boys in his class circling him like moths. He is smooth and brown as a chestnut in their midst, surrounded by a whiff of dusty sweat. His infamy is reaffirmed when the PE teacher punches him one morning when he refuses to change or train. He hardly moves a muscle when the fist makes contact and blood starts trickling through his lips. He balls his hands into fists, but does not hit back.

At school, Tommie hardly takes notice of Christiaan, but at night he takes him on his raids in the neighbourhood. Occasionally Tommie blows up a postbox with firecrackers; here and there he steals something from a garden. One evening he makes Christiaan wait in the street, hops over a wall and, after twenty minutes, brings back a radio, a box filled with records and a fistful of cash.

Christiaan has a shiny new Christmas bicycle; Tommie still rides his old one from primary-school days, for which his legs have become too long. They pedal up the hill. Tommie's body is swaying, his T-shirt flapping. It is almost completely dark.

When the road starts flattening near the top, Tommie is far ahead of him. The houses fall away. There are only black wattle trees and the occasional blue gum. Christiaan is pedalling as if in sand. The skin on his back is cold. He is an open target. Years ago, he recalls, there was a serial killer who hid in the hills and managed, for months, to evade the police. The Panga Man. Every now and then he would creep up on lovers in their cars and slice them up with relish.

Christiaan pedals until his lungs start burning.

At the big reservoir, Tommie is waiting for him. He drops his own bicycle next to Tommie's. They scramble wildly up the high wire fence. He reaches the top before Tommie, but when he rolls over the razor wire, it tears his shirt and draws a burning line across his ribs.

They clamber up an iron ladder inside a concrete tube. Tommie is in front, Christiaan below him, more wary now. The clanging of feet on iron echoes around them.

They emerge at the top and walk along the edge of the reservoir's domed roof, arms stretched out, to where they can see the city lying beneath their feet. Tommie takes off his shirt. Christiaan hesitates, then follows suit. They lie down on their backs, feet against the low edge. The concrete is still holding the afternoon's warmth. As always, the air is high and cloudless. The city is full of engines. Tommie lights a cigarette. He inhales the smoke. Then he brings it closer, until it almost touches Christiaan's skin. In the glow they study the bloody ridge across his ribs. He holds his breath, waits for Tommie to trace it with a finger, but Tommie grins and turns away, shooting his cigarette in a long arc above the city lights. Before he loses his courage, he reaches out for Tommie's temple, but Tommie jumps up. He crawls towards the middle of the dome. He gets up and stands on the high-est point like a statue. Then he disappears. Christiaan waits for him to return. After a long while – the concrete having cooled against his skin – he realises Tommie has gone.

When he scales the fence, more carefully this time, only Tommie's bicycle is there in the dust. The explanation to his parents the next day is that he has given his bicycle away. He refuses to say to whom. Neither he nor Tommie ever says a word about it again.

Another evening, a few months later. The last time, so he thinks, that he will ever see Tommie. Tommie and his mother will be moving out of the city the next day. When he asks where to, Tommie says they will be joining his father on the border, where he will help him fight terrorists. They are in Tommie's empty bedroom, among packed boxes. Tommie is lying with his back against a box, shirtless as usual, hands behind his head. He is telling Christiaan about the weapons his father has ready for him. An entire arsenal. They will show the terrorists who's boss. While Tommie is speaking, Christiaan reaches out without looking at him. He drags a finger through the hairs in Tommie's armpit. Tommie is quiet for a moment, then continues. The weaponry is becoming heavier, increasingly lethal. Christiaan brings his face to where his finger has just been, breathing in Tommie's scent. He stays like that for a moment, until Tommie gets up and pulls a wooden gun from a box. 'My dad has an Uzi like this,' he says, 'but much bigger; a real one.'

'I immediately recognised you,' Tom says, 'when we arrived here this evening.'

'Our youth is a no-man's-land,' Chris says, and looks away. How impossible, he thinks, to return to it. All that remains is a void to be filled with the wonders of the world.

For a while neither of them says anything. Tom takes his hand off Chris's neck. 'Your feet must be cold now,' Tom says. 'There's soup inside.'

He turns to the balcony door. It sticks when he pulls it, then yields. Dry leaves shift away like snow. Behind the shutters is a wall.

'Bricked up,' Chris comments. 'Back along the ledge it is.'

When he looks back to where he left his shoes by the tree, he is convinced he can see a face peeking around the corner. The Northern European from earlier, he thinks.

Yes, he is sure it is him: the man with the impeded body and the disobedient bones. He points towards the face, but Tom can't see anything.

They have been gone longer than Chris thought. Most guests have left. After another half-hour only Tom and Chris remain. Fred observes them from where she is carrying away plates. She decides they have to stay over.

'Too late,' she says, 'to order a taxi out here in the sticks.'

She lends the two men fresh trousers and shirts – Fred's for Chris and Tita's for Tom. Not a word is spoken about the event around the piano earlier. There is no trace of the earlier tension.

'Come and drink coffee here in our room!' Fred is leaning her head over the banister and calling down to the men. She is carrying a tray with a silver coffee pot.

Now Fred is sitting on the bed with her hands clasped around her shins, her face scrunched into a smile. Her neck is pulled into her shoulders and smoke is weaving slowly upwards from the joint between her fingers. A tiny coal drops onto the sheet and burns right through. The sweet smoke enters Chris's nostrils and the hollows of his skull.

Fred's shirt is taut over Chris's shoulders and the top button of his trousers won't close. Tita's shirt, on the other hand, is loose on Tom; his trousers seem quite roomy.

Fred notices the burn on the sheet. She lifts the sheet before her, the hole over her eye.

'What are you seeing through the ash?' Chris wants to know.

'The battered ones,' she says, and sips some coffee. 'The walking wounded left in the aftermath.'

'The aftermath? Of what?'

She does not answer. Tom smiles raunchily at Chris. An arm appears from behind the sheet and offers the joint. Chris takes a drag, then Tom, then Tita. Fred pulls the sheet around her face so that it tightens around her features. The hole moves over her mouth again. The joint is passed to her; she takes a drag. A trickle of smoke emerges from the black hole.

Chris turns to Tita: 'Tom wanted to know more about your research. Tell him about noise, about the hellishly noisy future.'

Tom leans towards Chris and Tita. His borrowed shirt tightens over his shoulders.

'Yes,' she says, 'that's where it starts. The Futurists expected a deafeningly noisy future, and were preparing to welcome it. They, in fact, wanted to invite it, to storm and destroy the traditional concert hall – the so-called "hospital of anaemic sound". Russolo armed himself with an arsenal of self-manufactured instruments. His Intonarumori – acoustic noise machines. Wooden boxes with a loudspeaker and a crank or electric button. With a turn of the crank or the press of a button one could make noise, and then modulate the tone with a lever.'

'Explain how it all worked,' Chris says.

'Well, inside it has – or had – a wheel that caused a string made of cat intestine to vibrate. The lever adjusted the tension. Glissandi or individual notes would then be led to a drum adjoining the loudspeaker –'

'Remind me of all the terrible sounds.' It is Fred, appearing from behind the sheet. Her eyes are wide. It looks as if pure noise could escape from her head.

'Well, there are six noise families, according to Russolo. First there are the roars, which include thunderings, explosions, hissing roars, bangs and booms. Then there are the whistling sounds, such as hisses and puffs. Following those are the whispers – murmurs, mumblings, mutterings and gurgling. The screeches, then, are the creaking sounds, the rustlings, buzzing, crackling and scraping. Further categories are the voices of animals and people: shouts, screams, shrieks, wails, hoots, heaving and sobs. Finally, there are the noises of percussion on, for example, metal, wood, skin, stone or clay.'

How he likes Tita! Chris thinks. When she speaks, it is with real concentration. She is focused on her listener: rather than imparting something, she is tuning her ear to his frequency.

'What's the subtitle of what you're writing?' Tom asks Tita, but it is Chris he is looking in the eye.

She looks down, as if wanting to divert attention from herself. 'Something like "Noise, War and Loss", but it's provisional. Something more subtle will present itself. But it definitely needs to involve war,' she says. 'For the Futurists, war was the height of artistic expression.'

'So, what I in fact intend to do is to trace the musical history of the twentieth century,' she says, 'searching for the moment' – she draws a line on the sheet and presses with her finger at random points – 'where all the major narratives, the big plans for the future, suddenly vanished like the morning mist.'

Fred removes the sheet from her face.

'The brave, cruel future . . . ' Chris says.

'And,' Tita continues, 'I then try to hear the echoes of that collapse, try to read it like tea leaves . . . '

'Is it too simple to say that moment was one of the two wars?' Chris asks.

'All those men – the music people and the warmongers – with their manifestos and tracts, their declarations and objectives!' Fred calls out.

'Oh, but their bravery was precious too,' says Tita. 'What they could not predict was what would follow noise, the silence that comes after collapse.'

Tom aims another wild smile in Chris's direction, as if wanting to undercut the pompousness of the conversation.

'We're starting to get old, aren't we?' Fred says unexpectedly, looking at the cold coffee on the bedside table.

She sits forward urgently, as if she has had an important thought. 'Come and live here,' she says, 'both of you, here with us. There's more room than anyone could ever need. Yes, and then we'll make' – she gestures excitedly to Chris, to Tom, to Tita, to herself – 'a house full of children. Imagine the scene: cacophony from morning till the eve, summer breakfasts by the canal, soccer in the garden at dusk, chapped knees and grazed elbows . . . and an orchestra, yes, enough children for an entire little orchestra!'

'I can see the orchestra before me now,' Tom pipes up drily. 'The four of us, on our passeggiata in the shade, happening upon them where they have petrified in the dusk: in complete silence, frozen screams on innocent faces. Arms and instruments reaching towards the heavens. A statue representing the heroic masses . . . '

His voice is unexpectedly dangerous. Both Tita and Fred look hurt for a moment. But then the lines of Tita's face sharpen. 'I have something to show you,' she says. 'Come!' She jumps off the bed and beckons.

They follow. Behind her, they climb the narrow wooden stairs that lead up from the bedroom.

In the attic they have to bend their heads away from the slanted ceiling. Tita looks as if she is bent double. A naked bulb is swaying between them, their heads close together.

'What follows now, a conversation with the dead?' Tom wants to know.

Tita ignores him. 'It is generally accepted,' she says, and her bone structure is casting sharp shadows, 'that all Russolo's Intonarumori were destroyed during the war. But . . . ' She pauses for effect, then lifts a black sheet from the shape between them. The wooden box is dust-free, the megaphone of the loudspeaker smooth and shiny.

'Don't!' she says, and lays her hand on Tom's forearm when he immediately reaches for the crank. 'It hasn't worked for a long time; the internal mechanisms are immensely fragile.'

'It is one of the smaller models,' she continues, 'but it is not the only one in existence, either. In the 1970s there was even a chamber orchestra that met in secret here in Milan to play on the handful of surviving Intonarumori. From all over performers assembled here, and at night, in abandoned warehouses, they would – '

'Bedtime,' Fred says suddenly, and blinks her little bushbaby eyes.

Chris and Tom's room is on one of the two unrestored middle floors, not on the canal side. The cast iron of the radiators is cool against Chris's fingers. He tries to open the curtainless sash window, but it sticks. A security light shines into the room from the industrial yard. When they stand opposite each other, naked now, their penises are heavy in the stale air.

Tom pins Christiaan against the mattress. As the air is forced from his lungs, he is flooded with joy. They travel across the bed in wrestling movements, taking turns to rise and push the other down. Their bodies, so Chris imagines it, are building fabulous towers. Slowly, Chris gains the upper hand. When his back arches above Tom's like a cat's, he can feel his spine exposing itself to the stars.

Sleep washes over Chris in waves. He dreams of a blue sky that is divided into mosaic tiles. Then it becomes murky, as if a cataract were shifting over it. In the dream, he realises that he is looking through the eyes of the dead child in Tom's story. In the canal, below the ice.

He wakes up after midnight. He should ask Tom for a photo of the drowned child. He tosses and turns, thinking of the nocturnal performances on Intonarumori in the seventies. He would have liked to hear more from Tita about this. He feels a kinship with these underground performers. Nostalgia is paralysing his muscles, as if he had been there too. His yearning for these people with their noise machines in unfamiliar industrial spaces causes his sex to stir like a snail against Tom's back.

Tom wakes up. His limbs move towards Chris as if through water. Initially he resists Tom. He relaxes and they accelerate: they become two smooth, pure objects, severed from their youth, from all ties and expectations; behind them, only the black heavens.

Later they wake up again. Chris thinks he can hear something: perhaps the water level in the canal is rising, perhaps the machine in the attic has started working.

'Who are you?' Tom asks in the dark.

'What do you mean?' Chris asks.

'Tell me.'

'Hmm, not sure what you want to know.' He considers an answer. One revelation would be as arbitrary as another. A man looking for his bicycle?

'I live in London. Academic. Art history, early modernist architecture and sculpture. Not a very fashionable field.' How cerebral, Chris thinks, even in this sleep-drenched moment.

'More,' Tom demands.

Chris can smell Tom, and there is something familiar and incendiary in the smell. 'If you must know, I'm working on an article called "Boccioni, Futurism and the aesthetic of Afrikaner Nationalism", Umberto Boccioni being a sculptor who worked early last century, of course.' Perhaps, Chris thinks, he should not have said 'of course'.

Tom doesn't say anything, just becomes more fragrant.

Chris breathes deeply and says: 'Yes, isn't it strange where ex-South Africans pop up these days and which subjects and worlds they join together?'

He still has difficulty gauging the right topics and level when talking to Tom. His last remarks, he suspects, make him sound like someone from the past, a messenger from a world gone by. He is disappointing Tom. He tries one more time: 'For Boccioni,' Chris says, and turns to face Tom, 'the rhythm of an industrial valve opening and closing was as beautiful as that of a living eyelid.'

'All this history . . . ' Tom says. 'I'm more comfortable with what's right in front of me.' His tongue is unexpectedly in Tom's left armpit. For a third time they intertwine, more tenderly this time.

Chris wakes early. Everyone is asleep. Only a slight glow betrays the coming dawn. Tom is lying with his hands behind his head, his armpits dark. Their borrowed clothes are piled up in a corner. Chris tiptoes to the bathroom across the hallway. He is unsure whether there is water here, but, when he opens the bath tap, it rushes out against the marble. It does not become warm, though. He waits until it is knee-deep and then stands in the cold water. On his legs and ribs he notices bruises. Like the stains in the marble, he thinks, as he immerses his body. His joints feel scratchy. He holds his breath, trying to slow his heartbeat.

It is hard to say how long he lies like this before the door opens. He sits up halfway, suddenly aware of his nakedness, even though the women hardly register it. His teeth are chattering.

'The noise machine,' Fred says, 'the Intonarumore! Tom has taken it. He must have crept through our room and simply carried it out of here!' She throws a hand in the air.

He is now sitting completely upright. 'It is hard to explain,' he says, and he is talking through lips that are numb, 'but . . . Tom ultimately gives more than he takes.'

The unhappiness does not vanish from Fred's face.

'It takes a long time to discover what it is that is being given,' Chris continues – and he realises that even he would take some time to figure out his meaning – 'to discover what the gains are that are yielded by losses . . . perhaps one never finds out – '

Tita starts smiling slowly. Something approaching joy is breaking through.

'It isn't a loss – we simply have to get it back,' Fred says vehemently.

But Chris's attention is with Tita. What he is reading in her expression is the beginning of understanding. All routes are left open, all uncertainties are held in equilibrium. An embracing graciousness is emanating from her. Everything that is irreconcilable, may, for now, be joined together. She can wait for as long as it takes for the connections to reveal themselves.

When they pull the door shut behind them, he takes out the plug. As the water runs out, his weight sinks into the marble. The cold enters his bones. Above the taps little blue tiles stretch to the ceiling. In the marble he can sense the vibrations of lorry engines.

If he has to interpret the ache in his bones honestly, it is a longing for Tom to return, and to bring with him a vanished world. He wants to fetch Tom himself, wherever he may be. But when you are frozen, you're unable to move; you can only wait to be found. And if it cannot be Tom, let it be the children who discover him – the little gang, huddling to gape at his open blue mouth. But there's a far greater chance that he will be lying here until spring arrives, until the ice gently releases him, and lets him drift down to the sea.

VAN

Sandrien is the only white woman in Bella Gardens. She is in fact the only white person in town. *An establishment for the accommodation of women travellers*, reads the website of Bella Gardens. *The most luxurious home for females*, reads the brochure in the dim entrance hall. One could mistake it for a refuge for unwed mothers.

Her hostess is Mrs Edith Nyathi, who introduces herself as a widow and retired matron of Frere Hospital. She never stops talking about her 'second life'. She raises her eyebrows and drops her head forward when pronouncing the phrase. The guest house is her pension, she says, 'my little egg'. The number of maids in her employ permits her to relax with a cigarette on the veranda during the day; sometimes, late in the evening, with a cigar. Mrs Nyathi does not raise her voice to any of the maids – a phalanx of demure village girls, ready to fry up sizzling English breakfasts or to polish baths and wooden floors to a high gloss. When she calls to one of her girls, it is in the same cooing voice she uses to address her guests.

The colonial veranda of the sandstone house offers a view over the village. Except for the college buildings at the top of the slope, the guest house is the grandest building in Vloedspruit. Corrugated-iron shacks hug the slope. Dotted between them are Basotho-style rondavels with thatched roofs. Lower down, where it is colder and where the watery waste collects, there are rows of government houses built of cement bricks, some with rickety lean-tos. Others have clay-plastered rondavels in the backyards. A village of *pondokke*, *kaias* and *strooise*, Sandrien thinks, but these are words from a different time.

In the mornings Sandrien walks up the hill to the training college of the provincial health department. She is attending a refresher course, lasting six weeks, to prepare rural nurses for 'the major challenges in primary health care today'. *Our Health Revolution* is the title of their newly printed textbook; it has laughing faces of different races on the cover. The classes begin at nine. At eleven, tea and sandwiches are served; at one there is a two-hour lunch break. In between, they fit in sessions about everything from vaccinations to smears to the physiological effects of different classes of antiretrovirals.

Her jaw drops when she sees the lunch provided by the college to the students and personnel for the first time. Samp, pap, rice, three varieties of vegetables, three kinds of meat. Deep, steaming pots.

'Is it all for us?' Sandrien asks the younger woman next to her.

'We have to eat, *meisie*,' she answers, and prods Sandrien with her elbow. The woman's earrings sway. 'Lerato,' she introduces herself, tucking an extra can of Coke under her arm. 'I'm a nurse from the Free State.'

The first few days Sandrien sits by herself on the steps. At first, she eats her food with a spoon. Then she starts using her hands, like the others. Why not?

On the third day Lerato joins her. 'You white girls don't get very hungry, do you?'

Outside the fence a few half-starved children with snot on their upper lips stand gaping.

When Sandrien hands some of her food to the children through the fence, Lerato clicks her tongue: 'Stop that!'

'But look at them! They're famished.'

'Just you wait. Tomorrow the whole town's children will be here.' Lerato points to the fence. 'Just behind that fence, all of them, tomorrow.'

'But then we must feed them. We have enough. More than enough.'

'Eish, you people.' Lerato clicks, more loudly this time. 'I know your type. You're like the crowd in my hospital. Charity doctors from Scandinavia. They don't know this place.'

Lerato gets up, her plate still half-full.

'I'm not from Scandinavia,' Sandrien says to Lerato's enormous back, 'I'm from the banks of the Gariep.'

'I admire the fact that you are dedicating yourself here; you must have had many other opportunities,' Sandrien says to Dr Shirley Kgope, the course leader, during morning tea, gesturing with her eyes towards the rows of shacks below the college buildings.

Shirley Kgope, although originally from the Eastern Cape, studied medicine in a drab city in the American Midwest, and is also a microbiologist.

'Why not?' says Dr Kgope, sounding weary of this kind of conversation. 'It is where I am most needed.' She takes a sip of tea. 'It would be more interesting to know what brings *you* here.'

Dr Kgope's cup tinkles in the saucer. Thick-rimmed porcelain cups, like in a teachers' common room.

'Why not?' Sandrien smiles. 'By the way, how did it happen that the training college here has such extensive facilities?'

'It was originally designed as a teachers' college,' says Dr Kgope. 'Everyone knew that all the teachers' colleges would be closed shortly, but the place was built nevertheless. It stood empty for a few years.'

'But why?'

Dr Kgope rubs her thumb over her forefinger like a cashier counting money.

'Bribes?'

'Draw your own conclusions.'

Dr Shirley Kgope bends down to straighten the lines down the back of her silk stockings. Tea time is over. They pick their way through goats on the veranda to get to the seminar room.

'We should tell Mr Mabunda to fix the fence,' says Dr Kgope, kicking goat droppings from the tiles.

'Why are you here?' Mrs Nyathi asks with sly, amused eyes when the two of them are drinking brandy alone late that evening.

The three other girls who are boarding at Bella Gardens, all nurses and fellow students, are out somewhere, probably in the shebeen further down in the village. Mrs Nyathi is small with a broad face, substantial thighs and cheeks across which baby skin is stretched beautifully taut.

Tonight she is smoking a cigar. Like two gents in a members' club they sit in deep armchairs.

'You're not the first to ask,' answers Sandrien. 'For the training, of course!'

Mrs Nyathi shakes her head. 'No, no, I mean why are *you* here?'

She gestures with both hands towards Sandrien's body. Towards her skin colour, in fact.

Sandrien sits back in the armchair. Two months ago, she had returned home to the farm at Dorrebult, her palate shredded by chemotherapy. She had spent three months in Bloemfontein. She stayed on her own in a guest house, within walking distance of the hospital. Her identical twin daughters sometimes came to sit with her in the afternoons after school, but she usually felt terrible and the two surly adolescents had little to say to her. On the first afternoon, after spending all morning in a daze, watching poison dripping into her veins, she even momentarily confused them with each other.

When she returned to Dorrebult, nothing was left of the weaving mill. The tables and looms stood there gathering dust. The yarn – the wool and the mohair – everything, gone. Just a few loose filaments on the cement floor.

'Where have they all gone?' She looked at her husband accusingly. 'Grace, Brenda, Xoliswe, the rest?'

Kobus shrugged. 'There's nothing left of the weaving business. What did you expect? You were the heart of it. Surely you know that.'

'But it was for them, as much as for me. How could they just let go of it?'

Kobus touched her elbow in passing. He put on his hat and drove off to his cattle. In the shafts of sunlight pouring through the windows, his footsteps had stirred up fragments of fibre that kept floating and shimmering.

Sandrien is surrounded by Mrs Nyathi's fragrant smoke. She is picking at loose threads under her chair cushion.

Over two years she built up the weaving mill. Poured a new concrete floor for the old barn, punched new windows into the walls for light. She went to work at a community weaving project in Grahamstown for a few months, acquainting herself with market size, potential sales points, marketing channels. Back home she met with each of their neighbours to assess attitudes. Most of the farmers were relieved about the opportunity for their labourers to earn an extra income, their burden of responsibility perhaps somewhat lightened. She spoke to the women on each of the farms, made sure the men were not present. The coloured women seemed more enthusiastic than the Xhosa women, but ultimately so many turned up that she could not take all of them.

She taught them what she had learned, weaving shoulder-to-shoulder with them until her hands were raw. Some of the women learned quickly; about half kept at it and became highly adept. Together with the five who remained, she developed the project. Colours and designs were adapted as she received orders from shops in Franschhoek and Dullstroom and Clarens. Blankets in natural, earthy colours; monochrome rugs with subtly varying textures. *Handwoven by women from the Eastern Cape* on the back of the label, underneath her brand name: *Glo-fibre*. A paragraph about Glo-fibre's environmentally friendly practices.

The business started growing; she was getting enquiries from Europe and the Middle East. When she learned the diagnosis, she called Grace in and told her. Grace was the only one of her personnel who had matriculated; she was bright and dedicated.

'I have to go away for treatment. While I'm gone, you must be the driving force behind the project, Grace, the linchpin.'

Grace promised solemnly, her tall frame tilting slightly forward.

There was little time. For two weeks, she trained Grace in aspects of administration and management. 'Showing you the ropes, no pun intended.' Grace did not laugh. Carefully she took Grace through the order books and her list of suppliers, showing her how to make entries, explaining everything.

Mrs Nyathi's eyes are shining. She is observing Sandrien, as if sharing the memory.

Sandrien considered asking Kobus to take over, but she knew he would not be able to manage it with the cattle. And he would not understand what it was that the mill demanded.

'Anyhow,' she said to Grace, 'it would run counter to the spirit of this if I involved my husband, or one of the other farmers' wives.'

She looked Grace in the eyes, pressed Grace's hands against her chest. 'I have trust in you. In your hearts you know the value of this, what it means.'

Grace arranged for them to sing for her when she left. She was embarrassed; it was not as if she was facing death. Prior to the mastectomy and treatment she in fact radiated health. When she got back and found the mill abandoned, it didn't take long to find out why. She was shocked at how ill Grace was.

She considers expanding on her answer to Mrs Nyathi's question. 'For retraining, of course; I'm rusty. Before, I spent years as a nurse in intensive care in a private hospital in Grahamstown. I want to work again. I have to earn money.'

Mrs Nyathi's screwed eyes are sharp.

Sandrien clears her throat. 'Perhaps,' she says and touches her throat, 'to become acquainted with the textures of loss.'

Mrs Nyathi laughs, her neat feet stir, her cheeks still as lovely as a baby's.

A thunderstorm wakes her. She pulls away the curtain. Lightning flashes across brown currents descending from the mountain. The currents branch out into a delta, flowing around some of the little houses and straight through others. She opens the windows; the curtains billow into the room. In her nightgown she stands before the storm.

After the incident with the children, Lerato no longer sits with her at mealtimes. Sandrien now heaps the food extra high on her plate every lunch and gives it to the children. She tries to hand them rolled balls of pap through the fence. Later she holds out the plate for them to take the food themselves. Their hands are smaller, move more easily through the tightly woven fence. As Lerato predicted, the numbers have swollen. There is a small crowd. Two of the littler ones have even wriggled through the hole made by the goats. Sandrien looks around. On the veranda a group of her fellow students are watching, hands on their hips. Then Lerato walks towards them, arms swinging, earrings jingling. She hits the fence with an open hand so that it rattles from one corner post to the other. The children scatter in all directions. The two small ones on the inside start crying. 'Bloody goats and children!' she shouts, but her anger is really aimed at Sandrien.

The smell of toxic gas enters Sandrien's nostrils. She walks away without a word, round the back of the classrooms. She will not shed a tear; she won't. In front of her a furrow has been dug into the hillside, directing water around the building. In the furrow there are two heaps of rubbish. One consists of hundreds of Coke cans, the other of smouldering plastic.

'I am Walter Mabunda.'

She quickly rubs tears off her cheeks. The man approaches and stands next to her, too close. He takes her hands between his. She stiffens.

'Why doesn't someone start a recycling project here?' she says, her voice more vehement than she intended. 'It could mean money, jobs.'

'Perhaps you should do it.'

'But I'm just here for a few weeks.'

He shrugs his shoulders. 'Managing this facility is a demanding task. I have only these two hands.'

She loosens hers from his.

'I presume you're staying in Bella Gardens?'

She looks at him. A charming voice. In his mid-fifties, she estimates, a good ten years older than she.

'Yes, at Mrs Nyathi's.'

'Hmm, such a good hostess. But,' he laughs lazily, 'she governs that establishment with an iron fist, I tell you. The girls who work there, they toe the line. Ooh, very scary,' he says in an unexpected alto voice, eyes wide. 'She can be withering,' he says, 'blistering.' He suddenly strikes her as somewhat camp. Below his beer belly, neat folds have been ironed into his slacks. His shoes are shiny.

'Mrs Nyathi has been a model of courtesy.'

'By the way, we must ask you not to lure the children.' His voice is sympathetic, soothing. 'They are a nuisance. We cannot take on responsibility for the entire community.'

The storms over Vloedspruit are fiercer than anything Sandrien has known. At night, lightning draws nerve patterns across the skies. Fountains burst from the slopes as if through a dam wall. Lower down, small buildings regularly wash away. The government houses remain standing, but mud is building against their walls. She is getting used to the rhythms here, even the storms. Her daily routine is not devoid of minor joys. Mrs Nyathi's fatty breakfasts, the morning classes at the college, the teas and lunches, the unpredictable – often perplexing – conversations with Mrs Nyathi at night on the veranda. She is getting used to the maids with their quiet eyes, furiously polishing or scurrying down the corridor, possibly instructed to remain invisible to guests. Her fellow students' social codes remain a mystery, though. As soon as she thinks she has started forming bonds of friendship, she is excluded again.

Sunday afternoons, when the other girls are out and she is not in the mood for Mrs Nyathi's company, or when the maids' unseen presences unnerve her, she goes for long walks. She breathes mountain air deep into her lungs after the rain. Children run naked through puddles and mill around her. They tug at her hands or clothes, search her pockets. She hands out money or sweets. She feels embarrassed, like the Western heroine in a Hollywood African fantasy: hand on the little khaki hat, children's profiles etched against her linen dress. Cows with bony rumps struggle up the slippery slope. One afternoon she realises most of the village market next to the government houses has been washed away.

Wherever she walks, little dogs run after the children and dart around her feet. They yap and yelp, dodging her footsteps.

'Why are there only small dogs here?' she asks Mrs Nyathi one afternoon.

Mrs Nyathi holds up her palms, as if saying: Isn't it obvious? She makes a gesture, as if bringing food to her mouth. 'They get eaten, don't they? The big ones.'

She is reluctant to call home. On a Sunday afternoon she calls Brenda, Grace's daughter, who is looking after Sandrien's elderly mother. Brenda is sulky.

'Missus Karlien is walking around with garden shears, trying to cut flies. She refuses to let me change her bedding. Sometimes she eats off the floor.'

The shadow of one of Mrs Nyathi's maids flits down the corridor. Sandrien regrets making the call, opening the curtain. Once a week Kobus calls from Dorrebult. He talks about his cattle, about their daughters in Bloemfontein. She invokes platitudes, talks about her accommodation, the nursing course, the storms. She keeps it vague. She wants to keep this place – this respite – separate. They do not talk about the illness, about the time she spent in Bloemfontein. That belongs to the past.

When Sandrien encounters Mrs Nyathi in the dim rooms of Bella Gardens, the same ritual always repeats itself.

'You still enjoying your wonderful stay, Mrs Gouws?'

Without fail, she answers: 'I am having the most wonderful time in this establishment of yours, Mrs Nyathi.'

Then Mrs Nyathi laughs, nodding her head as if they share a secret.

But this afternoon she catches Mrs Nyathi unawares. When Sandrien enters, she hears a loud voice in the bathroom. A new voice. It is Mrs Nyathi shouting at one of her maids in Xhosa. When Sandrien quietly passes by in the corridor, Mrs Nyathi turns around and smiles. The girl is in the shadow behind her. Sandrien can see the whites of her eyes. Mrs Nyathi pushes the door shut. Silence. From the bathroom, after a while, the unmistakeable sound of a slap.

The other nurses in Bella Gardens are polite, but keep their distance from Sandrien. In the mornings, when they stroll to the college, they cluster together, chattering. Around the table in the evenings the girls and Mrs Nyathi speak a mix of English, Sotho and Xhosa, so that Sandrien only catches the occasional snippet. On weeknights, they mostly retire to their rooms.

On Saturdays, Mrs Nyathi brings someone in to do their hair extensions in the sunshine on the veranda. At dusk there is chit-chat and giggling in the rooms of Bella Gardens. Vapours of perfume drift down the corridor. The maids sneak by on their toes, trying to get a glimpse of all things shiny and fragrant. With jingling bangles they trip through the lounge on silver heels. They make snake-like movements to the beat of inaudible music, initially ignoring Mrs Nyathi, who is looking on and keeping the rhythm. She keeps nodding her approval, over and over again, animated by an infectious exuberance. Then something strange happens: the air starts moving differently around the bodies. As if against their will, the girls start dancing to Mrs Nyathi's beat. They arrange themselves in relation to her, creating a formation with her at the forefront.

The taxi's hooter breaks the rhythm. To prevent mud getting on stockings, the driver picks up the girls at the end of the paved garden path. Music flows out when the white taxi door opens. Arms hang out of the windows once they're inside.

'Yes,' says Mrs Nyathi, when they are left sitting alone on the veranda, the village lights and fires below them. Her eyes are moist, searching for the taxi, its music fading amongst the houses. 'When I was a young nurse, there were also good, good times.'

Tonight she is wearing a headcloth, bright textile from West Africa.

'Where do they go at night?' Sandrien wants to know.

'There are places across the border in Lesotho,' Mrs Nyathi says, 'where you can have a lot of fun.' Her eyes widen and her head nods forward. 'A *lot* of fun.'

Mrs Nyathi looks askance at Sandrien, sips her brandy.

'How about you? You're still young enough. Don't you sing and dance, don't you sometimes seek out a little fun, fun, fun?' Mrs Nyathi shakes her head, pouting her lips as if talking to a baby.

Sandrien turns her head away, as if interrogating the thickening darkness. She uncrosses her legs, crosses them again. 'No,' she says slowly, 'my body refuses music. I only come close to singing when agony is at its worst. Then I make small noises under my breath. When I was ill, I sang like that, if you can call it singing.'

Mrs Nyathi stares at her. 'I sang for my patients sometimes, at night when they were dying.'

A tiny trail of sound, Sandrien thinks, illuminating the route.

Mrs Nyathi gets up and goes inside. She leaves her glass half-full on the table, perhaps annoyed that Sandrien has permeated the air with such sudden gloom. Sandrien stays until the fires of Vloedspruit burn out one by one. She is a revelation to herself in Mrs Nyathi's company.

She rolls around in her bed, then dozes off restlessly. Not long afterwards, drunken girls' voices wake her.

Mrs Nyathi stands in her bedroom door. 'He is here for you,' she says.

'Who?' asks Sandrien.

Mrs Nyathi winks.

It is Walter Mabunda. He has brought plums in a basket.

How squeaky clean the little rolls of fat in his neck are, she thinks when he bends over and delicately removes one of the fruit. He sits forward with a slight groan, holds it out to her between fingertips. She waves it away.

'Mr Mabunda – '

'Call me Walter.'

He bites into the plum with precision. It is the same colour as his lips.

'Walter, I don't want to make assumptions, but let me immediately clear up any possible misunderstandings. I am a married woman.'

He nods his head slowly. 'Oh, but a married woman of exceptional beauty!'

He looks at her shoulders.

She attempts to resist his gaze. From the corrugated-iron houses voices are carried uphill by the wind. A few large flakes of ash drift onto the veranda.

'I notice that the village market was almost completely washed away.'

'Yes,' Walter says, and shakes his head with a concerned frown. 'Unfortunately they built it on a flood plain. But I'm going to make an investment,' he says, and pushes out his chest. 'I'm going to erect stalls. The government will help with funding. Shirley Kgope's brother will build it for us. He was also the contractor for the college.'

His gaze rests in the vicinity of her chest.

A moth with false eyes on its wings descends on Walter's cleanly shaven head. It flies up as he bends over to her.

'Just be careful. People have their ways here.'

She does not know what he is trying to convey.

Then he talks loudly, his voice high, as if meant to be overheard. 'But, yes, my enterprises and investments are nothing. Your Mrs Nyathi,' he gestures with his head over his shoulder, 'she has her contacts, oh yes she does! It is thanks to her that the college was built. And look what she got out of it.' He gestures towards the house.

After Walter has left, when they are sitting on the veranda above the village lights and fires, Mrs Nyathi says, 'Yes, your

Mr Mabunda got himself a nice little egg with that college. He knows how to wangle things.'

Sandrien does not enquire further. She is thinking of the slap in the bathroom earlier.

As if in response to her thoughts, Mrs Nyathi says, 'There are things here that you would not understand, that aren't your business.' Mrs Nyathi smiles sweetly, holds her tumbler of brandy aloft in a vague toast to someone's health.

'Who built the original market at the bottom of the hill?' Sandrien asks, not to be deterred.

Mrs Nyathi thinks for a moment.

'Dr Kgope's brother,' she says, her eyes slits. Her pupils dart back and forth. Then her head nods forward and her eyebrows rise. 'She made a nice profit herself, our Shirley. Yes, that Shirley. Always so hush-hush.'

Sandrien is tired of Vloedspruit tonight. Apart from Dr Kgope's useful lectures about antiretrovirals and the prevention of mother–child transmission, she is not sure she is gaining any wisdom. She is relieved the six weeks are almost over.

'By the way, I'll be glad if someone could inform Mr Mabunda that I am not susceptible to courtship.'

Through the veils of sleep she is waiting for the precipitation. She can hear it rumbling in the distance. She wakes up; it has arrived. Thundering against the corrugated-iron roof and windowpanes. She jumps up and jerks open the curtain. The ground is white. Hailstones are bouncing off the roofs. She is standing there, her body like a lamp, waiting for the glass to break. Moments after Mrs Nyathi pulls her away by the arm from behind, it happens: glass flying where she was just standing.

The moment the hailstorm has passed, Mrs Nyathi summons some of her maids. They appear out of the rain to nail wooden boards to the broken windows. They clean up and dry the floors, change wet linen.

Sandrien fails to fall asleep again.

When she walks through Vloedspruit one last time the next morning, she notices the extent of the damage. Glass and blades of corrugated iron slice into the ground. A woman stops her at the market premises. The parts of the market that were still standing before have now gone too. The woman waves her arms. She is arguing animatedly, as if Sandrien is the cause of the floods, and responsible for repairing the market. Sandrien gives her money. The woman will not let her go. She sinks down on her knees in the mud, holding Sandrien back by her sleeve.

A downy feather descends on the kneeling woman's forehead. Sandrien looks up. Feathers are floating on the breeze. She shakes loose. She follows the feather trail. Like seeds at harvest time, down is hovering above the marshy area next to the river. Men are wringing the necks of herons and hacking off heads with pangas. Sometimes more than one blow is required. Dozens of water birds are dotted around, flapping with broken wings or trying to escape on snapped legs. The men do not even have to run to catch up with them.

'Your van is ready.' Sandrien clenches her fists after putting down the receiver: a minor triumph. The paperwork for her appointment at the municipal health department has been dragging on for more than two months. Since her return, she has been driving to the neighbouring farms with Kobus's pickup truck. He had to postpone transporting his cattle feed, had to walk to his herd of Ngunis. First of all she went to Grace, of course. She looked slightly better than when Sandrien had left for Vloedspruit. Her raw coughing fits could still not move the dust gathering in her lungs, but she was out in the sunshine, washing laundry.

For the umpteenth time she calls the municipal health director, her new boss. The phone just keeps ringing. She has to speak to the director to formalise her duties; she plans to drive straight to Aliwal North once she has received the vehicle.

'*That* thing? That's my van?'

The man from the divisional council shrugs. 'Dordrecht got a new one and threw this one out. It'll have to do.'

She walks around the vehicle. It looks almost like an ambulance, a pickup truck with a steel box on the back, yellow and red stripes down the sides underneath thick dust. When the doors at the back swing open, vapours of vinyl and iron emanate. The man helps her to hose off dust. The battery has to be jump-started.

Hardly a hundred metres away, the engine cuts out. She does not get out, stays sitting in the heat. Drops are evaporating from the windscreen. In the rear-view mirror, she sees the divisional council man approaching.

'The immobiliser,' he says, 'always been broken. What a time to start working.' He hands her a device, shows her which buttons to press, wiping sweat from his black cheeks with a white handkerchief.

*

54

In front of the municipal offices in Aliwal North there is a row of red geraniums. There is no one at Reception. She walks deeper into the building. The health director's offices are locked.

'We're getting a new director,' a secretary with a soggy chip between her fingers says. She puts it in her mouth. 'Come again next week.'

Back at Dorrebult she scrubs out the van. She checks all the medicine, throws out things that have expired. She washes the little cabinets, the steel floors and roof, scrapes old spots of blood from the examination bench. Plastic syringes that have baked brown in the sun crumble when she touches them. Kobus welds the rickety shelves firmly against the sides. She takes curtains from her laundry and hangs them in front of the back windows.

When she is done at dusk, she calls Kobus and they observe the vehicle in the bare yard. Except for the red and yellow stripes, it is almost white again, the Dordrecht Municipal Health Services address still on the back. Sandrien wishes it were pure white with a single red cross on each side.

Kobus nods his head.

'It is ready,' he says, 'your miniature clinic.'

His fingers are counting the vertebrae in her lower back. Her sleeves are rolled up. Her blood is flowing.

The corners of her demarcated area are Smithfield, Colesberg, Burgersdorp and Aliwal North. In the next two weeks, she drives to every farm in her district. In the mornings, she departs at dawn. After the first week, she is quiet over dinner, a slice of bread and a hard-boiled egg for both her and Kobus.

'I could not have imagined,' she says. 'Invisible, just on the other side of these hills. Like proverbial flies. Under grain bags in the dusk. Dozens of them.' She touches her forehead. The sore, sharp corners of bodies: they now populate her dreams.

Kobus says nothing, presses her hand underneath the table. She walks through the cool house, heading for bed without having eaten, ready for an early start.

When she enters the offices in Aliwal North, it is Lerato who is sitting there. She is leaning back in the chair, filling it.

Lerato calls out gregariously, as if old friends are reuniting. '*Meisie!*'

'Lerato?'

'But I'm the new director, *meisie!* See?' She points to the nameplate on the door.

'I had no idea.'

'We must talk, we must talk. You're one of my nurses, aren't you? A travelling one at that.'

'There are lots of things we have to discuss, yes.'

'Wait, wait, let's get a quick lunch.'

Lerato takes her to the Wimpy at the petrol station.

'See,' says Lerato when she has managed to get comfortable, 'this is a meeting. Get it? A me-eating.' She roars with laughter.

'Lerato, I have to get straight to the point. The situation is beyond belief. The numbers of HIV patients in my area are unimaginable. I don't know what my predecessor did, but nobody is on antiretrovirals and children aged five have not had any vaccinations. On most of the farms they cannot remember when someone last – '

'Wait,' says Lerato. She orders a milkshake from the passing waitress. 'Oh, and there's the mayor!'

Lerato waves. The mayor's car window shifts down. His head is as round as a bullet. He smiles from behind his sunglasses. Lerato struggles out of the booth with a sigh, instructs the waitress to pack her food and have it delivered to the municipal offices.

Over her shoulder, handbag tucked under the arm, she shouts, 'Send me your agenda, *meisie*, then we'll set up a proper meeting!'

Sandrien stays behind in the booth. At the petrol pump Lerato leans into the mayor's window. He says something and she laughs. Then she gets in on the passenger side. The dark window closes and they drive away. Sandrien pays the bill. An icy milkshake is left behind on the table.

That same evening she faxes a long report to Lerato. She requests clinic facilities in Venterstad one day per week. She lists requirements: HIV testing kits, vaccinations, a long list of medicines. The items at the top of her agenda are a discussion about the provision of antiretrovirals and strategies for the prevention of mother–child transmission.

A week later, not having had a response, she calls. The secretary answers. Lerato has allocated an office in Venterstad to her, the secretary tells her. She immediately drives there. When she finds it, it turns out to be a small storeroom. She drives to the farm again, where she collects a table and two chairs. Back in Venterstad, she arranges these as best she can. She then builds shelves with bricks and planks that she finds behind the building. Driving to the farm once more, she looks down Venterstad's white, dusty streets. The town buildings are mostly run down, nailed shut. The only movement is at the town bar, a small brick building with one window behind bars and a steel gate in front of the open door. A man exits and gets into his pickup truck. When he is gone, the street is empty.

'The entire team together again, aren't we?' says Dr Shirley Kgope, and smiles when Sandrien tells her about Lerato's new position.

They are sitting in Dr Kgope's air-conditioned office in Colesberg. Sandrien is excited to hear that Widereach is establishing a branch and that Dr Kgope has moved here to become the regional representative.

'The government policy regarding antiretrovirals has been so complicated and so defensive for such a long time, and there has been so much hostility towards NGOs who want to provide them,' says Dr Kgope. 'The policy of course changed some time ago, but in practice it's not simple. Let me get back to you on this. I'm still new and am trying to gain influence. Currently it is not Widereach's policy to provide antiretrovirals to government agencies, especially when we're not managing the infrastructure. Let's see how things work out.'

'But surely you understand the urgency of this matter, probably better than anyone else!'

'Believe me, I get it.' Dr Kgope's head nods slowly. 'We can let you have HIV testing kits immediately. But antiretrovirals? Much more problematic.'

Sandrien starts her rounds on Helpmekaar, where Grace lives. It used to be her parents' farm; now it belongs to her and Kobus. Here, in the outbuildings, was the weaving mill. At ninety-three, Ma Karlien is roaming through the half-remembered rooms of the homestead, wasting away. She refuses to move in with Kobus and Sandrien. Sandrien can recognise nothing in her mother of the woman she remembers. And it is someone other than Sandrien whom her mother is searching for in the dim rooms.

To prevent their labourers from obtaining lifelong tenure on the land, her parents let most of them go a few years ago. Only Grace, her daughter Brenda, and Xoliswe are left. Grace's other daughter, Alice, is dead. Grace is looking after Alice's baby. Brenda is looking after Ma Karlien.

Sandrien ties Grace's granddaughter to her back with a blanket while doing pap smears and drawing blood from the three women. When she is done, she sits down, right up against Grace. There is a small gust of wind. Grace's upper body sways slightly, and Sandrien feels the joints hinging inside Grace.

'I cannot stay for long; I have many other farms to take care of. I'll come again tonight.'

She rinses clothing for Grace, washes the child's cloth nappies, builds and lights a fire. Further promises are on the tip of Sandrien's tongue. As she drives away, she looks in her side mirror. Black veils of soot cling above the windows and doors of Grace's little house.

'At least I can do HIV tests now,' says Sandrien, 'thanks to Widereach.'

Lerato sits authoritatively behind her desk, arms folded.

'Look,' she says, 'the government also gives testing kits. But work with the Americans instead if you want.'

'I cannot get antiretrovirals from them.'

Lerato looks through the window. 'Have you heard,'

she says, 'that Walter Mabunda is now the provincial MEC for health? We must be careful, they want to completely provincialise health.' But then she brightens and continues. 'I've been invited, and the mayor too, for a hunting weekend at Twilight Lodge. A new hunting farm, a nice posh one. I'm not much of a hunter, but believe me, the mayor is – especially of girls!'

Lerato laughs as if she and Sandrien are conspiring.

'Can you please install a basin for me in my office in Venterstad? I have to sterilise my hands between patients.'

Lerato frowns. She picks up the phone. She looks at Sandrien while she instructs someone to order the basin. See, her expression says, I give the orders here.

'What is the situation with antiretrovirals, Lerato? We all know, after all, that the policy has been for some time to provide it universally.'

'Not so simple, girl. Issues of distribution, of infrastructure. Only doctors may prescribe them. And the issue of patient cooperation. We all know the risks if patients do not comply properly. We can only do what we can do. And what we have money for.'

'And if I can get it elsewhere, how do I get a doctor to prescribe it?'

Lerato frowns. She lifts her chin and looks down her nose at Sandrien.

'We have a lot of vacancies for doctors at the moment. Everything in due course, my *meisie*.'

Sandrien sits with her face in her hands opposite Kobus.

'Yesterday two of my patients died, in a single day. This morning,' she holds out an arm in front of her, 'I lifted a man on the examination table – a twenty-nine-year-old man – like a tiny bird. As I lifted him, the diarrhoea poured out of him over my arm, down my leg.'

Kobus remains quiet for a long time. He does not look up when he speaks.

'You're never here at Dorrebult any more,' he says. 'And even when you're here, you're not really here. You're becoming a stranger.'

When she arrives at her Venterstad clinic, the testing kits are there, compliments of Widereach. Her heart lifts. Each testing kit is in a little suitcase-like box, a clinic-in-miniature. Next to the queue of people in front of her door a basin is lying on the veranda. No pipes, no taps. She calls the works department, insists they come and install the basin today.

'If I haven't got a working basin by lunchtime tomorrow, I will complain to Lerato.'

The man laughs and puts down the receiver.

Late afternoon, after her last patient, she drives to Aliwal North. Dust clouds are emanating from the windows of the municipal offices. Scaffolding and canvas block the way to Lerato's office. A team of workers. Sandrien greets one of them, the husband of one of her sickest patients.

'Where is Lerato?' Sandrien has to shout to render herself audible amidst the din of brick cutters.

'We're renovating,' the secretary shouts back. 'We're remodelling! Lerato's office will be lovely! And double the size!'

She gestures excitedly in the direction of a set of textile samples next to a catalogue of sofas. She turns her head, holds up two pieces of cloth.

'What do you think? Isn't it a charming combination?' When Sandrien retreats, she calls with greater urgency. 'Look,' she gestures, 'look!'

She points to sample paint patches against the wall, shades of grey.

Away from the noise and dust, Sandrien pushes open the door of a cubicle in the ladies. Lerato is sitting on the toilet, skirt around her high heels. She is studying a sheet on her lap: a sketch of an interior.

'Sorry,' Sandrien mutters, and pulls the door shut.

She considers discussing the issue of the basin through the cubicle door, but then stumbles out.

'Wait!' Lerato shouts from the cubicle. 'Come and see the mock-up of my new office!'

When the coldroom's doors swing open, a cloud of vapour rises into the heat. The coffin appears from the cloud. Two men in overalls and gloves are pushing the trolley. The coffin is made of pine, but has been stained and varnished to look like ebony. It is topped by a bouquet of arum lilies. The chilled flowers look fresh and resilient. No sign yet of how fast they will wilt. The carriers lift the coffin and the mourners fall in line behind them. The men in overalls stand back and lock the doors, their delivery complete. Sandrien keeps at a distance. There is singing in the sun, a woman who collapses and has to be held up. The coffin descends into the grave. Afterwards she shakes hands with the family. They react with politeness, distance.

'What do you think of my fridge?'

It is Manie Maritz who has approached Sandrien from behind. The funeral is on Mara, Manie's farm near

Steynsburg. Manie is an acquaintance of Kobus's and one of the few farmers who hasn't sold out to the hunting-farm developers. She arches a quizzical eyebrow.

'There.' He points to the coldroom from which the coffin appeared. 'That's where we keep them fresh. We used to refrigerate slaughtered cattle and game in there. It needed only a few adjustments.'

'Good afternoon, Manie. I see you have some sort of business here.'

He smiles. 'Not quite what one had in mind, but one has to make do.'

Sandrien looks at the people still milling around the grave. Where before there was a field, there are now rows and rows of granite graves, some with turrets or cherubs.

'How do these people afford all of this?'

'This is only the beginning,' he says. 'There's a big feast coming.'

He points to a concrete surface on the other side of the graves on which a large tent has been erected. The mourners are making their way there. 'There'll be slaughtering now. I have two cows ready. They pay in instalments; it's a long-term business. One has to manage it carefully. I have arrangements with farmers to dock wages if payments become overdue.'

Sandrien leaves without saying goodbye to Manie. She will not be attending another funeral.

Sandrien and Kobus leave for Bloemfontein before dawn. She is going for her quarterly tests and scans. She had wanted to cancel her appointment, but knew Kobus would refuse. On the sonar screen in the oncology ward they see how the antihormone treatment is making the milk gland in the remaining breast atrophy. After the hospital visit, they pick up the twins at the school residence for lunch. When she sees them, she realises she has not spoken to either of them for over a month. They sit with the girls in a shopping centre over bland plates of food. The twins are sullen, as is usual these days. Sandrien suddenly becomes impatient to be back in her van, working. She forces herself to stay put.

In the car on the way back from the residence, Kobus peers at her furtively. He rests his hand on hers. 'You don't have to feel guilty about these privileges, even though there are people dying in the dust. The world is a broken place, but you did not create it.'

She pulls her hand from underneath his, looks out at the pale winter lawns.

On her way from one outer corner of the territory she serves with her van to the other, she stops at home.

'When last did you visit your mother?' Kobus asks. 'I was there this morning to take supplies, and she's not looking good.'

'What's wrong?'

'Have you forgotten, Sandrien? She's over ninety years old. She's fraying around the edges, she's drifting into oblivion. You've hardly been there once in the months since you've been back. And that little maid who looks after her –'

'Brenda, Grace's daughter.'

He shakes his head. 'It's not working. Too brusque, too little empathy.'

'I'll drop by.'

Her head is bent forward; she has started writing medicine labels at the dining table and sticking them onto amber bottles.

'You're not looking that good, either. You're losing weight.'

She keeps writing.

Kobus is on his way out, to church. He knows better than to ask her along.

'Surely one wants to be part of some community?' he said one previous Sunday morning.

She was sitting at the dining table, writing on vaccination cards.

'I have my community,' she said without looking up.

Now too she keeps on writing. Closing the door, he sighs quietly.

'It isn't looking good,' her oncologist says the following day on the phone.

'The enzyme tests are suggesting renewed cancer growth, but we need further tests to determine the location. Can we make an appointment for you?'

'It won't be necessary, thank you.'

He remains silent for a moment.

'Surely you understand the need, the urgency.'

'I appreciate your concern.'

For days on end she tries to get hold of Walter Mabunda at his provincial offices. As a last resort, she calls Mrs Nyathi.

'Do you still have contact with Walter?' she asks. 'Would you know how to get hold of him?'

'Of course,' says Mrs Nyathi, 'we talk often. He was once my husband, after all!' She laughs.

Sandrien remembers the set of friendly teeth. Mrs Nyathi always catches her unawares.

'No, that is news to me, Mrs Nyathi. I was under the impression that you're a widow.'

Half an hour later Walter calls Sandrien. She takes a deep breath. 'I am informed that you're an important man now, Walter.'

He laughs his lazy little laugh.

'You know, I serve the community according to my abilities, Sandrien. Make my contributions where I can.'

'Well, Walter, I similarly try to make my contributions. But there is one respect in which I feel myself severely handicapped.'

'And what would that be?'

'See, I run a mobile clinic in the municipal district of Aliwal North. And this brings me in contact with the ill, especially the large number of people who, as you know, have HIV or Aids in advanced stages. People are dying, Walter. My patients are dying in droves. How would I go about obtaining antiretrovirals for them? How do we turn things around? Government policy about this, after all, changed some time ago.'

'Hmm,' he says, 'Edith Nyathi told me what you were doing these days. You may know that we want to provincialise health. We could use someone like you well.'

'You know, Walter, I feel flattered. Politics aside, though, what about the antiretrovirals?'

'Well, you know, it's a complex matter, this. Funds, budgets, jurisdictions, infrastructure . . . You can imagine. Hmm.' The alto voice, the camp voice.

She remembers the finely stitched shoes, his beer belly underneath the perfectly ironed shirt. For a while neither of them says anything; they are contemplating the silence.

'You can come and discuss the matter with me here,' he says.

'If it would make a difference, yes,' she says. 'Port Elizabeth is far, though, and I prefer to be near my patients if possible, not to spend an entire day away from them.'

'Hmm,' he says. 'Why don't you come to PE for a weekend? Come and stay with me. I have a swimming pool and all.'

A feeling of despair takes hold of her.

When she does not immediately object, he continues: 'I have no doubt that you are still as beautiful a woman as always.'

She takes a breath. 'Walter, I am desperate to obtain medication. Over the last eight months I have seen eight people die. What can be done?'

'Hmm, come for a weekend. You won't regret it. A swimming pool and all.'

She visits Lerato once again. She is cool towards Sandrien. Has she got wind of the fact that Sandrien approached the province?

'I don't want to tell you something that you don't already know, Lerato, but there is enormous urgency. As I understand it, the central government policy is now clear, namely universal provision –'

'Understand one thing,' Lerato says, her finger tapping irascibly on the desk, 'we don't do hurry here.' She presses an index finger to her chest. '*I* set the pace.'

*

Seven days a week, she travels the dirt roads and tarred roads. The backlog on vaccinations has been cleared. Pap smears, blood tests and children's diseases make up the routine. She is waging a war against the odds with her Aids patients. She feeds them tiny spoonfuls of porridge. She looks after the children; helps the children to look after sick parents; helps orphans to look after younger children. She treats infections, tries to halt diarrhoea. She rubs feet. (Gently; the bone is just below the skin.) Early on a Sunday morning she loses another. A man, completely blind, walks straight into the veld. He falls on his face and stays like that.

'I think there is the prospect of a solution, Sandrien. I think we can stay at Dorrebult, make it work again.'

Kobus has returned from Venterstad's bar. His eyes are shining. As always after a few drinks, he is talkative and awkward, like a boy who has done something naughty.

'Manie from Mara was in the bar. He has a proposal. You know about his funeral business. He says you've seen his facilities. At first, he only set aside a hectare or so for graves. It's almost full – he's expanding. He's also an undertaker. He provides coffins, embalming, flowers, the lot. The coldrooms that they previously used for cattle carcasses now chill cadavers. These people's funerals are also feasts, you know, they slaughter cattle every time. The profits are phenomenal.'

She stares at him. His face is beaming.

'He wants to sell off land, and all his cattle, to invest more in the business. In the future, he wants me to be the exclusive provider of slaughter oxen.'

She does not say a word. He takes a deep breath.

'Sandrien, you know we are here on borrowed time. Even on Dorrebult and Helpmekaar together, we can't make a living from the land. When last did we earn a liveable income? Four, five years back? Input costs are going through the roof, prices are falling. All that works here now is game farming. And where would we get the capital to develop a game farm?'

'Why don't we just burn the dead in piles outside?' She hears herself, her tone calm and lethal. 'Then we'll live in eternal shadow, with a cloud of ash between us and the sun.'

'Be reasonable, Sandrien.' He is now pleading like a child. 'The dead must be buried. And what else? Do you think your endless driving with a steel box on dusty roads pays more than the children's school fees? All you're doing is alienating our neighbours. You're making the owners of the hunting lodges queasy, you're startling their guests. I can see how they suddenly fall silent when I enter the bar.' He sits back, his shoulders hanging. 'I must do *something*, Sandrien, we must live. One must adapt, one must naturalise. In this way, you start belonging here.'

When she speaks again, she does so slowly and emphatically. 'If you make as much as a cent from the slaughter, Kobus, I will never look you in the eye again.'

A shadow across his face.

Between Knapdaar and Burgersdorp the van swerves and skids some distance across the dust. It comes to a halt with the front end in a thorn bush. Her chest has hit the steering wheel with a thud. She gets out and walks around the vehicle. The left front tyre has burst. Oil is dripping through the grid over dry leaves. She pushes the vehicle a few metres back, almost collapsing from exertion. She sits down in the dust. On the horizon appears a cloud the size of a man's fist. She takes dust in her hands and rubs it in her hair, over her white uniform. It sifts through her lashes. When the silence releases the sobs, she stuffs a handful in her mouth, but it does not dampen the sound. The sobs multiply and roll in a cloud back to her across the plain. Her teeth grind on dust. She opens her eyes. The bush bursts into flame. It hisses like a blowtorch. She sits utterly still until it burns down to the roots, until the ash settles in a pattern around the stump.

She gets up.

Where the spare tyre should be is an empty hole. She drives to Aliwal North with rubber flapping around the rim. She parks in front of the municipal office. Lerato is pushing two combs in her hair in front of the mirror behind her desk. She observes Sandrien in the mirror, swivels around on her chair. Dust is sifting from Sandrien, her eyes are glowing.

'Sit,' says Lerato. She points to the chair.

'People are lying out there, dying,' Sandrien says from where she is standing, 'like dried-out hides. Where are my ARVs?'

'I have told you,' Lerato's face is hard, 'we can only do what we can do.'

Sandrien hits her open hand on the desk, so hard that small clumps of earth fall out of a plant pot.

'No!' Sandrien pulls in her fists against her stomach. 'We can do more, much more!' *We can find the divine fibres in our weak flesh, the undiscovered grace in our entrails!* she wants to add, but she has said enough.

Lerato gets up with less effort than might be expected of her bulky frame.

'Out,' she says in a deep, cold voice. 'If you can't show me respect, then you may as well go to Scandinavia. If you don't like your job, don't think we need you here.'

When she returns, Kobus is sitting in the dusk at the dining table. He has spoken to her oncologist. 'So, now you're going to sacrifice yourself for this cause with which you have burdened yourself,' he says. 'You're now going to obliterate your body.'

'It's not me, it is the course of the disease. I've tried treatment. Whether I want to endure further interventions is surely a personal choice.'

He swallows, peering into the dark corner of the room. He wipes his eyes. She does not say anything. The line of his chin hardens.

'What sense does it make to surrender everything for the sake of a struggle within a system that despises you?'

'The system is irrelevant, it's about the victims. They are my struggle. I don't want to reduce what's left of my life to the parochial sorrow of the privileged cancer sufferer.'

It is now almost completely dark.

'Do you remember,' he says, 'how a hunter's dog once got its paw stuck in a jackal fence here on the farm? When I got there, the leg was so infected that the dog would not allow me near it. I could let him suffer or could let myself be torn apart. I shot him through the head. In this way I brought relief. It affected me, but this was what I could do.'

She looks at his outline. The light glints on his eyebrows.

It is her turn. 'Do you remember the time when a dog made its way into the sheep-pen? How cruelly dogs play with trapped sheep? How we disinfected cotton thread and spent all night in the kitchen sewing up – no, weaving back together – shredded stomachs? How raw our hands were? How we didn't stop until they were whole again?'

She keeps her eyes fixed on the furthest point in the dirt road. She notices that when she keeps up the speed she stays awake. She keeps getting stronger. From here in her cab, her control room, she will be able to keep everyone safe. Soon she will be able to carry all the dying. She will hold them in the palm of her hand, the ill of the Eastern Cape – no, of the entire scorched hinterland. When she enters one of the game farms, she notices how the Americans with their shiny guns observe her from their Jeeps. Probably a pitiful sight in her dust-smeared van and soiled uniform. Probably just a matter of time before the owners forbid the mad woman with the wild hair from entering their land.

She is dizzy when she arrives at Shirley's office. She is now watching over her patients at night. She drips water through dry lips, lays damp cloths on hot foreheads. Now and then she takes a moment for herself, gulping fresh air outside, bathing in the cool flood of starlight. Then she stoops again, entering under low corrugated iron or reed-and-mud ceilings. Next to drums in which coal hisses, she sings shy songs she makes up to bring a little peace.

Shirley looks Sandrien up and down when she steps onto her office carpet. There is a voice on her speakerphone. She picks up the receiver, brushes over her pencil skirt as if it has dust on it too. She cups one hand over her mouth, cuts off the phone conversation.

'I'm afraid,' she says to Sandrien, 'our biggest donors have started shifting their funds to prevention. And in future, the emphasis will be on abstinence campaigns, rather than condom use. The distribution of antiretrovirals may well be phased out.' She shrugs her shoulders in an exculpatory fashion. 'These are the values of Middle America: we're talking faith-based organisations. Those are the ones now holding the money. And the donors elect our board. We have to move with the times.'

'On a personal note,' she continues, 'I'm on my way back to the US. Been offered work in Houston. I've been outside the laboratory for too long. Yes, probably less excitement than here. But Houston has good steaks, so I hear.'

She smiles unaccountably. Sandrien is certain the voice on the phone earlier was Lerato's.

Next to the television a woman is standing in the dark. It is her goatskin wristband on which Sandrien focuses. On the hissing television screen: electric snow. It is the first time in weeks that Sandrien is visiting the Helpmekaar homestead. It is six o'clock, the winter afternoon heat over, the curtains all closed. She was relieved to find her mother asleep. While searching for Brenda, she heard something in the erstwhile guest room. Then she encountered this stranger. And she knows what that wristband means.

'What are you doing here?'

Apart from the television, the room is almost unfurnished. There is a small soft hide (hare?) on the floor.

It's Brenda who answers from behind Sandrien: 'She has come to give medicine.'

Sandrien turns around.

'Who gives you the right to bring a sangoma here? What do you want to do to my mother?'

'Not your mother.'

'What do you mean? She's still my mother, even though you're caring for her, and irrespective of how often I come here.'

'What I'm saying, is that she's here for *my* mother. She's here for Grace.'

Sandrien's eyes flash. Now, only now, the fury is causing blotches to spread on her neck.

'If you so much as touch Grace, if you give her anything . . . '

Brenda steps right in front of Sandrien, looking her fiercely in the eye. 'She is not yours. What are you doing for anyone anyway? Everyone you visit dies. They die like animals, one after the other.'

They stare at each other.

'She doesn't belong to you,' Brenda says again. But without conviction. She shrinks back.

'So, when are you coming for a visit? Port Elizabeth is waiting for you.'

There is static on the line. As if a sparrow were sitting on the line, somewhere between Sandrien and the sea. She closes her eyes, imagines the little bird drying out and being scorched clean. In her mind's eye she blows off the skeleton with a single breath.

'I'm calling because I need something. Painkillers. Something stronger than the aspirin I get from the municipal authorities. Much stronger.'

Or perhaps an insect on the line, the feet of a gnat.

'Tell you what. Send a photo. We can always deliver something to your seniors over in Aliwal. Let's start with that. View it as a small investment. When you come to visit, we'll continue the conversation.'

'I want to have it in Venterstad, couriered to me directly. I know how influential you are after all, Walter. You are at the helm over there, aren't you?'

The line is rustling with the secret language of the most insignificant creatures, the little insects that are scattered by the wind.

'Hmm, it's tough. Medical protocol, legal implications . . . you know.'

'Do you want a picture or not, Walter?'

'Yes, yes, send it. I'll do what I can.'

'Give me your email address.'

She scans an old family photograph, taken from Helpmekaar's veranda. She trims it, cuts off Kobus, her mother and the two young daughters (not yet steady on their feet). Only she remains. She is young and her shoulders are bare. Her hair is glowing in the sun. Behind her the landscape is dry and bright. She enlarges the picture until her laughing features start disintegrating into pixels and then she sends it off.

Late afternoon she drives to Twilight Lodge, the new hunting farm north-east of Smithfield. It is a warm winter's day, even more scorching here than at Dorrebult. She remembers this place, she realises when she enters the farm through newly built stone gates. She remembers a picnic here with her school friends decades ago, in a lush gorge, when the farm was still called Twyfelsand. Twilight Lodge lies outside Sandrien's territory, but Xoliswe conveyed the message through Brenda that her sister lived there and was gravely ill.

The corrugated-iron shack stands on its own, away from the labourers' cottages. When Sandrien stops, a dusty child points wordlessly to the shack and disappears. No other sign of life. Not a tree or blade of grass in sight. She has to crouch to enter, a fluffy Glo-fibre blanket hanging over her arm. The heat is hanging thick in the gloom. The woman, she knows instantly, is not from here, nor is she Xoliswe's sister. She is painfully thin, with long bones and taut skin. Ethiopian, perhaps. Sandrien has difficulty breathing. The walls are black, the ceiling is black. Coal is burning ceaselessly in a drum. The bedding is black, the cast-iron pot on the floor is black. The water in the pot is black, so too the hessian hanging in the door opening. Apart from the bed and the pot, there is nothing. There has been no food here for ages, nor another human being. And the flies: the flies are the blackest of all.

All night the woman keeps making little animal noises. Sometimes Sandrien thinks there is a melody and sleepily hums along. At three o'clock the woman sits upright. A cold fire lights her up from inside. She laughs and hits Sandrien with the back of her hand, smack on the brow. When she falls back, she is dead. So it seems. But then she sucks her lungs full of air and starts singing or groaning until Sandrien dozes off.

A popping sound wakes Sandrien, a gunshot. Near enough to make the shack zing like a tuning fork in the dark. She looks at the black door opening in the black corrugated iron. Her heart races. An unambiguous warning.

Sandrien keeps her eye on the door until daybreak. She lays her hand on the woman's sternum. Where there used to be breasts, there are now ribs. The woman is still breathing, but her feet are cool. It will not be long now. Sandrien must be in Venterstad for the morning clinic. On her way back, she passes a man. He is waiting next to his Land Rover, sunburned arms folded (the landowner?). She lifts a hand in a greeting, but he just stares at her. She looks in the mirror. Her hair is tangled. Next to her eye, there is dry blood.

Before reaching the stone gates, she looks down into the picnic gorge. She catches a glimpse of the new lodge with its complex angles: glass and steel, decks overhanging the gorge; the silver water, above the treetops, of a floating swimming pool. A further memory of Twyfelsand, of that school picnic of her youth, comes to her. After the picnic, she remembers, the children went hiking with the farmer. From the gorge, they wandered to a huge flat rock formation in the hills.

'What would you say happened here?' the farmer asked. The black rock was scattered with bones. Sandrien deciphered the zigzag patterns of the bones and put up her hand.

'Is this where Bantus are fed to the vultures?'

'No, girl,' the farmer laughed, 'where do you get that from? Years ago, lightning struck the iron stone and killed a whole herd of zebras at once. It is their skeletons you're still seeing here.'

When the van exits the gates, Sandrien looks back fleetingly. A thin trail of smoke is trickling upwards. She could not say from where; she has lost her direction.

She has difficulty staying awake on the thundering dirt roads. She is not thinking of the nocturnal gunshot. She is pondering the riddle of the throw under which the coal woman was lying. It was drenched with smoke, but unmistakeable. It comes from the bed in which she herself slept as a child, in the Helpmekaar homestead. Ma Karlien used to come and tuck her in under this throw on winter evenings.

When she arrives in Venterstad, a little box is lying in the sun outside her office. She opens it and blinks in surprise. Ampoules of morphine. If only she had had them the previous night. The uninstalled basin has gone.

After her morning clinic in Venterstad, she drives to Colesberg. She sees the bank manager. It does not take long to increase their credit facility. Without fail, her parents repaid their debts to this bank over the years. So did she and Kobus. Two forms in triplicate and the money is available. She stops at their GP. She explains. He is reluctant. He has not seen any of the patients.

'*I've* seen them. I know their histories by heart.' His face does not change. She goes on. 'My father was your patient,' she says. 'My mother still is. Kobus and I are your patients. And my daughters. We have a history. And this is a matter of life and death.'

The doctor looks at her. She knows she smells. She can no longer get rid of the dust, no matter how often she showers, how she scrubs.

He relents. She gets a prescription on the condition that he would need to see the patients before the first month of treatment is over. She goes to the pharmacy and purchases antiretrovirals for all twenty-seven of her patients for three months. Then she goes home and sleeps.

Her cellphone wakes her. It is the first time ever that Lerato has phoned her. Lerato is overly friendly.

'What are you hearing from Walter?' she wants to know. 'Mrs Nyathi tells me the two of you are talking.'

Sandrien tries to wake up properly. It is as if Lerato is talking to her through a cloud of dust.

'He is the driving force behind the provincialisation,' Lerato continues. 'We have a big fight on our hands, *meisie*, a big fight.'

'I don't think it's my fight, Lerato.'

'No, no,' she says, 'you must help! The health of our people is important. You know that better than anyone.'

'What are you talking about, Lerato? You're unable – or unwilling – to even install one basin so that I could sterilise my hands – '

'Walter has laid a charge against Shirley. It's about money, lots of it. The government's money. He's got influence. The police are investigating it.'

'What does that have to do with you, Lerato?'

'Shirley Kgope is my cousin, surely you know that. And Walter ran to the police, telling them that she and I are in cahoots. She's going to disappear to the US. And yours truly will stay behind to face the music.'

'No, I didn't know you were family, Lerato. All these connections make me dizzy. And I don't know what my involvement is supposed to be.'

'Wait, I'll make you a deal.'

'I have to go, Lerato, my patients are waiting. I don't understand what you mean.'

'It's ARVs you want, isn't it? Well, I'll get them for you. As many as you want. It's government policy, after all.'

At first, Sandrien is too stunned to utter a word.

'What do you believe I can do for you, Lerato?'

'You have to talk to Walter. You must go to him in PE, go spend a weekend with him. He's got a nice, nice place. You know he fancies you rotten. Give him what he wants. And you have to convince him to let go of the corruption investigation. He'll listen to you.'

'By the way,' Lerato says when Sandrien does not respond, her voice now as light as a breeze, 'I hear you're going outside your jurisdiction. And you've caused a patient to die there. You were told your area, you know the boundaries. There are grounds for disciplinary, even criminal, charges.' She waits, lets it sink in. 'Let me know what happens in Port Elizabeth.'

When she enters the house at dawn the next morning, Kobus is waiting for her. He is standing on the slate floor in the entrance hall, a bank letter in his hand. With her body and one of the last remaining Glo-fibre blankets she had kept another patient warm through the night. There was a moment, just before sunrise, when she considered helping herself to the morphine. She smells of vomit and ash.

'You're getting us into serious debt, Sandrien. You're taking food from our children's mouths. What about their school fees, what about the farm? What about our lives, yours and mine?'

She ignores the wateriness in his eyes. 'If we take a second mortgage on the farm,' she says, 'we can pull my patients through until the government can take over.' Her voice is clear, her eyes fiercely blue.

'Your eyes have changed colour,' he says. 'They're now the colour of water.'

He leads her to bed, lets her lie against his chest until she falls asleep.

When she wakes up, a letter is waiting on the sideboard, her name in Kobus's writing on the front.

My dearest,

It is not impossible for me to understand something of the powers that have grabbed you by the heart. I too have a heart. The deaths in the hills around us touch me also. But the degree of your self-sacrifice scares me. And the obstinacy. Somewhere, the light of reason must shine through.

Let me ask you – devil's advocate – whether you're starting to take a certain delight in the misery? I ask myself: could the dogged tenacity of a Mother Teresa and a henchman look the same? Seems to me you want to collapse the pain and stench into one blinding truth. Where do you make the people behind the truth disappear to? And do they understand your abstract manner of saving them?

I don't want to make you choose between your patients and me. But we can't both collapse under the weight of the despair. Why join the ranks of the departing? Is the anguish awaiting us, you and me, invalid? Minor sorrow, you call it, parochial, but is it nothing? And when you've been extinguished, who will be doing the caring then?

Do you know, Sandrien, where I find the truth? In the silence of our bedroom, the flashes of lightning passing between our skins. In the moments when you and I are lying here, under this roof, searching for breath. It is small here, yes, but when I stick out my fingers, I am touching real flesh. And for me that is enough.

What you could do, assuming you wanted to save us, you and me, would be to choose one, one of those under your care, to save. You'll have to let go of the rest. Even that is more than the teetering formal structures could do. Those structures are locked churches. Outside the doors, the sufferers will be scorched to death after devouring the last blade of grass.

Choose one now, Sandrien, or let me go.

Kobus

It is Grace, on foot from Helpmekaar, who is bringing the news on a Tuesday afternoon. Ma Karlien has died.

'Grace, how far have you walked? You can hardly stand up!'

'I saw the house was looking cold,' she says. 'So I went to see. And then she was lying there.'

Grace is looking cold herself; she opens her mouth again, but then forgets to speak, or is unable to. She closes her mouth and waits.

Sandrien takes Grace back in the pickup truck, puts her back to bed. They search in vain for Brenda. Hours later Sandrien finds her where she is squatting behind the dam wall.

'As she was dying, she grabbed me with a mad power. Like this.' Brenda locks her hands around Sandrien's wrists.

'As if she wanted to drag me with her. As if she wanted to have a maid with her in hell.'

Sandrien sees the fear, sees a chance.

'Brenda, that woman you sent me to, she wasn't Xoliswe's sister. And tell me, how did she get the throw from the Helpmekaar homestead?'

Brenda turns away, her mouth like a prune. Sandrien takes Brenda's chin in her hand, forces the face towards her.

'Tell me what's going on here!' She has Brenda by the upper arm.

'They wanted her dead.'

'Who wanted who dead?'

'Everyone. Everyone wanted the black witch dead. The one on the game farm. The sangoma said, "Give her something from the one who kills everyone." So we give the throw. But still she does not die. She lies there in that black cage, breathing, she just keeps breathing. Then the sangoma says, "Send the white witch to the black witch, let the one who brings the plague go and touch her." And so it happened. You went. And you killed her. And my mother? You will do the same to her.'

Brenda tears herself from Sandrien's grip. She runs away over hard ground.

Early that evening, the logistics of death settled, Kobus gets into his pickup truck. The ambulance took hours to reach Helpmekaar. By the time it arrived, the body had become stiff. He returns late from the bar in Venterstad, mildly drunk.

'Ramotle bought drinks,' Kobus says apologetically. 'Only he and I were there.'

He is sitting across from Sandrien, looking down at the table. The alcohol, so it seems, makes him want to drown the words of his letter in a torrent of other words.

'Ramotle has all kinds of news. Blurted out big secrets after a few. You remember I attended the launch of Twilight Lodge a few months ago, and was so surprised they'd managed to get all the planning and environmental approvals? And what a place! Right through to the presidential suite with glass floors above a waterfall. Anyhow. Big story. Believe it or not, after the soccer World Cup, the winning team will be coming to Twilight Lodge to relax for two weeks. All hush-hush. Well, not that discreet. The guys here are arranging parties to which everyone will be invited – municipal and provincial officials, cabinet members, business types, pop singers, you name it. There are even rumours the president will be here, but all low profile.

'The funds are almost unlimited, it seems. They're all getting contracts, the local officials, the lot of them – supply of game vehicles, catering, luxury transport, entertainment, the whole lot. There'll be dancers, acrobats, fire-eaters, a veritable circus here in the hills. They're even importing some grand boat from Austria for a function on the Gariep dam. Originally built to navigate the Rhine. And it all keeps getting bigger. Ramotle was here today to inspect more game farms, looking at the quality of accommodation. The famous people apparently all have a huge entourage. Everyone has to get here, sleep somewhere, eat somewhere . . . And everyone, so it seems, has to party.

'Arrangements have been in process for months. You can imagine how elated Ramotle is about the prospect of so many celebrities and politicians here in his sphere. A real coup, as he refers to it . . . '

He stops, looking swiftly up at her, shy like a schoolboy.

Sandrien remembers Mayor Ramotle with his round head. She saw him at a petrol station in Aliwal. She says nothing of her night at the Twilight Lodge or the warning shot. Her mind is working rapidly, even though her eyes are clouding over with exhaustion.

'Come to bed, Sandrien.'

But she walks into the dark guest room. She does not switch on the light, falls asleep in her clothes.

On Wednesday morning Sandrien leaves for her rounds later than usual. Even in the early morning it is warm. Approaching Helpmekaar around a bend, she notices a car in front of Grace's little house. She stops and gets out the binoculars she inherited with the van. Three figures are trembling in the heat. Brenda is one of them. Next to her is the woman with the goatskin wristband. The third figure, she is convinced, is Lerato. The face is hazy, but the shape unmistakeable. Lerato is handing something to the other two.

Sandrien puts the van in gear. She rattles over the dirt road. When she enters the road turning off to Helpmekaar, Lerato's car is well ahead of her, speeding away towards Burgersdorp. Sandrien turns off. At the end of the straight road, Brenda and the sangoma are standing motionlessly. The sangoma then dashes off to the right; only Brenda remains, standing alone, in the middle of her windscreen. Sandrien pushes down on the accelerator. Thick dust spews out behind the van.

When she stops and gets out, the dust envelops them. Brenda is barefoot, her dress thin, fists against her sides.

'Open your hands!'

Brenda puts her hands behind her back. Sandrien grabs her by the upper arms.

'Show!'

She brings her hands forward and drops five crumpled R100 notes in the dust. Sandrien screws her eyes.

'It's her, isn't it, it's Lerato who had me sent to Twilight Lodge, who bribed the sangoma to play on your superstitions?'

She looks Brenda in the eye. A crafty little operator or a superstitious pawn?

With folded arms, Sandrien awaits Lerato on Thursday morning in the municipal parking area in Aliwal North. Lerato is late; Sandrien has been standing in Lerato's parking spot for hours. On her way in, Sandrien filled up at the petrol station. Through the Wimpy's window, she saw Lerato eating breakfast with Manie Maritz. She considered going in, but decided to come and await her here instead.

'Have you been in PE?' Lerato asks when she sees Sandrien.

'Forget PE, Lerato, forget everything. Just tell me why?'

'What do you mean?'

'You're plotting with sangomas and paying people off. It was you who had me sent to Twilight Lodge.'

Lerato looks at her watch, shifting the designer handbag under her arm. She looks important and bored. Lazily she removes her sunglasses.

'Sangomas also have their place in the public health system.'

'You used me, Lerato. You wanted to threaten me with disciplinary proceedings so that I would help you to influence Walter regarding the corruption allegations, and help you fight your political battles. And on top of that, you wanted to undermine my credibility with the community.'

Lerato looks through Sandrien, at things way beyond her.

Sandrien continues. 'Let me tell you now. If you don't provide ARVs to my patients, then I'll make a formal complaint.'

Lerato throws her head back. She crows with laughter until the tears start rolling.

'*Ag, meisietjie*' – she shakes her head, still overcome with hilarity – 'and to whom will you be complaining? Whose interests do you think are at stake?' She pinches Sandrien's cheek playfully. 'If only you had an idea of the scale of things, of how puny you are.'

Sandrien pushes Lerato's hand slowly but firmly out of her face.

'I have a better idea than you might think. I know of the big plans, about Twilight Lodge.'

Lerato stiffens, her face hard now. She tucks the handbag heatedly under her other arm.

'Let me tell you how things work, *meisie*. Nobody likes death. And you,' she comes closer still, her index finger against Sandrien's chest, 'shove it into people's faces. Shortly we'll have important guests. You have no idea who you're irritating. Be careful, *meisie*, be careful.'

Lerato turns around, walks away.

*

From Aliwal, Sandrien drives to Mara. Upon entering the farm, she sees two men with their hands in the soil. They are digging small holes, like graves for birds. She stands outside the house, so that Manie has to come outside. He greets her stiffly.

'Geologists,' he answers when she asks about the men. 'Where the graves are currently located, the ground is as hard as stone. A bugger to dig there. And bloody expensive. Soil structure determines profit. I'm looking for the most appropriate place for expansion.'

Sandrien does not answer, turns her back towards the graves and the diggers.

Manie starts relaxing, points out outbuildings on the other side of the house. 'Look,' he says, 'a new crematorium. I converted the ovens where we used to smoke meat.'

She turns towards him. 'What are you up to with Lerato, Manie?'

'Sandrien, you are meddling now. But, if you must know, I'm having discussions with her about formal permissions for the expansion. This kind of business is strictly regulated. And so it should be.'

'It's not only permissions she's wangling for you, is it, Manie? What else do you pay her for?'

He is quiet for a long time. Then he speaks softly. 'Business is business, Sandrien. And survival, survival.'

She nods, speaks with a deep and slow fury. 'I understand,' she says. 'Your business is death. And the condition for survival a steady supply of cadavers.'

He turns around and enters the house, closing the door behind him.

*

Sandrien misses Vloedspruit's storms, the waters rushing down from the mountain and the violence overhead. She misses the way in which the electricity in the sky incites the skin. The storms have something to do with why she calls Mrs Nyathi that Friday, why she is looking for answers from her, for consolation or explanations.

In her mind's eye, she can see Mrs Nyathi in a rocking chair in the lounge, throw over her knees, her legs too short to touch the floor.

'Mrs Nyathi, I don't want to involve you in all of these things, but let me tell you anyway – '

'Oh, I'm hearing all the stories, you know. Yes, I have my sources – Walter, Shirley, the rest. I heard how Lerato and her hangers-on lured you. But her henchman couldn't go through with his job and just warned you in the end.'

Sandrien can hear how she carefully takes a sip of her brandy.

'Henchman? Job?'

'Don't err about motives. The forces are greater than you reckon. You're nothing to them, just a thorn in the flesh to be got rid of.'

Sandrien can hear someone whispering something to Mrs Nyathi in the background. Mrs Nyathi suddenly strikes her as a puppet master. Her instinct is to put the receiver down, and that is what she does.

Ma Karlien's funeral is arranged for the weekend. Saturday, after the service, refreshments are served in the homestead at Dorrebult. Sandrien asks the twins, home for the weekend, to look after the guests. She only stays for half an hour. When she pulls away in her van, her daughters look at her with the same expressions as when they arrived at Dorrebult for the first time in months, no longer as children, but as guests. The punctured exhaust drones. She has become the district's batty woman, she realises. She does not give a fig. Her people are waiting elsewhere. Let one of her patients come here, let him fall over like a stick, a piece of driftwood amidst the scones and rattling saucers. Let them see. She does not look at Kobus where he remains standing, helplessly, on the veranda. The departing with the departing, Kobus. Thus we join the ranks.

On Monday they move Grace to the Helpmekaar homestead, she and Brenda. Who, other than Brenda, could help her? They carry her into the house between them on a sheet, slip her onto Ma Karlien's iron bed. Over the weekend Grace has weakened suddenly. Sandrien bends over and turns her ear towards her, the breath barely noticeable against her temple.

'You've become as light as a leaf, Grace,' she whispers.

The blankets under which she is lying are the first two that they wove together. Sparks crackle and chase across the wool when she pulls one blanket over the other. For a second, Grace is surrounded by a pale glow.

Sandrien prepares a bed for herself in her old room. Her creaky childhood bed has long since been replaced. The throw that used to cover it has been cremated or buried with a woman from Ethiopia. The window frames, originally wooden, are now made of steel. But it is still her room.

She walks out to the van to pick up her medicine chest. The morphine, she realises, has been left behind at Dorrebult. The van's headlights do not work. In the dark she drives back with the help of the moon and her memory. Not a single light is on in the house. The door is open. Kobus is sitting at the dining table in the moonlight.

'Sit, Sandrien. Grant me a moment.'

At first she remains standing stiffly in the door, then she sits down. There are four of them: she, Kobus and a blurry face underneath each of them reflected in the shiny wood.

'So, you made your choice,' he says hopefully, but without conviction. 'You've selected one.'

For a long time she does not answer.

'When Grace goes,' she says, 'I'll be bringing the entire district's orphans to Helpmekaar. Not one will be left behind.'

Kobus moves his hands, sits back. For a while he says nothing.

'There is only one way for us to afford that. To make it possible for us to ultimately stay here at all. You know that.'

Back at Helpmekaar, Sandrien sends Brenda away and injects Grace with morphine. She flattens the blanket with her hand, feels the shape of the arid landscape underneath. She imagines a granite lid weighing down on Grace's face, resting on the brittle tips of her cheekbones. She averts her face, leaves the room. She wanders through the interconnected rooms as if over a wide plain, ending up back at Grace's bedroom door. She looks at the ampoules on the bedside table, feels the veins in her own arm.

She sits down on one of the benches on the veranda, back against the wall. Her parents built this house, this veranda with its ironstone pillars. A dry wind starts blowing. On the bench next to her there is a movement, a rustling. She cannot see her – there is only a dark hollow – but she knows it is Ma Karlien. A few swallows slip by.

'I guess I should say sorry, Ma.' It sounds as if she is speaking into ice. 'I forsook you, let you waste away alone in this ramshackle place.'

The wind blows in dark gusts through the garden.

Sandrien holds out her hands, palms up. 'What I can say is that I tried to be of service with these hands. Look: the skin is rubbing off my palms. I am becoming dust.'

Her mother is sitting too far away, in a vacuum over there.

'Here come the swallows now,' she hears her mother sigh. And so it happens. The black birds swerve between the pillars, skim along the veranda ceiling and back out. Swish-swish, they sweep, and their numbers increase, time after time they come, half-possessed, in and through and out and back.

Her voice is hoarse, the dust has settled in her throat. 'I have to go, Ma. Perhaps the birds have come for Grace.'

But there is nothing. The birds have gone. And it is Ma Karlien who has gone with them.

Inside she bends over the bed, her ear against Grace's lips. Her breathing is shallow but regular.

In the kitchen she stands in front of the sink. She smells the thinly worn bar of Sunlight soap and the evaporated staleness from the drain. Her skin crawls. She is occupying the same space as the ghosts of maids who have washed their hands raw here over the years – the maids from her childhood, those of Ma Karlien later. In vain she searches for faces in the windowpane above the sink – faces as worn as the bar of Sunlight soap. Grace's is the only one that appears. She hopes they can forgive her, the ghost-maids and Ma Karlien.

Sandrien keeps a keen eye on the black windows as she wanders through the house, through the chain of rooms, around and around. Thanks to the game farms, so many predators live in the hills these days. Out there, beyond the circle of light, they are already lingering, their saliva like diamonds in the dark. Perhaps she should drag a bench in front of the veranda door and keep watch. One cannot be too careful. If they want to get in, they will have to eat through her first.

But when the weight of granite settles in her mind again, she knows: it is time. Yes, she will pre-empt the predators. She will lift the body from her mother's bed, the body that no longer belongs to Grace. And when she walks out of here (inching her way along, not to scare away the beasts), it will lie lightly on her hands. She will stretch out her arms to the edge of the light, where the yellow eyes dart, and offer what remains.

'Here,' she will say, 'I know you are waiting for us; here she is at last.'

It will be swift, the cleaning up. Just a little bag of snapping bones.

She walks out on the veranda, notices the distant lights of a convoy of vehicles – nocturnal hunters with infrared visors. She rubs her knuckles raw against the ironstone. With a flash of the hand she will summon them tonight: an army of ghosts, ready for battle.

A MASTER FROM GERMANY

Shortly before his mother's death he sees her naked for the first time in his life.

He enters the bedroom. The bathroom door has been left open, in case she should fall or lose consciousness. It frames her: the body shapeless, the small towel she quickly presses against herself too small to cover her lower abdomen. Each pubic hair with a drop of clear water clinging to the tip. They both look away. Later they pretend it never happened.

Let's first go back in time, a few months, to where he is standing, halfway down the cellar stairs, looking up at Joschka. Joschka is hesitant, calling him back, a large old-fashioned key in his hand. They are staying at Joschka's brother-in-law's castle, Burg Heimhof, in the Oberpfalz, not far from Nuremberg.

The castle sits on a rocky promontory, overlooking a quiet little Bavarian valley through which a Harley Davidson roars once or twice a day. The castle has a waterless moat on one side; on the other side it overlooks the edge of the cliff. The moat is overgrown and scattered with rubble. There is an eighteenth-century gate with metal-plated doors and ornamental carpentry. The part of the castle in which they

are standing dates from the eleventh century. It is five storeys high. The oak floors have partially collapsed. The stairs,
too, are broken off in places: as you ascend, they suddenly
vanish. If you look down, you can see through three floors,
all the way to the stairs descending to the cellar. If you look
up, there are pigeons beneath heavy beams, light radiating
through holes in the roof. The broken lines of the floors
and stairs and beams form a three-dimensional diagram,
an optical illusion. It is hard to get a grip on scale. Through
openings in the wall you can see fragments of the valley
and surrounding hills and forests, the hamlet at the foot.
On the metre-wide sills there are birds' nests.

Joschka's brother-in-law, whose parents bought this
castle from the German government for a song shortly after
the war, has been restoring one room on the middle floor
for decades. Painfully precise: wall paintings of knights and
unicorns, floors and ceilings of reclaimed Southern German
oak, torches on the walls. A knight's armour stands in the
corner with a lance clutched in the gauntlet. You could
imagine that he is still in there.

A strange sensation: standing in a beautiful room, but
when you open a door, you are in a ruin.

Or let's go back a week further. Berlin. They are staying
with Joschka's friends Aarik and Wilfred in Kreuzberg.
Joschka lived in Berlin for a few years before moving to
London, where they met. It is Joschka's opportunity to
show him his Berlin, everything from the sublime to the
abject. Mostly the abject.

On the first evening there, they go out on the town.
They move from bar to restaurant to party to bar to party

to underground event to nightclub. They meet friends of Joschka's, and acquaintances. And friends and acquaintances of friends and acquaintances. Joschka snorts too much cocaine in toilets. He moves with purpose, as if heading somewhere, as if his feet are lifting off the street. There are taxis, long walks through wide streets, lifts in speeding cars. From Kreuzberg to Schöneberg to Mitte, to Prenzlauer Berg and back to Mitte. They join people and take their leave, meet and move on: a night of greeting and departure, of random trips and changes of direction. He drinks too much himself, swallows or snorts things he is offered without knowing what they are. There are times when they linger – sometimes it feels like an eternity, sometimes like seconds – in apartments all over town. The places of friends and acquaintances – or those of strangers. Fragmented conversations, shared cigarettes. Apartments overlooking courtyard gardens, one on the Landwehrkanal, a penthouse by the Spree, a place in Mitte deep inside the Hackesche Höfe, another next to the gardens of Schloss Charlottenburg. A place in a massive Communist-era block by Alexanderplatz. Here he stands on a little concrete balcony next to a blonde nymph dressed in metallic tights. The Fernsehturm's sphere hovers above them like a disco ball.

Everywhere there are people; all of them know Joschka. They remember him or know of him, have something to say about him ('*ein wilder Junge*, this guy of yours,' or someone nodding in Joschka's direction, a kind of hero worship in his eyes: '*Der dunkle Prinz des Nachtlebens dieser Stadt, dein Freund*'). Joschka as the dark prince of Berlin nightlife: he is not all that surprised. He meets all of those milling around Joschka, immediately forgets their names again. In one place there are Ulrich, Aloysius, Ebermud, Detlef, Ida and Petra. Elsewhere there are Arno, Theodulf, Finn, Christian, Ava, Till, Lauri, Eriulf, Hilderic, Reiner and Ervig. In diverse places they encounter Sven, Nardo, Hugo and Wolfgang. And then there are also Ladewig, Kai, Adelfriede, Leander, Monika, Arno, Irnfried . . . Or similar names. There is no end to the list.

Later he will be unable to recall large parts of that night. In reality it was probably two or three nights, people and events having since merged. Like shadows observed through a smoke-blackened pane.

There are nevertheless chunks of time he remembers clearly, jutting out like shards of glass.

At some point in the early evening they are at a bar in Kreuzberg. They park on a bridge, descend the stairs and walk along the canal. Ahead of them, lanterns are hanging over the water. Wooden floats are anchored to the banks. On these, people are lying and sitting on cushions under sweet marijuana clouds. Next to the open-air bar counter, someone is spinning über-cool Berlin lounge music. The floats wobble as they walk across them. He gets the feeling, and not for the first time, that Joschka is leaving him behind, that he cannot catch up with him. He can only follow. He looks at Joschka's proud shoulders from behind. It belongs to him, this city, to Joschka. He takes a puff on a stranger's joint, thinking it might help.

'Peace,' the young man says from beneath his fringe when he takes his joint back, as if it were California, circa 1964. The marijuana paralyses his limbs.

Joschka is like a charged wire. The cocaine makes him quick and hard; he walks with heavy feet across the wobbling floats. It is as if he has somewhere to go, something to do. A monumental destination and a heroic act, something requiring superhuman effort. Far ahead of him there appears to be a vision – radiating, blinding – of another city. That which is here, right in front of him, is not enough, just an obstruction in the wide, straight road he is on.

He tries to ignore Joschka for a moment, focusing his attention on the blonde girl next to him (one of many that night), sunk into a pyramid of cushions. A perfect young Aryan specimen. They smile at each other, at first without saying anything. The air is like honey between them. He mentions it. There are fireflies around his feet, and around hers.

'Shhh,' she says, and giggles a little.

With a finger on her lips, she points at the fireflies and whispers: '*Sie möchten Honig trinken.*' They want to drink honey.

She takes him by the hand, pulls him down onto the cushions. He stretches out and starts relaxing, his head against hers, the tips of her hair against his cheek.

'*Wie heisst du?*' she enquires about his name, her sweet breath in his ear.

His tongue is sluggish. '*Was bedeutet schon ein Name?*' What's in a name?

She shudders, folds her arms against the cool air.

'The dew,' she says, 'is falling asleep in the folds of my clothes.'

They both look languidly towards her friend, who is blowing soap bubbles through a plastic ring. The three of them stare with exaggerated astonishment at the shiny little rainbows on each bubble. The blower extends her hand, attempting to catch the bubbles. She fails, then bends forward, slowly, as if burrowing through molasses, and drags her fingers through the reflections of buildings on the water. Underneath him, the float is rocking. He is floating on the shimmering city.

Bubbles keep gliding and bursting. Just the slightest soapy spray remains of each bubble when it disappears. Joschka is behind him unexpectedly, his fingertips resting lightly on his head. It is when he draws back, he knows, or now recalls, when he stops following, that Joschka comes and finds him. He keeps forgetting. His skin erupts in goose pimples. He looks intently at his own sleeve. While he is staring, a drop condenses there, on the black leather. Out of the honey-like air.

With a thick tongue, without looking up, he says, 'How slowly the dew is forming, Joschka: like lava hardening into a landscape, a continent breaking apart . . . '

His eyes close while he is speaking, then open slowly when he forgets his words. Fog is approaching across the water, from below the bridge. It changes the air around the floats, brings a certain restlessness. He tries to look through it, at what is drifting behind it. Joschka's fingers, he realises, are no longer on his head.

' . . . like a pearl growing in an oyster.'

Joschka is not within hearing distance any more.

Other clear fragments: A small restaurant on a busy street in Mitte. Spanish hams hanging above the counter, swaying in the air-conditioning. Joschka is smoking with someone outside – an Ebermud or Wolfgang or Camilla – and crowing with laughter. He is alone in here. The lights are too bright and he is hungry. He keeps looking at the hams. They leave without eating.

A brief interlude at a party in a Jugendstil apartment in Charlottenburg. The ceilings are four metres high and there are wide sash windows on each side. He stares at the graffiti on the ornate ceilings, at the crystal chandeliers, dim with dust. Joschka is standing on his own in the double doorway between the connecting rooms; he has stopped speaking. But his dark beauty is enough, his mere presence. The crowd is still swirling around him, now more than ever. Around his long, thin legs, small buttocks, high, broad shoulders, around his cheekbones, almost Asiatic, sharply chiselled below his black eyes.

An underground party in Kreuzberg. They struggle to find it. The man with them in the taxi will get them in, even though they are not on the guest list. These things are secret, such squatter parties in empty public buildings. At the first whiff, the *Polizei* will come and break it all up. The man is on his cellphone, engaged in endless conversations, trying to establish the exact location. In between the man is giving directions to the frustrated driver. He is talking at breakneck speed. (Is he on amphetamines?) A few harsh words are exchanged. They arrive at what must be an old school or government building. The man on the phone is still getting instructions as they walk. He has a torch; they slip in through a side entrance. They get lost, walk back and forth through corridors and a courtyard; over and over again they turn back and into other corridors. It must be the wrong place – there is no sign of life, just more corridors and windows nailed shut with chipboard.

Then they feel the heavy bass of the music in their bones before they can hear it.

Later, in the early-morning hours: Berghain nightclub in an old power station. The music is hardcore Berlin industrial; it has a sharp silvery velocity, a frequency just short of frenzy. Narrow stairways cut upwards through the colossal central space, in different directions, to different floors. High against the walls are windows, old pulley systems and transformers. Behind the bar: counters, chunks of greasy machinery. On one level, just next to the dance floor, there is a long row of elevated cells. What the original use of these might have been, he could not say. Now couples are standing in these little cages, kissing, visible from two sides. Like something from a science-fiction film: robots learning human emotions, or a laboratory in which the state monitors and controls reproduction. A man climbs out of a cell right next to him. The girl gets out on the other side. The man turns towards him, addresses him:

'*Ich kann mich nicht an deinen Namen erinnern.*' I can't recall your name.

He has never met the man, he is not one of Joschka's crowd. '*Name, mein Freund, ist Schall und Rauch,*' he responds. A name, my friend, is just smoke and mirrors.

Joschka is behind him, wary and suspicious of the stranger. Joschka's eyes are blacker than usual, with lightning in them. Joschka takes him by the hand, leads him to the heat of bodies on the dance floor. They do not move, they just look at each other. Amongst the dancers accelerating like phantoms, they slow down. He rests his head on Joschka's shoulder. Joschka's cool palm folds around the back of his head. Against Joschka's bare chest gleams a slender silver Jesus. Any tension there may ever have been between them, or ever could be, is resolved in such moments. Joschka's other hand is searching for his. There is distress in the hand. Within a split second the entire world falls into place.

A car ride through a deserted Potsdamer Platz with someone, an architect (Kai? Leander? Sven?), pointing out the different buildings. Like a disinfected piece of North America amidst the grittiness. He looks up at the buildings. The rising sun flashes against glass cliffs. There is no one else on the roads.

Back in Aarik and Wilfred's flat. They close the curtains against the morning glow. The curtains are thick, shutting out the light completely. After a few minutes in the dark, Joschka rolls over towards him. There is a vehemence about Joschka. He holds on tightly, his feverish night trip finds a purpose. Joschka directs his head down towards the Jesus on his chest. Two shaven heads like moles in the dark room. The heads bob and nibble, fall backwards and gulp for a different kind of air: the thinner, higher atmosphere. Joschka's straining, all night long, towards something utterly distant, is at an end.

'This is where you've been heading,' he whispers to Joschka. 'I can feel it in you.'

He is infinitely tender towards Joschka, as always. The tenderness is gulped down thirstily. Joschka is visibly flooded with calmness; within seconds he is asleep, head in the crook of his arm. Joschka's short hair under his fingers is as soft as fox fur. *He*, however, is lying with his eyes wide open. The clashing signals in his blood short-circuit his synapses.

Not long after, Joschka is awake. The gleaming city on

the horizon has moved further away yet again. Joschka is searching for a new destination, one inside another body. They are both on their knees on the bed, devouring. Then he tastes iron. Something is wet on his lips and chest. Joschka is undeterred, but he detaches himself. He opens a slit in the curtains, lets the sun in: Joschka naked on his knees on the white sheet. Over his face and chest, bright blood in wild brush strokes. He looks at himself in the mirror. The same. As if he has been tearing at prey.

'Where is it coming from?'

Joschka looks down with amazement, touches his nose, from which, it turns out, blood is pouring uninterruptedly.

'It's me,' he says, 'from me.'

Like the aftermath of an accident, so it seems, or a fight. He looks down too, touches his chest. The silver Jesus has carved him. Two short, deep cuts. Painless.

'And from me.'

Through the slit in the curtains and the open window golden light is shining. A few leaves whirl through; one clings to his upper back. A dove perches on the window sill.

'How darkly he is staggering aloft, how intoxicatingly, your dragon-prince,' the dove says. 'You can expect a terrifyingly beautiful death.'

He is astonished that he can suddenly understand it, the language of birds. Too astonished to engage the dove in conversation.

We are back in Bavaria now, a few days later. Saturday. Joschka locks the oldest part of the castle, *die Ruine* as the family calls it, behind them as they exit. Joschka called him back up from the cellar.

'Who knows,' he said, 'what one might encounter down there.'

The large key is comical in Joschka's hand, a prop for an *Alice in Wonderland* film.

The child, Joschka's nephew, eleven-year-old Maximilian, is showing them the rest of the castle. A serious child. A stout-hearted miniature guide. There is a well-preserved seventeenth-century section, more knights standing heavily in corners, old swords hanging from hooks on the wall. Pointed Gothic windows with lead glass as murky as silt. Maximilian climbs on a sofa with his Nike sneakers and points out Alexander the Great in an oil painting. The Nike-feet keep disappearing in front of him, around corners, up steep stairs carved from stone. Maximilian shows him the three-hundred-year-old toilet. It hangs out over the abyss. Through the stone bowl, one can see all the way to the bottom of the valley. How unlikely his relationship with Joschka is, he thinks while peering down the ur-toilet. In London their lives are light years apart. For eight years he has been a management consultant at one of the prestigious multinational firms. In the beginning he did not think it would last. It would be a role he endured temporarily before switching to something that better suited his temperament and natural rhythms. An academic post, perhaps, or a job at an international NGO. But over the years your resistance to the corporate common denominators weakens: the narrow spectrum of values and driving forces, the agendas and manoeuvres. It seeps into you. You allow your productive capacity to be hijacked. You build a fort. You look after your interests. You accumulate wealth. You make your alliances, you reconfigure your alliances. You plot your route. You persuade, you withhold, you buy off. You play the game. Well, he has had enough of the game. It bores him to death.

And his social circle in London? Of this too he has had more than enough: the small bourgeois clique of ethically minded types. The Oxbridge and Ivy League champagne socialists from Islington and Camden with their polite vegetarian dinner parties where the financial crisis, global warming, Middle Eastern politics, auctions of mid-century Danish design furniture and the Royal Opera House's productions of contemporary opera come up in conversation.

Joschka was the antidote to the whole lot. Joschka awoke him from his slumber, where he was lying on the bottom like a fish with gills hardly stirring. Made him shoot upwards and break through the surface, gulping. Everything that felt self-satisfied and predictable and stale and worn was cast out, all with a snap of the fingers. Joschka does not own a penny and has no interest in pounds. No mortgage, no insurance and no private medical care. He rents a room in the heart of London. He has hands that are capable of anything. Hands that start shaping each day when it breaks. Hands that track the shape of whichever body may be at hand that day. Hands that knead and mould dough. He works as a pâtissier in a Regent's Park restaurant. Each day he throws himself into his work with utter surrender, the creation of things that are sweet and full of visual drama. Handmade chocolates, metre-high French wedding cakes of stacked profiteroles, almond mousse as light as a feather. And more hearty, earthy things: lush cheesecakes, dense and nutty Levantine pastries from which honey drips, heavy English puddings soaked with brandy or custard.

He too became an object of Joschka's complete dedication. There was enough scorching light behind Joschka's eyes, enthusiasm like white heat, to propel them both like a rocket. There were, admittedly, many other forms of self-surrender; this he understood early on – ways in which Joschka sought sweet oblivion. *Vergessenheit*. The signs were there: the ways in which Joschka instinctively knew the underbelly of the city, could read it immediately, the snippets he divulged about his life in Berlin. There were fiery and unknowable impulses just below the smooth skin. A frail bravado, an unsettling unpredictability. Above all, he possessed a hungry kind of beauty. Simultaneously vulnerable and careless. Glowing and chiselled. The eyes of a stag. Tattoos from Pacific islands on veined forearms.

Joschka came to cook for him in the winter darkness, in his spacious apartment in a converted warehouse on the Thames. Heavy Middle-European flavours floating through the spotless minimalism and out over the brown river: soups with dumplings, rabbit, schnitzels, liver. The clinical kitchen was being put to use for the first time since he had moved in. He could see that, for Joschka, it was a joy to have such a virginal kitchen to himself. Joschka was baking, his head bowed forward in concentration. He was caring for him. This was but one of Joschka's faces, the man fixated on his cakes. There were several Joschkas: the careless one, the caring one, the baking one, the one with the velvet eyes who would sometimes simply disappear in the city, in the streets, for days on end, not answering his phone, who would thereafter sleep for two or three days non-stop before rising and appearing again, a little paler and leaner, but more glowing than ever. He did not ask Joschka questions about these absences. For reasons he cannot explain, it did not matter. There were few things about which they asked each other questions. That is how it was. Only in Berlin did he start gaining a better understanding of Joschka's surrender to lost time, the vanished days.

'Why do they not live in this part of the castle?' he asks Joschka when Maximilian leads him out into the courtyard, where there is a patch of grass, dead flowerbeds and a deep well. 'It looks quite liveable.'

'There's no heating,' says Joschka, 'and, apart from the antique toilet, no bathroom.'

The castle complex consists of several buildings from several periods. It is built in a ring and faces a courtyard garden. On the outside, the walls are thick and there are small windows overlooking the moat and the valley below. The family live in the smallest building, a nineteenth-century house with a steep pitched roof. A small place within a large place. Joschka's brother-in-law works as an insurance broker, his sister as a nurse in the American army base nearby. Even though they live in this rambling place on a clifftop, they are like any German family in a cramped village house. There is a small backyard, just a shard of concrete above the abyss, enclosed with a wire fence. Inside is a Doberman. Through the fence it has a view over the valley. It barks at every movement below. Or, sometimes, for no apparent reason. The animal is sick, it seems. The ribs show, the tail remains tucked between its legs. Foam has dried around the mouth. Its bark is dry and raw.

Joschka's mother calls and announces she is coming to visit. Joschka stiffens when his sister tells him. Tension descends over the house. It takes an hour before she arrives;

she is coming from somewhere near the Czech border. A neighbour is bringing her.

'I must warn you about my mom,' says Joschka. 'She is basically a tramp, a *Landstreicherin*.'

During the visit, the house is filled with uncomfortable silences and impenetrable dynamics. The woman is unkempt and short and wide. She does indeed look as if she sometimes roams the countryside, as if she is sleeping rough. He cannot but wonder how such an unattractive woman could have given birth to such a beautiful son. An alcoholic, that is clear, and perhaps on various kinds of pills too. Her speech is slurred, her dialect, Bavarian, is in any event too strong for him to follow properly.

After the visit, Joschka is visibly disturbed. They take Alice's magic key and escape to the room in *die Ruine*, away from the little family, the little house. They stand in front of the small window, houses like toys in the valley below them.

'Tell me about your mother.'

Joschka looks fleetingly at him and away again.

'What's there to say? She wasn't a mother.'

Joschka says nothing more. He probes. Joschka shrugs his shoulders moodily.

'It's not an interesting story. Nothing new, nothing unusual.'

He goes on reluctantly. Almost from the beginning, she was alone with the two of them, his father having vanished early on. For as long as he can remember, she drank. His sister, just two years older than him, packed his schoolbag in the mornings and made breakfast. He recounts how his mother would often disappear, sometimes for weeks, how they had to make do on their own, had to ask neighbours for food, or his aunt in a neighbouring town. One evening, he continues, after she had been away for a week or so, he heard the front door opening. He jumped out of bed and there she was, in the corridor. He locked his arms around her waist, refused to let go. 'Are you back now? Can you please never leave again?' He made her promise, and she did, repeatedly. 'I'm back. Here with you. Forever.' She loosened his arms, put him to bed. He lay there, listening to her fussing in her room. After a while, just before dozing off, he heard the sound of the door-latch. A car engine. He jumped up, ran out. Too late: she was gone. She just came home to pack a suitcase. This time she did not return. For a month they managed on their own, but, in the end, when they ran out of food and there wasn't a pfennig left in the house, they went to live with his aunt.

A call for him late afternoon on his cellphone. It is his own mother, from South Africa. He shifts from one corner of his mind to another, through all the rooms in between. His parents still live in South Africa, even though all their children have left the country. They own a farm there. An old family farm, inherited. They rarely go to the place nowadays; it is no longer safe. His mother harbours a deep nostalgia that nevertheless draws her back there. On the farm is a newer house, as well as a crumbling hundred-year-old farmhouse.

In front of the old farmhouse, next to the half-collapsed sandstone pergola, there grows an old crabapple tree that she remembers as a young tree, before the new house was built. She remembers the shade, has often told him how she played underneath it as a child. Now it is old, knotty. In summertime, when the fruit becomes too heavy to carry, branches tear and collapse in the dust, apple clusters and all. When he was young, apples were steamed and stewed for lunches in the new house. Sugar was added to counter the sourness. When served as part of a plate of food, it was brown, half-caramelised. Sweetly sour. Nowhere else has he ever encountered exactly such apples. When raw, they were inconceivably sour. One's face involuntarily screwed up when you bit into it.

'The tree is dying,' she now says over the phone, 'branch by branch.'

They took a cutting to a botanist, she explains, and he had never encountered the species. She is having it grafted. They are using the trunk of a hardened European apple tree. Notches will be cut into it and buds carved from the crabapple tree will be inserted. Then it will be wrapped in cloth, like dressing a wound with bandage. They will replant the new tree at the new house when the grafts have taken, when it starts budding with the new season's blossoms.

'Is that all you called to say?'

Usually she only calls when there is important news, whether good or bad. His parents are not of the Skype generation. Long-distance calls are not for conversation, but for conveying information. Sometimes more than one call is required, sometimes the ground has to be prepared first.

'Yes,' she says, 'that is all.' (He doubts it.)

The jump in his mind to South Africa is too great, too fast. He returns to Bavaria, to the Oberpfalz. To Joschka, of whom his mother has never heard and never will.

Joschka wants to cook a large dinner for them all. They are standing in Kaufland, a supermarket on the fringes of

Nuremberg. It is the largest supermarket he has ever been in. The dairy products disappear into infinity. It is fresh and bright in here, like spring. Joschka looks intently at the refrigerated shelf, as if searching for an ingredient.

'There is something,' says Joschka, 'I have to tell you. About the blood, the other night.'

He can feel the cool air against his temple. He waits for the rest.

'You should get tested.'

For a few moments he is silent.

'Are you saying what I think you're saying?'

Joschka turns away, starts packing things into his basket, things they do not need. He looks at Joschka as he is walking away, through the fog that is rolling from the fridges. There is a tingling feeling in his upper back.

Back at home, Joschka takes the key and they ascend the stairs in *die Ruine*.

'Where can I have myself tested?' His voice is pinched.

He does not ask Joschka other questions, about his history, whether he is on medication. He is considering his own options. Too late now, anyhow, for post-exposure prophylaxis.

'There's a clinic in Nuremberg. It'll be open on Monday. We'll have to wait.'

'Wait? Wait!'

His voice penetrates the walls. Somewhere higher up, pigeons flutter between oak beams.

Joschka looks down at the floor, speaking slowly. 'It wasn't easy, you know, having to tell you . . . '

'Enough, please.'

Until now it has always been possible to declare any seed of doubt, any sign of indifference towards him from

Joschka, void. The slightest touch between them would exorcise any uncertainty regarding their connection. The touch would make him understand Joschka's quirks, made him endlessly patient with him: his bravado, his instinct to pull away feverishly and be deeply needy at the same time. Perhaps that is what Joschka found in him. And a hesitant promise of safekeeping. And what did he find in Joschka? Apart from the fact that Joschka came to redeem him from his worn world, there is a lot which he draws from Joschka, but he understands little of the mechanisms as yet; he will still have to work it out for himself. For the time being, he can only understand Joschka in strings of images. Joschka ignites a blowtorch in his chest, that he knows. Joschka lifts his heart, lends him a comet's speed and brightness, makes him as weightless as a bat. With Joschka he has been simultaneously untouchable – immortal – and a target for danger. Simultaneously armour-plated and flayed.

Now he sees Joschka stripped of imagery. He avoids the smoothness of Joschka's skin. He is filled with urgency and disquiet, worry about himself mingled with concern for Joschka and the implications of his disclosure.

He is playing with Maximilian in the courtyard garden. They are kicking a ball back and forth, sometimes too far, so that it bounces off thick walls. Joschka is sitting in a rusty garden chair, watching. Back and forth the ball goes. The child cannot get enough of the game. They do not utter a word. They throw, then they kick. An hour passes. The sun is baking down. The child does not smile, does not say a thing. The game is all seriousness. He kicks the ball too hard; it ends up in the well. They both look over the edge; it is lying at the bottom, a red dot on a heap of rubbish.

'*Warte hier*,' says Maximilian, asking him not to go. Running into the house, the boy looks over his shoulder to make sure he stays.

He brings two plastic swords and shields from his room. They cross swords, again and again. Stand back, charge. Joschka is sitting in the sun. Blades are clashing with a clacking noise. On the other side of the house the Doberman is barking. Incessantly, hoarsely. He looks at Joschka from the corner of his eye, mouth tense, muscles increasingly tightened. The blunt swords keep on smacking, against the shields, against each other. Joschka jumps like a wound coil from his chair.

'I'm going for a walk,' he says. 'Come with me.'

'I'm playing.'

Maximilian looks, sword by his side. Joschka exits the gate, the heavy door swings open, he disappears alone over the moat bridge.

He holds his sword aloft. Maximilian too. They start again.

Half an hour later, Joschka is back. He and the child are sweating, but they do not stop. The swords hit each other with a rhythm distinct from that of the dog's thirsty bark. He gains ground, retreats, lets Maximilian move forward. They stop, hold the swords in the air, start again, take turns driving each other back.

Joschka has a sheaf of yellow wild flowers in his arms, carrying it like a child against his tattoos. When Joschka passes behind him, he can smell the forest outside the thick walls. The instant consolation offered by the shadow falling over him, as soothing and intimate as moss, makes him want to sob. Their shadows slip through each other and then Joschka is gone, inside the house.

'Let's put away the swords, Maxi.'

Joschka puts the flowers in an earthenware ewer in their room. He does not remark on it. Joschka avoids looking at him. Within a day he will have forgotten Joschka's eyes. Already he has trouble picturing them – sometimes so black, at other times so transparent.

Maximilian had to vacate his room for him and Joschka; the boy is sleeping with his parents in the only other bedroom. The room is filled with children's things. Books with stories about knights, an encyclopedia showing different types of knight's armour, swords and shields. A book about the forging of blades in previous times, about castles and city states of the Middle Ages. One containing children's versions of Germanic and Nordic myths. There is a Lego set with plastic panels for building castle walls, little pointed flags for clicking onto the crenellations. A miniature trap door, operated with a crank between the index finger and thumb. A garrison of knights on horseback, arrangeable in battle formations. In a corner there is a box with lances and plastic swords in sheaths.

They sleep on bunk beds with children's bedding. The duvets are virtually the only items in the room without a medieval theme. His has a pattern of aeroplanes on it, Joschka's has red racing cars. He gets the top bunk, Joschka the bottom one. Before switching off the light, they lie in silence for a long time. They cannot see each other. His feet are sticking out from under the duvet, over the end of the bed. Joschka's are probably hanging out even further.

They sleep restlessly amongst the toys, with cars and planes beneath their chins. When he gets up to go to the bathroom, he bends over to look out the small window. The dog is still barking ceaselessly. Above the back door there is an outdoor light. On the bright cement, the animal is contracting into spasms when the noise tears from him, as if he is vomiting. Is it not bothering anyone else? He looks in Joschka's direction, but he is invisible in the dark. Is he sleeping or are his eyes open? Is Joschka looking at him as he is looking back at the dog? The ribs suck in, the desiccated body convulses. The eyes are glassy, the mouth foaming. When the dog notices him, he stops for a moment, looks down the quiet valley and then starts again. Like a tubercular cough. He looks at the outlines of the hills surrounding the valley. The barking is projected onto the entire landscape. Everything looks like the sound from the dog's dry lungs.

When he returns to bed, he sees that Joschka is lying with his knees pulled close to his chest, curled up tightly against the barking. He thinks about how everything will end after this weekend. He thinks of Joschka's shadow, soft and cool and intimate. Of how that is all that will remain.

Sunday. He does not eat breakfast, Joschka neither. Joschka's sister and brother-in-law left early with Maximilian for the morning mass in the white baroque church whose spire rises above the pine trees at the other end of the valley. The fridge is droning and the wall clock ticking.

'Shall we get out of here for a while?' Joschka asks.

'I'm not really in the mood.'

'How about Bayreuth?'

Before they came, he told Joschka he would like to visit Bayreuth to see the opera house and Haus Wahnfried, Wagner's villa.

'Come,' Joschka says, 'come.'

He gives in. They drive in silence.

They walk through Haus Wahnfried. The sacred atmosphere would normally irritate him, the way in which the place is curated so as to render one complicit in worshipping the master, but his attention is elsewhere. All of this makes no impression on him. He is listening to his own footsteps, and Joschka's. In the main room, the salon-cum-music-room, they walk along opposite walls. The room protrudes into the garden, in a half-circle with large windows. Here they meet, here they come face to face with each other, each with a hand on the grand piano. They look out into the garden, to the granite grave of the god himself. Far back, beyond a fountain. Joschka looks down at the piano.

'Will we never look each other in the eye again?'

It is Joschka who says this, before moving away. On the piano, on the black lacquer, the shape of his hand remains for a few seconds in a whisper of vapour before it disappears.

After lunch, back home in the castle, they visit Joschka's aunt. She is ninety-two. When Joschka first asks him to come along, he says: 'You go. I don't feel up to it.'

He is lying on the aeroplane-patterned duvet, facing the wall.

'Please,' Joschka says behind his back. 'I told her about you. She's expecting both of us. She wants me to come and show you to her. Please.'

They go. The aunt is small and fit and shy. Never married. Her speech is nasal (a split palate). She would go to pick chanterelles at dawn, on her daily wander through the woods, before swimming twenty-four lengths in the pool at the American army base. The house smells yeasty, of the fresh mushrooms, of soil. And chocolate cake. Chlorine, when one gets close to her. In her presence there is a new Joschka, softened to the core.

'I taught him to bake, this *Junge*,' she says while taking the cake from the oven, Joschka beaming behind her in the heat. There is apple tart too.

They come from her garden, she tells them. The apples.

To demonstrate, she opens the window and picks an apple from one of the branches abutting the house. She is wiry, as he sees when she bends over. A forest woman, a survivor. She offers him the apple.

Back home, he says, 'I am going for a walk.'

'I'm coming with you,' Joschka says.

'No, alone.'

Outside the gates, he walks along a curved footpath, further up the hill. He walks past a small wooden hut, a forest ranger's house. He stops for a moment, looks out over the next valley, parallel to the one overlooked by Burg Heimhof. Downy seeds drift around him, catching the sunlight. There are white butterflies around his feet. The path turns increasingly wet and slippery where it approaches the forest. It reminds him of an Anselm Kiefer exhibition he and Joschka saw in London, in the white subterranean cube of a Mayfair gallery. Canvases ten metres wide layered with paint and mud as deep as the span of a man's hand. One could not refrain from touching it. It was not the *representation* of a landscape of mud and sludge. It was the landscape itself.

Then he is in the forest.

When he closes his eyes, he is no longer in a pine forest, but in the cliché of the German forest. A dim place of antique oaks with interlocking branches. He wants to feel all the things that hover here right on his skin, wants to shift them across each other like a quadruple exposure: myths and music, history and landscape. A richly decorated *Szene*. It is becoming colder the deeper he goes. In this air, one could perhaps even, with sufficient concentration, stir up all the twentieth-century European horrors. He stops, opens his eyes. It is just a dead forest. Absolute silence. The signs are hidden, the codes illegible beneath the floor of pine needles, antique blood seeped deep into dark soil. Out there, from where the light is filtering in through the forest's edge, the Vierte Reich reigns: American military bases, BMWs and highways like deep blue rivers. It is the outside realm that gives the forest meaning, not the other way around. It renders the forest small and harmless. The force drained from everything, the claws filed blunt.

His cellphone rings in his pocket. A muted sound amongst the pine needles. He is surprised there is signal coverage here. It is his father.

'It is about your mother,' his father says, his voice unsteady. 'She wanted to tell you yesterday, but she couldn't.'

'What is it? What did she want to say?'

'She wanted to tell you, but couldn't.' His father's voice is strange. He utters a wild sob. 'She is ill. Liver cancer. It's spread to the lungs. And the brain. There won't be treatment.'

His father puts down the receiver. He leaves the path, deeper into the forest. As he walks, the tears come.

A miniature scene is all he is capable of. He can only put together the small pictures, in a chaotic fashion: he and Joschka, fragments of the castle, the house with the room full of plastic swords, the fragments of forest around him, his own worry and sorrow. His mother: she stays on the edge of the photo, too over-exposed to recognise, the continent where she finds herself too cut off from everything northern.

He stops, looks up, listens for birds. All he can hear are the lines, something from his school days, which he now starts reciting:

> *Über allen Gipfeln*
> *Ist Ruh,*
> *In allen Wipfeln*
> *Spürest du*
> *Kaum einen Hauch;*
> *Die Vögellein schweigen im Walde —*

The voice of a bird, somewhere above the pines (they will not venture into the dead dusk down here), sweeps away the calm peaks and windless treetops of the poem: '*Sie bricht herein! Sie bricht herein! Die dunkle Nacht der Seele . . .* '

'Don't bother,' he says, 'with the warnings and the mockery. It's already enveloping me from all sides.'

He gets bored of being lost. Time to go back; soon the sun will set. He crosses paths he has probably walked on before, encounters a pile of pine trunks he is convinced he recognises. Sometimes he sees light and thinks it is the forest edge, but then it turns out to be a clearing. He crosses open areas with wild flowers that look familiar, a square of blue sky above him. He is starting to get worried. Occasionally he encounters a viewing tower for fire watchers. He climbs the ladder of one such tower, hoping he might be able to see Burg Heimhof on its rock amidst the forests and valleys. When he has almost reached the top, he finds the trap door above him locked shut, confirmed with a sign: *Zutritt verboten*.

He wanders around for another hour, searching for light. Then he hears the bass line of music. He follows the sound. Furious German rap. He imagines a skinhead next to a boom box, tattooed on his neck or shaven temple. Then the music is joined by light. He is out. In a dark fold against a northern slope, a small village with featureless modern houses. Right up against the mythical/non-mythical forest. Two young men with spits in their hands. They are roasting bratwurst over open flames, the music emanating from the house. He needs to cross a corner of their garden. They look at him. He does not look at the spits. He walks along a tarred road, there are road signs, he emerges in the valley below the castle. He sees the place from a new angle. From down here it seems like an extension of the cliff.

Upon his return, the little house in the castle smells of baking. Joschka is at work in the kitchen. He avoids the kitchen, goes to lie down on the plane-patterned duvet.

Later, Joschka comes and lies down too. He tells Joschka the news about his mother while looking up at the ceiling. He does it reluctantly. It feels wrong given their newfound strangeness towards each other, but there is no one else to share it with. Joschka is quiet for a long time.

'I would be lying if I said I know how it feels. As far as I'm concerned, my mother has been dead for a long time. I don't remember.'

He catches an early-morning train to Nuremberg. First he visits the clinic, then gets a taxi to the airport. From there he will fly to Frankfurt, where he will wait a few hours for the evening flight to South Africa that he booked the previous night.

He is waiting to board in Nuremberg airport. The airport building displays the kind of watered-down architectural modernism that has become the common denominator of airports everywhere in the West: row upon row of structural glass plates in a steel frame. One could be anywhere in the extra-sylvan world, in the Vierte Reich. And yet, in the distance beyond the runway, the hills are briefly visible, and the dark green of pine forests, before the fog closes in.

He has a box of biscuits with him, German biscuits that Joschka baked and shoved in his hands when he left. He just looked at it without saying anything.

'Let me know when you're coming back to London,' Joschka said, eyes still avoiding his own. Joschka's hand is burrowing into his, like a small forest creature in distress.

We return to where we started, the nude scene in the bathroom. As mentioned, neither he nor his mother says a word about it. It is as if it never happened. Something has changed, though, something has become raw. The breach between now and then, the time of innocence, has been brought into sharper focus. Or maybe he is imagining things; maybe it was nothing more than it was.

When he arrived in South Africa a month ago, he made a call to London and resigned from his job. It was long overdue. His former assistant packed up his office, shipped the boxes. He asked a friend to empty out his flat and let it out. He did not say goodbye to anyone in London, gave no one his new telephone number or his parents' address.

The rhythms of his mother's illness catch his mother and everyone around her unawares. For a few weeks, she looks better than ever, radiating inner light. One could imagine the diagnosis was a mistake. Then the decline follows, much faster than predicted. It progresses with such speed that one cannot keep up. Soon she has intense pain. Accompanying the pain is protest, refusal. She declines pain medication. She wants to maintain control. ('I want to know what's going on in my body. Want to be all there when it all happens.') Her condition changes daily, there are new kinds of pain, pains she cannot describe.

The more she becomes lost in thought, and the worse the pain, the more she does. She gets up and cooks on a large scale. She is waging a war on the scattering growths inside her. She'll show the pain. For hours on end, she cooks and bakes, as if determined to fill a freezer from which everyone whom she has ever loved can eat for the rest of their lives. She cleans the floors, dusts, polishes windows and prunes potted plants so that no one else will ever have to do it again. She drives off to buy clothing for his father, bringing back pullovers and thick socks for *him* too, for all his future winters in the north. Everything will be clean, everyone will be warm and fed and cared for. So it will be. For ever and ever. (Amen.)

Later, still without painkillers, she is lying, motionless, amidst the regularity of domestic sounds: the drone of the fridge, the ticking of clocks. When one enquires cautiously, she insists there is no pain. Judging by how serenely she is lying there, one could almost believe it. But now and then something travels dimly through her eyes. She talks about taking a trip to the farm with him. She wants to show him the grafted crabapple tree, wants to see for herself how it is growing. Wants to sit in the sandstone pergola again. She is sure she can do it; they can stack a pile of cushions in the back of the car. His father must come too. He nods, but he knows it is not possible, knows it will never happen.

One evening he brings her back from the hospital after she has undergone a procedure. An attempt at brief relief – in the intestines of this most unembittered woman, the bile had dammed up to bursting point and required surgical drainage. She is sore. They drive through wet streets and he tries to understand the nature of pain. It is a strange evening. It has rained unnaturally heavily. It has stopped now, but the idea of rain hovers in the dark. The pain makes his mother speechless. It is a blade cutting them from each other, a presence in the car that dominates them in different ways, makes them absent from each other. In himself there is an echo of her pain, black and shiny and enormous and soundless. But it is not pain itself. Outside there are so many lights: street lamps, houses, cars, shopping centres. It surprises him how powerless all the bulbs are against the dark, how little they infringe on it. He looks at her: she is blind and frozen. The pain inside her is a strange country, an impenetrable language. Not a Germanic language barked in a menacing voice, but a set of soundless signs.

Like aleph, the unvoiced Hebrew consonant. Or what one hears when the birds fall silent.

It is during this time that he gets such an unprotected view of his mother in the bathroom. The retina will not let go of the image, he realises after a while. It stays with him. He wonders what it means, the lingering. Yes, it does carry something in it of *then* and *now*, the man before and after the event. How he is to construe the respective selves, however, he will never know. But he knows it is a dividing line, a flash of light in the blindness of which all protection is torn away. And it superimposes her body indelibly over his German trip, a defenceless landscape on the edge of collapse. It is also on one of these mornings that she gets up and walks out into the garden. She takes the spade from the gardener. He stands back slowly, respectfully. His forehead is shiny, he has taken off his woolly hat and is turning it around and around in his hands. She puts a foot on the spade, pushing it into the soil. The man's eyes are turned downwards. She totters. The gardener steps forward, gently adds his own foot. Together they manage to turn over a sod. On the underside earthworms teem and twist.

'At least one spadeful,' she says with rasping breath when she sinks into the sofa. Perhaps she wants to dig her own grave, one sod per day.

'You can bring it now,' she says. 'Administer the oblivion.'

He helps her into bed, lifts her feet gently onto the sheet. He covers her lightly with an angora blanket. She surrenders, accepts the morphine. In the coming days, she insists on increasing doses, much more than prescribed.

The care becomes exhausting. He and his father take turns with the night shift. By his mother's bedside he searches inside himself for all the tenderness he possesses. Nothing is kept in reserve.

During the first week or three he and Joschka occasionally exchanged emails. But Joschka and the entire northern world – London, Berlin, Nuremberg, the castle above the valley – feel so utterly removed from this strange continent. From this place of his childhood that has nothing to do with him, that never really left traces on his consciousness. Their electronic epistles are devoid of substance, impart no concrete news. They are stiff and unnatural – nothing feels the same from here. The menace of his mother's illness dominates his thoughts, so that the events around Joschka in the previous months look increasingly distant and implausible, like something remembered from a story. The emails start trailing off. In his state of intensified emotion, while his mother is sunk so deep into her pillow, he does, nevertheless, write to Joschka again one night. Lack of sleep has made him scratchy behind the eyes.

Josch

You have, I realise tonight, taught me a few simple lessons (is there any other sort?) and for that I want to thank you. What are these lessons? In no particular order:

1. That one must learn to live with open endings.

2. That we like grafting our painful little stories onto other, greater narratives, onto stories filled with deeper trials and more intense pathos. Even though we want to weigh them down with meaning, they just remain what they are: our own stories.

3. One may linger in a beautiful room as long as possible. One does not have to open the door.

4. That everything is of short duration; we are permitted but a brief sojourn in a shadowy landscape.

5. I am (still) here. I am alive.

6. Pain is a soundless language, a different language to the birds'. (On reflection, this lesson may have come from my mother.)

7. That I owe the gods gratitude for a mother who loved me (loves me, if love is still possible). A mother who never forsook me, who cherished and protected me.

8. To keep the gleaming distant city fiercely in view, without a hand against the brow to shade the eyes.

What I taught you, if anything, I do not know. Perhaps just how tenderness feels when it bleeds through fingertips.

Tschüss, bis später.

He receives no response to his list of lessons. The correspondence ends.

One day, when he awakes from an afternoon nap after a long, gruelling night, he looks out the window and sees his father in the sunshine. When he goes down to his parents' room, the bed is empty. He exits through the veranda doors. The light is sharp, the sun white.

'What's going on?'

'She's gone. They've come to take her away.'

'Why on earth didn't you wake me? I wanted to be there.'

His father shrugs his shoulders, keeps looking at the stirring leaves. 'Meaning does not, after all, lie in the end. It's just a moment like any other.'

He wants to grab his father by the shoulders and throw him onto the lawn.

We move a few months ahead. He still thinks of Joschka sometimes, more so now that his mother has died. Via a distant acquaintance, he hears that Joschka has moved to Bavaria, that he has renounced London and Berlin. He now lives near his sister in the Oberpfalz. There was a forest ranger's hut close to the castle, he remembers, by the foot-path, on the edge of the forest. Perhaps Joschka moved in there. Perhaps he goes wandering in the mornings, climbing one of the fire towers at dawn, looking out over the fog-shrouded valleys. He could not say, they no longer speak. These days, when he tastes something sugary, he imagines feeling the tips of Joschka's fingers on his head. Just for a moment, but still. Sometimes, when a long shadow falls over him, it feels sweet and cool, like Joschka's, with the same texture of velvet. And often, when he wakes up, he expects to see planes on his duvet.

He wishes it were true, the idea of Joschka as a Bavarian ranger, in a forest hut close to Burg Heimhof, the child of his aunt. But this account turns out to be apocryphal. By chance he comes across one of Joschka's Berlin acquaint-ances one day. The man is on holiday in Cape Town. It is one of those names from his and Joschka's Berlin nights (Ritter? Wolfrik? Tabor?). The man remembers him even though he would never have recognised the man. The man tells him that Joschka returned to Berlin shortly after he returned to South Africa when his mother had been diagnosed, that he has cut himself off from everyone, that he stopped his medication shortly after his move and is withering.

He retreats while the man is speaking. He holds his hand above his eyes, seeking out the shade.

So, his mother's pain did not belong to her alone, it also had to stand in for Joschka's. It had to fill in his imagination, had to give content to lost time.

What about him? *Es geht*, as Joschka would say. Life goes on. Things could be worse. He never found out the result of his test. Anyhow, we all know how an ending looks, or have some notion of it. His father was right. Endings are all the same, everything ends up in the same place. You would rather linger in a beautiful room, the room of which you now often dream, a cube within a cube. From the corners of the colossal ur-cube, cables are stretched to the corners of the smaller cube. And there it hangs: a box within a box. You keep the door locked. Outside the threshold, you know, the floor falls away. No stairs lead here. Nothing supports the floor. Should you look down into dizzying space, you would see cellar stairs disappearing into the darkness below. Should you look up, you would see pigeons flashing through columns of light. Elsewhere, tumbling beams and floors. Remarkable, the proximity of the two things: the perfect and the abject, the room and the destroyed space. In here, on the heavy oak table, there are wild yellow flowers. In the corner, there is a knight's armour into which you could climb. Through the walls you can hear the pigeons and, behind that, an undertone that you could cut out if you carefully adjusted your ear: the barks emerging from a dog's barren intestines.

One morning, upon waking from the same dream once again, he gets up and opens his bedroom door. He sits down at his computer and books a ticket to Berlin.

WAR, BLOSSOMS

Later on he will see it differently, but it starts as a kind of war. Or, at least, a series of escalating skirmishes.

He is caring for his mother. Cancer is growing in her intestines. She is going to die. The only unknowns are the moment and the precise route. The markers are set out for him: the self-poisoning body, the distending organs, pain, starvation and farewells.

The war, when it begins, is about food. It is a soundless war, a collection of mute battles. She hardly speaks any more. It deprives him too, of speech and breath, the disease.

He registers its progression in fragments.

The day dawns when she stops eating. The oncologist had explained this would happen. The last phase. It is important for the patient's psychological state, he had elucidated, not to intervene. Let 'the thing' take its course, do not try to coerce.

But when her refusal comes, he does not accept it. He too refuses. He is constantly in front of the stove. He has rarely before had to cook. He is clumsy, inept. Even so: here he stands, steaming chicken, then shredding the flesh into strips along the grain. He also cooks pale, watery vegetables. He juices pineapples, adding the pressed juice of limes. He makes toast and thin chicken soup. It is not helping. Nothing helps. He carries the untouched plates back to the kitchen.

He leaves his mother on her own for a while. She is calm, she is sleeping. For the first time in a week he goes outside, sits down in the autumn sun. He has forgotten that autumn in the Highveld is so beautiful, even though here it is bounded by a suburban garden surrounded by crime-ridden streets. For many years he has restricted his visits to summer so as to escape the northern winter.

Out of the blue he gets a phone call, on his British cellphone, from his Japanese friend Hisashi. How long is it since they've spoken? At least a year.

'This is unexpected.'

'I'm here.'

'What do you mean, Hisashi?'

'I've come to visit.'

'Here in South Africa?'

'Here in South Africa.'

'And you're here already?'

'I'm here. In Johannesburg.'

Just before his departure from London, he sent all his friends an email, notifying them that he was on his way here. It contained all of his contact details. He was in a hurry to get to his mother's bedside, couldn't take proper leave of anybody. Hisashi had moved back to Tokyo from London a year before, but was still on the list. Typical of Hisashi, to arrive at such an inopportune moment, without warning.

The air is moving. The leaves of the pin oak are falling ceaselessly, their stems impaled in the lawn. The tips of the leaves tremble in the breeze like nerve endings.

In the course of an afternoon, his mother's complexion changes from grey and transparent to yellow. The vomiting commences. It doesn't stop. She has not eaten for days; there is only bile. It is as if an external force is controlling her, making her shudder to her fingertips. Even her eyes are yellow: the eyes of a devil.

Food, when he tries to eat, congeals on his palate. He sits on his own at the kitchen table. Ultimately he has to spit out the grey masticated mush onto the porcelain.

The freezer is overflowing. While she had the strength, she spent her days cooking. Baked puddings and loin of lamb, trifle and stuffed shoulder of venison, oven-roasted chicken with a lemon where the bloody intestines used to be. But these are not for her; they're a legacy. She has now forsworn the body's banalities, the lower functions. He is standing in front of the freezer, chilly fog billowing onto his feet. There are plastic bags, aluminium dishes and plates Serried in rows, the contents unidentifiable, everything furred with frost. Nausea wells up in him. A cupboard full of cadavers. Fossils of the future. He works up a fury against his mother. The ice age has dawned.

He meets Hisashi in the French embassy in London, about two years before his return to South Africa for his mother's last months. They are introduced to each other by a mutual acquaintance, one of Hisashi's French colleagues, Philippe. Philippe is engaged in a uniquely French version of conscription. Or, rather, Philippe chose 'community service' as an alternative, which entails travelling between French embassies across the world marketing champagne on behalf of French regional authorities. He organises glittering events in lavish interiors in London, New York, Beijing or Kuala Lumpur for guests clothed in expensive textiles, impeccably cut, where the champagne, flanking bowls of *fraises*, fizzes against crystal.

Sometimes he wishes he were French too. The joys of what is not immediately useful, of the mellow delights and nurturing of an old culture, could have suited him well. Better, at any rate, than the diaspora of fearful, grim, white children from South Africa of which he forms a part, like it or not.

He doesn't really know what Hisashi does at the embassy – generic administrative work of some sort. Nor does he know what the driving force of the friendship between them is. There is little common ground. Be that as it may, before long they are planning a trip together to Vietnam and Japan. At first, in fact, only to Japan. He has long been interested in an eclectic variety of Japanese things. From Kabuki and Noh theatre to manga in all forms and travesties. From the woodcut prints of the Floating World and writers like Mishima, Ōe and Murakami, to underground bands from Tokyo with names like Ghost, Angel'in Heavy Syrup or Acid Mothers Temple.

Perhaps it is simple. Perhaps the unlikely friendship is fuelled simply by the fact that Hisashi is Japanese. An old-fashioned kind of exoticising. And, because he so carefully preserves Hisashi's strangeness in his own mind, he doesn't really know what Hisashi in turn might be drawing from the friendship.

The Vietnamese extension to the trip is inspired by Philippe, with his second-hand nostalgia for the former French colonial *territoire*. One notices it immediately in

Philippe, the inherited memory. The sedimented layers of historical reminiscence. He is often struck by the way his European friends remember places they have never known.

In Philippe's flat there are photos of his great-grandfather in Saigon during the Franco-Siamese war of 1893. Another of his grandfather in the first Indochina war. A grandmother in Hanoi, in a garden full of flowers that look familiar to Philippe, but that he cannot name. Inherited artefacts on a sideboard, a drawer full of little objects of silver and silk: handmade trinkets that conjure up a vanished world.

For his European friends, the dead are alive and the vanished places still exist. Loss is in their blood, the boundaries of time permeable. How different it is for him, a naïf from the remote Third World. For the recently dispersed with their encumbering passports. To them everything is new; everything has to be discovered and experienced and lost from scratch.

He pleads, holds out half-teaspoons of soup towards her pursed lips. Nothing.

He does not stop cooking. He reduces the portions so as not to overwhelm her. Smaller and smaller the mounds of food become. At one point he kneels before her bed as before an altar, offering crumbs as if to a sparrow-goddess.

He thought the battle was about getting her to eat, but no. It is, he now realises, about who is caring for whom. She wants to look after him from her bed. Sometimes she is too weak to speak, but she is obsessed with what he is eating, wants to know what he is taking from the freezer and preparing for himself. He is, after all, her child. And he persists in bringing her small offerings.

He stops eating too. He makes sure that she knows it. Refusal is easy.

When he walks out into the garden, the trees are bare. A carpet of pin-oak leaves covers the lawn. Days have passed since he last set foot outside the house.

Hisashi calls. He has made it clear to his Japanese friend, as politely as possible, that he must maintain a reasonable distance, that now is hardly the best moment for a visit. He has sketched only the broad outlines of the situation. Even so, Hisashi calls him once a day. He doesn't say much. Just calls and then waits for him to initiate the conversation.

'As I said, Hisashi, I'm sorry I can't show you around. It just isn't possible at the moment.'

'I'm managing. I have a car. I have a hotel. Don't worry.'

Cheerful silence.

Hisashi's imperturbable good cheer irritates him, rubbing up against his own despondency. What the Japanese man is doing in this dull provincial place he cannot fathom. There's nothing to see here. Nothing to learn. Nothing to lift the heart. One does not travel here to civilise oneself.

By the time their trip to Asia comes around, Hisashi has already moved back to Tokyo, where he now works at the Alliance Française. He himself is still in London. They fly out to Vietnam: one from the west, the other from the east. They meet in Hanoi. They book into a modern hotel. The air is grey and murky. The streets are rivers of scooters. When you cross, the scooters open around you like currents around an island. Hisashi is mistaken for a Vietnamese, even though he is in fact too large to be either Japanese or Vietnamese. He is from the southernmost corner of Japan, from the countryside, not far from Nagasaki. Peasant stock. His forebears were scorched brown on the watery rice paddies. Over centuries their feet have become waterlogged, swelled and lost their shape. Hisashi is heavy, bigger than he. Dark. His feet fleshy.

They want to do different things. He wants to visit the art museum, take pictures of the Buddhist-Communist kitsch of Ho Chi Minh's grave and the French colonial buildings, visit the street with dog restaurants. Hisashi wants to sleep during the day and then wander around endlessly at night observing people, visiting karaoke bars and drinking Vietnamese coffee in cafés filled with teenagers. Before long, misunderstandings arise. Hisashi's English is surprisingly limited for someone who has lived in London for a few years. Sometimes they try to converse in French, but Hisashi's French is even worse than his own.

During the day he goes about on his own, Hisashi staying behind at the hotel. He goes into a dusty shop selling Communist propaganda posters from the old days. He buys one inciting the young proletariat to make pig farming the future of the socialist Vietnamese state. The poster shows a young man and a young woman, both of implausible proportions, the perspective from below, rays of sunlight fanning out behind them. Each is clutching a heroic piglet under the arm. Each with a fist in the air.

That evening, when they are out walking, two Vietnamese girls on a scooter drive right up to them on the pavement and offer themselves in shrill tones, shouting out prices in English for a menu of obscene acts. He holds himself aloof to get rid of them, but Hisashi banters with them. Hisashi confuses them because he looks vaguely Vietnamese, but doesn't speak Vietnamese. The situation becomes increasingly uncomfortable. He walks ahead on his own. The girls heckle him from behind.

Later, back in the hotel, he takes a shower. When he comes out of the bathroom, Hisashi is sitting on the bed wrapping a few trinkets that he has bought on a street somewhere. When he comes closer, he sees that the strips of paper being used for the wrapping are torn from the propaganda poster he bought earlier.

'What the hell, Hisashi?'

He mentions what he paid for the poster. Hisashi looks astonished, hurt.

'Thought it was just a piece of newspaper. Forgive me.'

Hisashi remains sheepish for the rest of the evening. The Japanese man makes himself small, watching him furtively. He withholds forgiveness.

He is relieved when they leave Hanoi, but he resents not being on his own. He doubts whether they will complete this trip together.

A respite, a fragile ceasefire. He makes his mother's bed with her best linen. A handwoven blanket, white as snow. Things she has not used since her wedding day. Up to now she has been sleeping on the sheets on which his father died a few years before.

He washes her hair. Every thirty seconds she has to take a break. He holds her hand mirror in front of her while she brushes her hair and applies make-up, for the first time in a week. She rests between every movement. He rubs foundation lightly over her upper cheek with his forefinger. His stupid fingers are becoming cleverer.

Then they intensify, the skirmishes. He tries to veil his attempts at feeding her as an extension of the freshening of the bed. He takes out the best porcelain, silver-coated cutlery. Heirlooms unused not only by his parents, but also their parents. He arranges a delicately embroidered linen cloth on a tray. He does his best with the cooking.

She awaits her tormentor at every mealtime. One can sense the tension in the air when the aromas float from the kitchen to the bedroom.

'I can't digest the food,' she says softly. 'It's physically impossible, surely you know that.'

Once or twice, when he feeds her, she does eat a mouthful or two. It gives him an opening, creates a precedent. The battle becomes increasingly determined, the object of it progressively smaller. Now sometimes just a grain of rice, a bread crumb. A sugar crystal.

An unequal battle, he realises. But he does not relent. He towers above the bed, the light behind him. She is lying in his shadow. Her own shadow has already departed.

I will match you, he decides; what you eat, I will eat. Gram for gram. Morsel for morsel.

Sometimes she asks him to put on some music. Always the same. Medieval German church music. He considers trying to get her to ingest something while it is playing. Perhaps her resistance is lowered then. He sees how her face relaxes while she is listening, knows he would be able to catch her unawares with a spoonful, even two. He decides against it. He cannot assail her last redoubt.

He walks out into the garden, looks up.

These days have a barely audible undertone, like the music she listens to, an underlying note that is sustained and trance-inducing. A divine presence is thus made audible, say those who are knowledgeable about such music. *He* thinks it is the sound of breath forced through the vocal chords while the body is disintegrating. The sound of inconsolability.

They are in a flat-bottomed boat, he and Hisashi, on a wide, brown river. A small, wrinkled chestnut-coloured woman with a Vietnamese straw hat is rowing. Every now and then she jabbers as if they can understand her. Otherwise just silence and water against oars. They are a half-day trip away from Hanoi, in the mountains. The river meanders among massive rock peaks, overgrown with foliage in the mist. Palm trees, water buffalo. The destination is the Perfume Pagoda – the forty-ninth temple. En route they will pass forty-eight other temples. On the banks amidst the bulrushes. On stilts above the water. Between treetops. Against slopes. Simple temples of antique wood, larger ones in the Chinese style. Old and new. One by one they slide past. He is counting.

It is a Buddhist holiday. The river is packed with boats overloaded with pilgrims. On a normal day, the route up the mountain to the cave where the Perfume Pagoda is located takes, say, three-quarters of an hour. Not today. Where they moor, thousands of pilgrims are congregating under strings of small multicoloured flags.

They move with the crowd. Here too everyone seems to think that Hisashi is Vietnamese. He himself is also attracting attention. Some pilgrims have never seen a Westerner. They point at him and laugh, holding their hands in front of their mouths, touching his shaven hair. They think he is a monk, he imagines, or perhaps a thin, pale Buddha, sliding in the mud. He repels the pilgrims' attention with a stony face. Hisashi is patient and acquiescent, giggling with the people.

The path is becoming steeper, and narrower. He has to cling to the roots of trees. Among the pilgrims there are ancient, shrunken figures. They can hardly stand upright, are being dragged towards the peak by the current of people. Hisashi picks up a child who looks as if she is going to be crushed. She immediately smiles at him, strokes his face.

The path is becoming increasingly slippery. The pressure is forcing the breath from his lungs. Everything is coming to a standstill. The bodies pressed against him smell of something he doesn't know. A stampeding disaster is imminent, he thinks. And yet an unfamiliar kind of patience and tolerance reigns. The wind is playing through the prayer flags over the path.

'Enough,' he says to Hisashi. 'Meet you at the bottom later.' He slips and stumbles through the crowd, against the current, to the foot of the mountain.

The world is shrinking. His routes are contracting: from his mother's bedroom to the kitchen to the garden to his own bedroom. Now and again to a shop. Only the order of the destinations varies.

He is sleeping in the bedroom right above hers. It is only her rising cloudlets of warm breath that hold him up, he thinks in the moment before sleep overtakes him.

He holds his own breath. In the morning, when he enters her room, the winter sun is falling over her white sheets. She does not want him to draw the curtains at night; she wants to see the sun for as long as it shines.

When he is not with her, he thinks of her as tumbling – with the sluggish, unnatural movements of an astronaut drifting away from a ship. But that is not how it is. She is just lying there, entirely still, hands under her chin, angled at the wrists like a mouse's feet. There is a bell to ring when she needs him, but she has never used it. During the night, through his sleep, he listens for the tinkling, should it ever come.

She is saying something. He has to listen with his ear against her lips.

'Terrible pain,' she says. 'Deep. From underneath the foundations, from the soil.'

On a different occasion: 'A barbel,' she whispers, 'in the sludge.' Nothing further.

He exchanges her morphine plaster for one with a higher dosage, 50 micrograms.

Later that morning, for the first time in more than a week, she asks for food. She would like some cottage pie, she says. A reconciliatory moment, something she can still do for him. Or perhaps it's a cruel trick, a new tactic. If it is that, it's working. His chest fills with bright light at the mere thought of her asking for something, even though he knows in his heart of hearts she will not eat it. He goes out to buy tomatoes and potatoes. He drives to the shop at speed, then rushes back. Out of the packed freezer he takes lean mince. He leaves it to thaw in the sun on the veranda.

He sits down inside. He looks around him, tries to imagine how her absence will change every object, every piece of furniture and every ornament. He tries to imagine how a world without her would look.

He gets up and goes outside, feels the mince. It's half-thawed. Watery blood is dripping onto the floor tiles. When he comes back inside and looks up, she is sitting on the sofa where he has just been, in his stead. Like her own future ghost. He is startled. He blinks.

'Hello,' she says softly, all innocence.

One corner of her mouth twitches into a little smile. She has noticed his consternation and patently understands what he is thinking. It's the last time, he thinks, that she will remember how to smile.

Late afternoon the phone rings. The landline this time. Hisashi. He should never have given out the number.

'I'm here now.'

'Where?'

'In a guest house.'

'Where?'

The new lodgings, it turns out, are just around the corner.

Why? he wants to ask, but he contains himself. He curses himself for ever giving out the address. He does not invite him to the house, but agrees to meet him somewhere nearby for coffee.

'Unfortunately, I have only ten minutes,' he tells Hisashi.

They meet at a coffee shop in a shopping centre where the muzak and human noises drift up to the high glass ceilings, creating a constant undertone.

'Do you remember Philippe?' Hisashi asks. 'He is dead.'

'What? When? I didn't hear.'

'Month ago. Someone at the Alliance mentioned. Somewhere in Asia, drowned in a hotel swimming pool.'

He wants to hear more, but that is all Hisashi knows. What a banal end, he thinks. Too much champagne in the blood, perhaps – the accumulated residue of years of sipping the nectar of European civilisation. There is silence while Hisashi chews his cake.

'I can help you here,' Hisashi says in between crumbs. 'Allow me.'

He is instantly furious. How dare he? What is it that's driving this clumsy Japanese man's behaviour, that's keeping him here? Is there nothing, or no one, waiting for him in Tokyo?

'No, Hisashi, you can't.'

'Come on, let me help.'

Does the man have the thick hide of a walrus?

From the Perfume Pagoda they travel to the coast, to Halong Bay. Dragon Bay. A large expanse of water, with two thousand islands. The islands resemble the rock peaks inland around the Perfume Pagoda. Steep and pointed, rising like mountains from the water, tropically overgrown. In between, wooden junks are navigating like warships: sails aloft, dragon heads spewing flames at the bows. He and Hisashi negotiate a price and sail out on a junk. They get a cabin. They will spend the night on the water.

The air is murky and turbid. Some little islands have inlets with floating villages. Rows of floats with wooden houses and moored boats. A woman is sitting on her knees on the edge of a float, gutting fish. Scales drift away from her in silver patterns. She bobs up and down in the junk's wake, not looking up.

The anchor is dropped. Kayaks are lowered into the water. He and Hisashi row around one of the islands. On one side is a low entrance, so that, at ebb tide, one can only just row through. You have to pull your head into your shoulders, the rocky roof against your crown. When you can tilt your face to the sun again, you gasp: a perfectly round lake, inside the islet.

'This island is a doughnut!' Hisashi says, and laughs.

Steep, tropically overgrown slopes around the lake. Absolute silence. Something moving in the hanging branches. A tail appearing and disappearing amidst the foliage. He has read about the generations of shy monkeys that spend their lives here. They know every tree, every branch, even before they are born, a map of the slopes etched into their genes. He cannot get a proper view of any of them. Just flickerings of movement from the corner of the eye.

He hears a splash behind him. Then silence. When he looks around, Hisashi's kayak is lying bottom up. The boat is in the middle of the lake. Ripples move towards the edges and the water settles again. Only he is left. And the invisible monkeys.

For a moment he enjoys the peace. Then he takes a deep breath, rolls over and dives down into the cold water. He gropes around, grabs onto a soft arm. He drags the weight to the surface. At least the fatty are lighter in water. Hisashi gulps for air. He bursts out laughing, spluttering and coughing. He himself finds nothing to laugh about.

Rowing back, they are chilled to the bone. In their cabin, he and Hisashi take turns in the shower. 'You first,' Hisashi says. His eyes are shiny.

His throat constricted earlier at the thought of the two of them together in this little cabin, but a calmness has come over him now. He is being emptied; his thoughts fill with water. He showers, wraps himself in a blanket. Hisashi takes too long and his shower is too hot. Steam fills the small room. The Japanese emerges, naked and shiny like a seal. He looks at the large smooth surfaces of the dark body. It is the first time he has thought of Hisashi as sensual. Hisashi stands there smiling; steam keeps rising from him. Hisashi stays standing like that until he pulls the blanket tighter around his shoulders and walks out onto the deck.

Hisashi follows after a while, now also wrapped in a blanket. A child is approaching them slowly out of the mist, rowing a small boat standing up. He offers his wares: cans of Coke, a glittering fish. He quotes prices in dong and dollar. Hisashi leans forward, towards the water. He and the child have a conversation without understanding each other.

Out of the murkiness, more children come rowing towards them. The little boats cluster against the junk, bumping gently against the wooden hull. The children look up, stretching their hands towards the two figures in blankets, as if towards gods. Hisashi reaches out to them, their fingertips touching. The blanket slips from his shoulders. The children's clothes are thin and dirty, their feet flapping in leaked water like misshapen fish. Children of the floating world. Water monkeys.

Shadows rise up from the water. Dusk. When he looks

up, the haziness lifts for a moment. The current has fanned out the scales from all the villages' fish scrubbers into a veil drifting from the bay, following the sun. Beyond the islets, the deep sea is gleaming. He suddenly wonders what the inhabitants of the floating villages do with their dead, whether they just quietly slip them over the edge. He can feel the earth tilting into darkness.

He wants to rejoice, drop onto his knees and pray into the empty winter wind. Yesterday he did not think she would survive the night. This morning she ate a scrap of toast the size of a thumb. And three black grapes. He counts the stems to which shreds of grape flesh still cling. Over and over. Like a child learning numbers. The number three: one plus one plus one. It moves him to tears.

The more she ingests without vomiting, the more his hand is strengthened. There is no longer any excuse. He looks over her shoulder while she loads rice onto her fork, grain by grain. She puts the fork down. Slowly, she shifts the plate towards him across the bed. It is almost too heavy for her. The pile of rice remains almost untouched, as white as the sheet stretching between them like a frozen sea. They look at each other. He is adamant. A tear runs down her nose. Slowly she props herself up on an elbow, stretches out a hand. With a fingertip she picks up a grain, brings it to her lips. She falls back.

'There. I can't do more than that for you.'

She is hardly audible. He leaves her in peace.

In the kitchen he looks at the plate. For all the toil and struggle and strategising, she has, over the last week, eaten less food than would fit into the palm of a child's hand. The euphoria was misplaced. He is losing.

He relents. For the rest of the day he stops trying to feed her. He can see the pain taking hold of her. He keeps asking how she is feeling, how much it hurts, over and over. Every other minute, until she can no longer answer. Initially, the answer stays the same; later it becomes just a movement of the head. He ascends the stairs to his room, back down, through the kitchen and out to the garden. The familiar route.

The gate bell rings. There is a video intercom for keeping out danger. It is Hisashi's face that appears on the screen.

'Hello!' Hisashi bellows into the microphone, his wide forehead against the camera.

Then, louder, so that the speaker inside vibrates: 'Hello?'

He lets him in.

'And now?'

'I'm dropping by to see how things are going!' Even jollier than on the phone.

Hisashi walks further into the house, looking around avidly.

'She's sleeping, Hisashi, it's not a good time – '

His mother's voice from the bedroom, stronger than before: 'I'm awake. Show the guest in.'

Hisashi walks ahead of him down the corridor. Then he stops, bends down. On the wooden floor, Hisashi finds an insect wing. Green and red with black spots. That of a locust, the kind that sweeps in swarms through wheat fields leaving not a grain behind. He holds it against the light, stretching it between his fingertips like a fan. In the bedroom his mother is waiting.

*

From Hanoi they fly together to Tokyo. Hisashi's flat is so small that one has to fold away the kitchen counter to access the bath. It slots together like a three-dimensional puzzle: the water from the kitchen sink drains into the bath, the little dining table slides away on a track to allow the bed above the study corner to hinge out of the wall. Like a Rubik's Cube. Click-click. A flap in the kitchen is lowered to reveal the bathroom mirror. Lights tilt in different directions. Doors slide away. Television and computer screens swing from niches. Paraphernalia fits into drawers.

He and Hisashi have to fold and brush past each other too. Each of them sleeps on an edge of the double bed, facing outward. He sleeps badly, dreaming that the bed snaps into the wall with them in it and that he is smothered together with Hisashi. He wakes up with Hisashi's sleepy breath on his neck. The Japanese man has turned around and moved closer.

They spend as little time as possible in the flat. They attend a Monday-afternoon Kabuki performance. As tradition dictates, the male and female characters are played by men who have for decades acted the same role, their acting polished to perfection. The stage movements are stiff, stylised. The theatre is filled with Tokyo housewives who gasp with joy when an old man with swollen feet and a prominent Adam's apple changes into a delicate young girl right before their eyes. The audiences know the piece, they anticipate each movement, each word, each note. They could see it another hundred times. Or a thousand. It will never bore them.

When they walk back to the flat, Hisashi pulls him by the sleeve.

'Come, I want to show you something.'

They walk up a narrow staircase. At the top, a young woman is awaiting them. She smiles a broad smile. She takes him by the arm and leads him deeper into the building, but Hisashi gesticulates, no, it is he himself who is the client.

'Ah!' she says, as if having an epiphany.

She makes Hisashi sit down in front of a mirror. She holds up in front of him a catalogue with photos – coquettish schoolgirls with an index finger in the mouth, middle-aged housewives, bashful geishas, office ladies in pencil skirts. A short conversation follows, a negotiation. Hisashi points decisively at a picture.

She takes the make-up palette in her hand and starts working on Hisashi's face. He is standing to the side, watching. From time to time she stands back, admiring her handiwork. Moves closer to add a detail or scrape something away. Then Hisashi gets a wig. Black straight hair styled in a bob. Excitedly, she pitter-patters to the next room. She is dragging Hisashi – a shy hand clutched over his mouth – behind her. He follows the giggling pair. She disappears between rows of clothes hangers and reappears with an outfit – a frock of cerulean silk. Then shoes. Hisashi undresses, standing there in his underwear, his face carefully made up and white against the shapeless brown body. Once he is dressed, they trot in single file to the next room, Hisashi now in high heels.

In this room, there is a runway, like at a fashion show. She makes Hisashi practise his walking in heels, one hand on the hip, mirrors all around. He is doing his best, but she shakes her head, claps with her hands, repeats her instructions emphatically. She shrugs her shoulders, turns to him as if he could help. She gives up, leaves the room muttering. The transformation is incomplete. Hisashi is unperturbed, looking at himself in the mirror over his shoulder, at his substantial derrière cocooned in silk.

They are back in the flat. Hisashi is himself again. His own face, his own clothes. The place transforms like a machine. Kitchen becomes bathroom, living room becomes bedroom. One can travel between rooms without moving an inch. Panels snap open and hinge and slide and swing. Drawers fit in their niches. Clasps click shut.

He is lying awake; Hisashi is snoring. When at last he dozes off, he dreams of Hisashi lying in a rice paddy, slowly swelling into enormity as gallons of water ooze into him.

Hisashi sits down in the room with her. He now keeps arriving unannounced at any hour of the day, simply making himself at home. Coincidentally, it happens whenever she is having a better day. She talks to him. She sits up, asks for tea, even eats a tiny corner of toast without prompting.

He withdraws, sits down outside in the garden. He opens up a blank notebook on a table of steel mesh under a red chestnut tree. Now and then a leaf falls on the page. Sprinklers switch on automatically, wetting the lawn. He wants to write a belated journal of his and Hisashi's trip two years ago. A thorough report, day by day. He is trying to remember, to figure out what happened during the trip, if anything, and what it has to do with what is happening here now. The silver drops from the sprinklers hypnotise him. His pen hovers above the page.

*

On the surface it could well look like something else, this struggle of minute movements and intense strategy. Owing to unknown causes, his big toe has become infected. Overnight it has swollen like a clown's nose. His mother notices it when he walks into her room barefoot. (Little escapes her gaze.) She is deeply concerned; she becomes fixated on the toe.

'In the pantry,' she says. 'Epsom salts.'

'It's not important,' he says.

'Bring it.'

She makes him prepare a strong solution in a bowl with boiling hot water. It is virtually scorching him.

'Keep it in.'

For almost an hour he has to sit like this under her supervision. Only once does she send him to fetch more boiling water. His wet sole leaves the single track of a cripple.

'Let the solution draw out the infection.'

She flickers up somewhat, talks a little while his foot, so it feels, is sucking up water rather than expelling the impurity. He wants to take it out of the bowl.

'Not yet. Wait.'

The next morning, when he wakes up, the toe is back to normal. She is sick as can be. Vomiting. Pain. Tiredness absorbing her into the earth. She exposes her shoulder with the morphine plaster. A little square of transparent plastic film. She pulls it off and drops it on the carpet, where it curls up and disappears in the sunlight.

'And now?'

'Doesn't help anyhow.'

He presses his knuckles against his teeth.

'Pills then? Even just paracetamol?'

She turns away. The struggle has entered a new, brutal phase. Scorched earth.

'It's not important.'

He opens his mouth to say something, but she waves away his words with her hand.

'No pill ever again. Never anything again. My body still belongs to me.'

War beyond war.

She asks him to switch on the music and turns her back on him. The chant of monks. The droning bass behind it could be God's voice, or the voice of the deep sea.

They go on an excursion. From Tokyo they will travel south-west. The ultimate destination: Itsukushima Island, near Hiroshima. They book tickets to attend a Noh theatre performance on Itsukushima. Hisashi is not in the mood for it.

'Boring, elitist stuff,' he complains.

He persuades him. They travel by night to avoid the worst of the traffic. When they return, it will be by day, so that they can get a view of Mount Fuji's snowy peak.

Hisashi is driving – singing and humming to stay awake. For his part, he is trying to sleep, but is forced to listen: off-pitch fragments of French chansons, British pop, impenetrable Japanese songs. When Hisashi switches on the radio and it belts out Kylie Minogue, sleep finally deserts him.

Just before midnight they stop at a service station on the highway. They refuel, then park next to rows of lorries. He aims for the little, brightly lit restaurant where waiters are waiting behind polished glass, like wax dolls, but Hisashi says, 'Let me show you something.'

They walk around the building to a different entrance. Behind the first door is a slot machine. Hisashi inserts coins. It is warm and stuffy here. A little window swooshes open and two towels and magnetised cards slide out on an electric tray. They walk through a second door. The steamy heat takes one's breath away. A dressing room. They undress and, with a swipe of the cards, lock their clothes in two steel lockers.

They walk through a third door. In here everything moves at a languorous pace. Fat, naked lorry drivers are immersing themselves in baths or arranging themselves on deckchairs around the edges. Boiled red, like crayfish. Some leave their towels and slip into the water. It is scorching. The men look at him from under heavy lids, at his white body. Nobody says a word. In such steam, while you are slowly being boiled tender, it is not possible to speak.

When they arrive back at the carpark glowingly revitalised, he notices, for the first time, the rows of plastic cherry blossoms blooming on electric wires criss-crossing overhead.

He is sitting on the veranda. Hunger makes him alert. He has not been strictly implementing his threat to eat no more than his mother does, even though he makes her believe it. He nevertheless has difficulty taking in much, so that he is starting to feel transparent. The transparency enhances his senses.

A lukewarm winter breeze is blowing. His ears are tingling with birdsong and the wind is moving through the branches. For weeks his mother has been reluctant to go out, even though he has offered to drag her bed out here, so that she can lie with her feet in the sun. He will have to find a way to bring the birds and the singing branches inside, to her. Her sheets are too white and silent.

Dry leaves brush over the veranda floor, past his feet. Winter wants to sneak into the house. Perhaps he should stay here to keep out the plundering season, to catch every leaf and crush it, until his hands themselves turn to dust.

Later on he is sitting in a garden chair, in a shaded corner under the red chestnut tree. From here he can see his mother through the window, in her bed. And she can see him. His travel journal is progressing. What he has forgotten, he makes up. It is coming to him, faster and faster. His pen takes them to places they have never been.

He is there with her at every turn, at each crossing of another little boundary: when she can no longer lift her foot high enough to get into the bath, when a glass of water becomes too heavy and slips from her hand. At her request he brings paper. She wants to write a few last letters. She tries, but trembles so much that she can only make ink marks. It upsets her more than anything to date. More, perhaps, than the cancer diagnosis. For hours, she does not say a word. He leaves her alone.

'I'll write,' he says later in the afternoon. 'You dictate.'

'Later,' she says. (Never, that is.)

She turns her back. He stays. She asks him, after a silent spell, what he is writing out there in the garden.

'I'm struggling to finish it,' is all he says.

'Shall I read it and suggest an ending?'

He hears something in the house. He walks to the lounge. A bird is fluttering about, up against the ceiling. Some greyish suburban bird or other; he has long since forgotten the names of birds here. He tries to chase it out. It keeps flying into corners. He opens the double doors to the veranda. It flies out, sweeping over the frost-dead lawn into the white sky. Bird shit stays behind on the interior walls, like crooked letters. Like Eastern calligraphy. Maybe that is an ending. Let the birds write it.

He had been trying to keep Hisashi away from his mother. He thought the Japanese man would exhaust her. But she inexplicably perked up when he peered into her room.

'How are you doing, Mommy?' Hisashi asked.

He wanted to point out to Hisashi that one does not address someone else's mother in that manner in English, but she got in first.

'Bring me a cup of tea and then we can have a chat,' she whispered.

When Hisashi returned with the tea, she was drowsy, but she took a sip or two.

'I'm going to come and cook for you,' Hisashi said to her.

He wanted to explain that his mother was no longer eating anything, and that he was looking after her anyhow, but again she was too quick for him.

'Something new, please. Something I've not eaten before.'

The gate bell rings. Talk of the devil. When the front door opens, the food smells reach him instantly. They are emanating from the little tower of plastic boxes Hisashi is carrying against his chest. He wants to wax indignant about the repeated invasions, but his stomach is empty and his mouth watering.

'We'll be eating outside,' Hisashi says, marching in.

'She won't go outside, Hisashi.'

Hisashi just smiles mysteriously. He unpacks the food in an orderly and precise manner, not on the veranda, but in the shade under the red chestnut tree. On the rusty steel-mesh table he sets out miso soup, bowls of rice, a chicken and noodle dish, and vegetable tempura.

He just stands there, looking on helplessly. There is green tea. Hisashi is disappointed that they don't have Oriental mugs. He has to pour it into ordinary teacups.

'Where do you get all these things, Hisashi?'

'Cooked it!'

'The ingredients, I mean.'

'Tried delicatessens nearby. Shopping centres. Useless rubbish. Japanese ingredients, but expensive, useless rubbish.'

He explains how he ventured into the run-down city centre, how he tracked down a little shop selling real Japanese products. The kind of things one would find in Tokyo.

'Now we carry her outside.'

Hisashi is smiling as if everything here is a secret and inexhaustible source of joy. The smile is as tormenting as the undertone in his mother's music. He shakes his head.

'She doesn't want to, Hisashi. I've told you, haven't I? She hasn't been out for weeks. She's too weak even to sit up.'

Hisashi keeps smiling, leading the way into the house.

She agrees to be carried outside. They help her from the bed into an armchair. The skin is hanging loose from her bones. Without a word they carry the chair between them, out into the sun, towards the smells of food.

*

Slowly, very slowly, the masked actor glides across the stage of cypress wood. Apart from the stylised representation of a pine tree, the stage is bare. With the flick of a fan and the tilt of a mask, the actor becomes a beautiful woman. One forgets that there is a man behind the second face, the wooden one.

Noh, so his travel guide informs him, was originally called Sarugaku – monkey music. The first actors, according to the guide, were supposedly monkeys impersonating the gods.

The actor's fan is laid down once he has assumed his position, and is only taken up again when he walks off the stage. The stage hands, clad in black, hand over props. They remain mutely on stage.

The themes are conventional. In the first scene a young woman in love and a desirable warrior appear. The love remains unrequited. In the second scene the woman is a ghost. More beautiful than in life itself. Earthly ties and desires have been transcended.

Hisashi is fidgety. Once he has had enough of the shimmering gown of silk brocade, he finds it all too stilted, too slow. This he imparts by means of a loud whisper. The performance consists of several dramas and lasts the entire day, but they leave after the first piece.

Hisashi stands around looking bored while he is buying a mask in the tourist shop. The kind worn in the play, a *Noh-men*. He tries on a few; there are a number of traditional designs. He chooses one that expresses a spectrum of emotions depending on the angle at which the wearer faces the audience. A bowed head shows joy, a smile. As the wearer gradually lifts his head, the light now catching it differently, the expression gradually changes. Surprise, then anger. At last, when the onlooker is faced squarely, there is undisguised anxiety.

They drive back. Hisashi is behind the wheel, where he is most comfortable. He is sitting turned sideways, away from Hisashi. He is reading in his guide about *rōjaku*, the final phase of a Noh actor's development, when, as an old man, he refines the art of eliminating all unnecessary sound and action, until only the essence of a scene or the action imitated remains.

'Fuji next,' Hisashi says.

'And Aokigahara.'

Hisashi looks at him quizzically.

They stop at the baths next to the highway again. Hisashi goes off to soak himself. He, however, undresses and stands in front of the mirror in the dressing room. He is trying on the *Noh-men*, dropping his head, practising the angles.

In one sitting she eats more of Hisashi's dishes than the sum of what he has managed to get her to eat in weeks. And she keeps it in. Hisashi's visits have a remarkable effect. She is truly improving. She gets up and walks short distances again, as in a New Testament miracle: to the sofa in the living room, once even to the door leading onto the veranda. For a moment she remains standing there, but the frosty breeze against her cheeks makes her teeter.

'Have you seen,' Hisashi asks, 'how transparent?'

'What do you mean?'

'She is now a ghost.' Hisashi ogles him; unexpectedly, there is lasciviousness in the Japanese man's heavy fingers.

'It's time for you to go, Hisashi.'

He leaves.

He keeps an eye on his mother from the garden. She is like a marionette when Hisashi arrives. The air in the house changes, stirring her limbs. When he leaves, she falls back onto the pillows like a rag doll.

Outside the bathroom window, the mesh of grey winter twigs creates complex patterns. He is bathing her, not for cleansing, but against the pain, which briefly flees before the warmth. The knobs of her knees are outlined against the white enamel. He pours piping hot water over her, aims it at the pain.

He wakes up in the early morning hours. The tinkling of a bell. Unmistakeable in the nocturnal winter air, the air that is crystallising around him and his mother. The silver sound brings relief. He recognises it instantly. He walks down the stairs. He finds her in the kitchen, sitting at the table in her white nightgown: in electric light, in front of an empty plate.

'No,' she shakes her head when he asks whether she has rung the bell, 'it's in the bedroom.'

The voice is hollow. It is coming from afar. She starts keeling over, weightlessly. There is nothing left of her.

'Sea of trees': that is what Aokigahara is often called. But here in the pine forest, where he and Hisashi are walking along a footpath, Hisashi hesitant behind him, it does not sound like the sea. It is the quietest forest in Japan. Perhaps that is why people come here to kill themselves. About fifty bodies are found in the forest every year. Notices are pinned to trees, in Japanese and English, trying to dissuade those planning to commit suicide. A small bouquet of flowers is tied to a random tree. Areas to both sides of them are cordoned off by blue ribbon. Volunteers come to scour the forest each year, according to his travel guide. The ribbons are put up to delineate search areas.

Through the treetops, there is the occasional glimpse of Fuji. The sky above the snowy peak is the brightest shade of blue he has ever seen.

'Have you seen enough? Can we go back?' Hisashi wants to know.

He shakes his head, striding ahead. Here and there a figure is visible at a distance, on other paths, through the trees.

They sit down to rest for a moment. The silence penetrates the skin. He reads in his guide that *ubasute* was practised here up to the nineteenth century – the practice of leaving an old and enfeebled parent in a remote place to perish of hunger or exposure. There is a reference to an old tale of a man carrying his mother up a mountain on his back, planning to abandon her there, at the peak, to the elements. On the way there she snaps off twigs, scattering them behind them, so that he will find his way back down and not perish with her.

'Shall we turn around now?' Hisashi asks.

He shakes his head. 'I want to go further.'

They have hardly started walking again when a figure appears against the light, some distance to their left. Not on a path, but between the trees. The figure stops, then remains quite still. They stop too. Something in the silence compels him to open his backpack and take out the *Noh-men*. The afternoon sun is shining through the leaves. He wants to put on the mask. He will adjust the angle, lift his chin all the way from below. He will know exactly what the effect is of every degree of tilting. But the mask stays in his hands. The figure just keeps standing there, as if petrified.

Then the figure lifts his arm and points. He looks around. Behind him, Hisashi has lain down flat on his back in the path. Motionless, eyes open.

Hisashi is sitting next to her on the bed. He is standing around, as if supervising.

She points to the wild gardenia growing near her bedroom window. 'Go and pick me one. Please.'

Hisashi trots outside elatedly. The flowering time is in fact over; there are just a few flowers left. The slightest draft causes more to drop. He keeps an eye on Hisashi through the window. When his thick fingers stir the small shrub, a spray of flowers sifts down onto his feet. He brings one inside. She smells it, shakes her head slightly.

'Nothing.'

He goes and picks another, and two more after that, until she detects the last whiff of summer and smiles quietly, eyes shut.

In a week's time it is his birthday.

'By that time, I'll be walking around again,' she insists.

The corners of her mouth are pulled downward by the pain. She wants to know what is left in the freezer for a birthday meal. He feels paralysed, unable to formulate an answer. Everything, is the answer, the entire colony of misshapen cadavers. He closes his eyes. He can imagine the last words, when they come, sometime or other in the next few days. As has become his habit, he will bend over her, lower down this time, to catch the last puff of her breath: 'Take something from the freezer,' she will say. 'Let it thaw for dinner.'

Since Hisashi's meal in the garden, she has not eaten again. The era of food has passed.

'I would love an ice-cold glass of lemon syrup.'

He drives from one cottage-industry shop to another. At last he finds home-made syrup with bits of lemon peel floating in it. He fills a rippled glass with ice, dripping syrup over the cubes and diluting it with water. She takes a sip, or rather, dips the tip of her tongue. The nausea overwhelms her. She falls back, trembling, with a weak, apologetic smile.

Water is his last hope.

'Tap water has a metallic aftertaste,' she says.

He goes out to buy her carbonated water of various brands. He serves it with a few strawberries, cut in half and sprinkled with sparkling grains of sugar – not to eat, but to reflect in the bubbles and lend colour to the water. He holds it to her lips. She throws up. She reckons it is the carbon dioxide. He goes out to buy still water. She does not hold that in either. The last line of defence falls.

It is night-time. He is by her side. He has difficulty staying awake – he keeps the overhead light on to create the illusion of daylight. Earlier, the pain was so intense that she bared her shoulder for a new morphine plaster: 75 micrograms. She is now travelling freely between sleep and wakefulness; the border fence has been removed. Boundaries between his mother and himself are fading too. He no longer knows which side he is on. He has been concentrating so long on feeling the illness in his own body. He wanted to become the perfect echo chamber. Wanted to be her from the inside, to make her pain entirely his own. But as soon as he thinks he is approaching the slippery mass of the pain, he looks in her eyes, sees how far ahead of him she is. Her boundaries have shifted unimaginably. He must now give up.

Even so, he cannot. This is what he now asks for in a prayer, the first in years: drive out the evil. Let it enter me. Make me the host, like a possessed swine from Gadara. Or it might be a moment of perfect beauty that sucks the evil out of her. No matter how hard he has to search, or how far or randomly he has to travel, find it he will.

His chin touches his chest, he cannot stay awake. She is whispering something. Or he thinks she is whispering. He brings his ear closer. Nothing. There are times, especially at night, when he wonders whether she will ever say anything again, whether she can still speak. He is able to measure what he has left of her in two ways: in days or in the number of sentences she will still utter. She is moving, she wants to go to the bathroom. He didn't think anything was being processed any longer. She shakes her head at the bedpan offered to her. She wants to get up. There is a remnant of will, a welling up of insistence. He clasps his arms around her chest, under her arms. He walks with her, an endless journey to the toilet. Or no, he is the only one touching the ground; carrying her. Her feet and arms are are rowing in the air, slowly and weightlessly. His mother the water-treader: she thinks she is walking, but she is swimming towards the light. He lowers her over the porcelain bowl. A few drops of urine, the colour of a forest pond.

On the way back, her resistance hardens. She extends an arm, struggling towards the door. 'I'm leaving now,' she says, and he knows immediately: it is the last sentence.

Everything that she still has left is invested in the refusal – the force of a raging crowd.

'Please,' he begs, 'please lie down instead.'

Initially he thinks it is the medication that is befuddling her, but when he looks her in the eye, he sees that she knows and means what she is saying. He has to apply coercion to get her under the sheets.

She slips away and he too slumbers in a chair by the bed, leaning forward, his head against her feet. In a dream he sees her against a slippery cliff. She is pulling herself up with great effort, on a rope with forty-nine knots. He wakes up when a raspy sigh escapes her. Like a gust of wind flipping through the pages of an open book forgotten on a summer lawn. The pages rustle and turn to the last word.

Hisashi's visits are unpredictable. Sometimes short, sometimes long, any time of the day. Sometimes twice a day, sometimes not at all. Hisashi watches critically when the oncologist arrives to set up a mechanical syringe driver. The needle goes into her chest. The plastic tube is filled with an amber-coloured mixture of morphine and sedatives. The little machine is wound up and placed on her pillow. It ticks like a bomb while slowly forcing fluid into her. When the oncologist has left, he pushes Hisashi aside gently. He feels his mother's pulse and, with his other hand, his own. Elsewhere in the house, the wall clock is chiming more slowly by the hour. It has not been wound for at least a week. Like metronomes running down at different speeds, all these rhythms, the interrelationships between intervals increasingly complex.

Hisashi is doing his little things: sometimes he just stands looking at her for a long time, talks at her in jolly Japanese, cooks something, becomes engrossed in some incomprehensible little ritual. On the whole he is ignoring Hisashi. He now often sits outside, in the rosy light filtering through the red chestnut leaves. He observes the white bed through the window. He writes in his journal. This is how he thinks of the writing: he is trying to give texture to the surface of a strange planet. Perhaps this will enable him to start exploring the textures around him, the most mysterious of all surfaces. Often, when he is writing in the garden, Hisashi sits or strolls near him, stealing glances at him. He still has no idea what Hisashi thinks his role here might be.

The morphine mixture is now draining all movement from her limbs. She is slipping into a semi-coma. Even Hisashi, during his unexpected visits, can hardly make her stir. He scatters small winter flowers from her bed to the veranda door, out across the veranda and in a winding path through the garden.

'What are you doing, Hisashi?'

'It's a route; I'm encouraging her to walk again.'

Hisashi keeps walking and tossing flowers.

'Look after yourself,' Hisashi says from where he has stopped at the end of the flower trail, only a few left in his hand. 'You're becoming a ghost too. You must follow the path yourself.'

For an hour Hisashi watches him intently as he writes at the steel-mesh table. He does not look up, just clenches his teeth ever more tightly. At last Hisashi averts his gaze.

'I'm flying back this weekend. I'm going to confirm my flight for Saturday morning.'

The blind fear entering his heart catches him entirely off guard. He knows very well he only has to say a word and Hisashi will stay. But he cannot.

No, he will test Hisashi. Saturday, when the morning sun starts falling into his mother's bedroom, he will throw open the front and veranda doors. He will go and stand in front of her cupboard. He will take out one of her night-gowns and put it on. In her bedroom he will smear a daub of make-up on his face. Then he will lie down next to her, there under the white sheets, and curl up like a monkey. Their faces turned to each other, eyes open, everything in perfect symmetry. In silence they will wait for Hisashi. To come and care for them. To come and feed them like a mother feeds her twins: a spoonful for him, and then a spoonful for her.

And if Hisashi does not come? Then no one would have to refuse, or threaten to refuse, ever again. He will see to it that his desiccation and departure coincide with his mother's. The leaves will blow in through the doors. The garden birds will fly in and whirl around their heads, will write an ending on them. Sharing a boat, they will row through to the secret lake. With a white flag at the bow.

VNLS

'Sounds like a venereal disease, that name.' On the veranda Mrs Nyathi's eyes blink in the moonlight.

Ondien half-smiles. 'Yes, I guess, like something that would have meant insanity and death for a woman a hundred years ago.'

She leans over towards Mrs Nyathi's cigar, smouldering on the edge of the ashtray. 'May I?' Ondien puffs on it, blows the smoke in little clouds towards the village lights below them. 'It stands for "Victorian Native Ladies' Society". An attempt, originally, at ironic allusion – '

'Gosh, they were rotten with venereal diseases, the women, when I was a nurse in Frere Hospital! Ooh, you should be careful, girls of your age!' Mrs Nyathi clicks her tongue. 'The men do just what they want, they don't care.'

She wriggles in her chair, lifts her puffy feet in front of her, looks through screwed-up eyes at Beauty, sitting deeper in the shade. Lying under Mrs Nyathi's chair are two dachshunds, like twins.

'Yes, you young girls with your voices like honey and the music in your hips. You are the candles and men the moths,' she continues, nodding her head.

'I don't think,' Ondien says drily, 'our music gives off the sort of heat that the moths might be hoping for.'

Mrs Nyathi is not to be dissuaded. 'Oh, you'll see over the weekend in Lesotho. They won't be able to keep their eyes off you.'

In the room Ondien moves her travel-worn suitcase and the little box of VNLS CDs off the comical four-poster. Satin is draped from above in salmon pink. 'Here in Bella Gardens you can expect luxury, everywhere just luxury,' Mrs Nyathi insisted on the phone. Since it is the only guest house in Vloedspruit, there was in fact no need for sales talk. The 'Regina Suite' was allocated to Ondien. The *R* on the room's nameplate, she noticed later, had at some point been scratched out (by a mischievous guest? an aggrieved employee?) and replaced with a *V*.

Ondien can hear little noises from next door. She knows Beauty's sleeping routines well. First she rubs cream in little circular movements on her face. Slowly, she then folds the sheets back, testing the mattress before entrusting her weight to it. Nungi has been lying asleep on the single bed next to Beauty's since dinner, when Ondien peered into their room: clothes scattered around her, hips wide and self-assured under the sheets.

Ondien takes out one of the CDs, holds it under the reading lamp. She smiles a little. The production values of the cover design are dubious, like the quality of the recording itself, which she had made at her own expense in a musty Long Street studio in Cape Town. She is standing in the middle, plucky in drag: an early British-colonial uniform. Beauty and Nungi, in Zulu skirts, are kneeling at her sides, their breasts exposed, complete with beads and little patches of leopard skin. *VNLS* in an arc of large lettering at the top. Like a vaudeville handbill, an advertisement for a Victorian spectacle.

A storm is building outside the open bedroom windows. Ondien is tossing and turning amidst billowing satin. She gets up, creeps across creaking floorboards towards the veranda. She stands in the wind, looking out. A backward little frontier town. At the top of the slope is an official building, a school or college of some kind. Then there is this ramshackle nineteenth-century house where they are staying, Bella Gardens, with its ornamental ironwork below the veranda ceiling. Probably an old farmhouse. Otherwise the village consists of shacks that seem to be perpetually washing away. There is nothing here. She has to laugh at herself, stuck in this outpost. She allows herself a flash of memory of her former Parisian life, but stops once she starts thinking about Thierry.

Something is moving at the edge of the veranda. The dachshunds' little bodies stir where they are lying under a chair, as if Mrs Nyathi's feet have been left behind, disembodied. Sleepily the two trot into the house, one behind the other, to snuggle up under Mrs Nyathi's sheets.

Ondien stands with an index finger in one ear, cellphone against the other. Inside, Mrs Nyathi has put on another record. The record player is built into a high-gloss wooden cabinet, like a coffin. Their Mistress's Voice. Miriam Makeba is singing. For their presumed enjoyment. Hers and Beauty's and Nungi's. 'Amampondo!' Makeba sings, and there is heaving and clicking, heaving and clicking. The throat, the intestines and the knotting stomach muscles: all flesh serving the rhythm, inducing hypnosis.

'What about the sound system and the sound engineer? Did you get my email with the mock-up of the poster?!'

Beauty is sitting on the veranda step, listening to Ondien's side of the conversation. Mrs Nyathi is stroking the dogs on her lap. Trixie and Mixie, they are called, she informed Ondien the first evening. 'Got them last month. Some pleasant company. It's lonely for a widow here in the mountains.'

'Wait, give it to me. I understand the language.' Nungi wants to take the phone from Ondien. Ondien turns away. Miriam Makeba is becoming louder, more insistent – one of Mrs Nyathi's maids is turning up the volume inside. The phone cuts out.

'Bloody telephone lines in Lesotho!' Ondien says, and rolls her eyes. 'The goats probably chew them to shreds. Just have to hope for the best. And drag as much of our gear with us as we can.'

In two days' time they are performing in Lesotho. About half an hour's drive by taxi, their hostess informs them. She looks as if she wants to go along, does Mrs Nyathi; as if she has not felt music in her limbs for some time.

'It's "Pata Pata" time!' Mrs Nyathi shouts out with Makeba, her eyes now screwed shut in entrancement. Trixie lifts her wrinkly neck and slurps little mouthfuls of whisky from Mrs Nyathi's glass.

Ondien submits to the waiting, to the forlornness of the little village. One afternoon she walks down the slope, through all the poverty, to the flood plain by the river. Fish are lying on the ground after the previous night's floods, barbels flapping in the mud. Children are running around, collecting fish in plastic shopping bags, touching Ondien's hands as they pass. She smiles, not really present, hands out a few coins.

She is happy to be here, on the edge of everything. She could only stomach the Cape Town music scene for a few months. Initially it provided a shot of energy after London and Paris's insincere politeness. New influences made the VNLS sound even more complex, more chaotic. The music had found a new niche. Or, rather, new niches to smash. *Her* music – she, after all, is VNLS's image-maker and driving force; Nungi and Beauty have the voices and the rhythm, but they just follow.

Earlier, VNLS's sound was a reasonably coherent fusion of Western club music with instrumentation from North and West Africa, with kwaito and township elements in between. Gradually, they had to start packaging and underplaying the *éléments exotiques* – the multitude of influences – to retain their mainly white Parisian audiences. Ethnic was passable, as long as the listeners could make them out, in a recognisable way, to be *Zoulous*. In Cape Town the elements multiplied swiftly: Nigerian soul layered over London electro-pop, influences of ragga. A little funk and hip-hop. Lyrics in Cape Afrikaans. The musicians with whom they collaborated rotated as fast as the music mutated. There was a brief Cape gang-rap phase, but Beauty was too scared to work alone into the small hours in grubby Long Street studios with the men with their golden teeth and prison tattoos. Ondien started listening to Lucky Dube again, Yvonne

Chaka-Chaka and Brenda Fassie. She listened further and further back into history. A long time had passed since abandoning her academic interest in ethnomusicology, but now she was listening to kwela and marabi again, was singing along to early Mahotella Queens, starting to make a thorough study of mbaqanga from the 1760s. She pushed her ear right up against the speaker. The old recordings crackled with static.

After one of their Cape Town performances, a record company representative came up to her. He ignored Beauty and Nungi and looked Ondien in the eyes.

'Some astonishing moments and sounds,' was his judgement, 'but it doesn't gel, there's no identity. A hodge-podge. There's something we could work with, though. I like the ethnic thing.'

He offered to buy drinks, but looked annoyed when the other two did not want to come along. It turned out his intention was an intimate drink in his hotel room. For the three of them.

'I think you are misunderstanding the complexity of our intentions.' Ondien's tone was as chilly as only a European could manage – her lessons had been learned in the wintry north.

The multitude of sounds milling inside her skull had unpredictable – and probably irreconcilable – influences on VNLS's music. Her own musical reactions became unpredictable too. Sometimes they would hit upon a chord or stanza that suddenly made her choke on her tears. Initially, she thought she might be approaching cacophony, but when she closed her eyes and listened more deeply, she could make out prime chords behind the noise. Something that was gravitating back, to the beginning. She reminded herself that she was unable to endure anything other than skimming over the surface of this country; that this was the reason for her original departure. To make the music move forward, she had to avoid origins. She had suddenly become averse to Cape Town cool, to the city itself. Whenever Ondien noticed VNLS's audience getting going with the dancing, she would improvise, working against her own rhythms and melodies. On impulse, she would harden her ear and interlace small quotes from ancestral music. The high priests of European bloodlessness were honoured in this manner. Precise little fragments of Schoenberg or Webern would find their place. Alien in the bright sunlight. She insisted on translating English lyrics into Afrikaans and Zulu, combining the Afrikaans with the most unresolved, self-cannibalising music – songs that were pulling apart at the seams. Their performances descended into exquisite chaos. Fellow musicians stormed off the stage. Audiences booed. Beauty and Nungi kept dancing in their Zulu skirts with apparent joy, singing into their microphones.

Their last night was a perfect Cape Town November evening: everything shimmering, perpetually moving, something nervous in the air. But how absurd the city looked to her when she and Beauty and Nungi returned to their hotel room after the performance – this city with its wild oceans and sandy flats, its corrugated-iron shacks in the fog, its self-satisfied enclaves with neo-modernist villas cantilevered over the waves. She stood there, looking out from the balcony on the eleventh floor, and thought: it's time to go. As always, Beauty and Nungi followed. For a few months thereafter, they stayed in guest houses and down-at-heel hotels in villages in the Western Cape and Free State, played where they could, for white as well as black audiences. They were penniless, and had to support themselves with what, after their Parisian adventure, Ondien had left of a modest inheritance from her parents. Ondien adjusted the music according to where they were. She was as nimble as a fox, reading audiences and veering in new directions. (A *rousserolle verderolle*, Thierry called her between his sheets in his Marais *appartement* shortly after they had met: a marsh warbler, the migrating northern bird that can impersonate seventy species from Africa.) By this time, Beauty and Nungi knew her so well that they could follow seamlessly.

The white audiences were suspicious. Art-festival types: thin-lipped parents with obstreperous children, important women with important hair, thirty-something yuppies with German-style spectacle frames, acned teenagers misinterpreting the fashions of more civilised parts of the world, clean-faced Free State university students. Mostly Afrikaans-speaking, sometimes with cynical expressions when commenting behind their hands amidst the noise. Even though Ondien felt strange here – kept herself strange – the sense of menace that she would sometimes experience in front of black township audiences was absent. There she had to wear the 'ethnic thing' like a mask to outface the listeners until, at last, she could reach them. It took something for a white woman to soften them, to render them defenceless enough to be entertained.

The first Christmas back in South Africa Ondien spent with Beauty and Nungi. Ondien's parents had died two years earlier, within two weeks of each other. She could attend only her father's funeral. It was to be her last visit to the farm where she grew up. She had hardly set foot back in London when her mother collapsed over her little gardening fork in a bed of nasturtiums. Ondien could not afford to fly back again. Shortly after her mother's death the farm was sold.

The only family member still left in South Africa was her sister Vera. In an Italian-style villa in Bryanston with security cameras in the garden. But only just: she and her husband were spending most of their time on business trips to Dubai, the children looked after by au pairs. The last time Ondien saw them was at the funeral. They wanted to establish themselves in Dubai as soon as possible, they explained over and over again.

'Not that different to this place,' Vera said, gold flashing on her fingers. 'Just safer. Sunshine. Homes the same size. Swimming pools. International schools, tax advantages. It's not really all that strict either. Westerners are allowed to drink alcohol. And you hardly need have anything to do with Arabs.'

No, she would not be spending Christmas with Vera. Vera did not even know that she was back in the country. And, who knows, perhaps the tide had turned, perhaps Vera and co had decided, after all, to make cultural concessions and give up Christmas, in anticipation of their utopian existence in the Middle East.

Her brother the banker she had seen only once when she was still in London, in a restaurant filled with City men in suits. The place made her feel frumpy. Her kaftan with ornamental stitching around the neck was a mistake. She found herself wondering whether she smelled of the small grey nest of a council flat that she shared in South London with a Ghanaian photographer and a Japanese ballet dancer.

'When will you be moving on from the academic stuff?' Cornelius wanted to know. 'There's a big world out there, you know. You have talent. You could easily requalify in, say, finance or law.'

When she tried getting in touch again afterwards, a series of women – secretaries or lovers – answered his phone each time, explaining that he was travelling. He was either in Tokyo or Moscow, in São Paulo or Sydney.

Her younger sister, Zelda, was in Phoenix. She was divorced from her psychopathic American husband. The psychopath was unemployed and she had to support him. The American courts had forbidden her to take the child out of the country for more than two weeks per year. Zelda would not be able to return to South Africa. Ondien had not spoken to her since their father's funeral. Zelda had been so run-down by her working life, the long flight and her maladjusted, brutal child with his Arizona accent that they had exchanged no more than a few sentences, and half of it in English. It had surprised her how Zelda's Afrikaans had become diluted. Ondien was sad about Zelda. They had been bosom sisters in their youth, just two years apart. Walking together from the farm to the village school in the mornings, they had always smoked a cigarette on the sly in the red grass. On one such morning, Zelda had accidentally set Ondien's sleeve alight. The burn was still visible on her arm. Yes, she missed Zelda. But she was also grateful that Satan's child was trapped in America. She had no desire herself ever to set foot on that continent, and the ocean between her and that little psychopath was hardly wide enough.

So, over Christmas it was just them: she and Beauty and Nungi. They were in the Karoo, having rented a small cottage on a farm. The farmer and his wife cast each other furtive glances, trying to figure out the relationship between the three of them. Ondien cooked a goose that she had bought from the farmer's wife, stroking the scar on her upper arm absent-mindedly as she stood in front of the stove.

'You are now my family,' Ondien said later, as they were eating, and lifted her glass.

A moment after she said it, she sensed that her tone had been misplaced. It was as if the false note reverberated for the rest of the evening, as if it made the air ebb and flow all night. One moment they were strangers to each other, the next sisters, then strangers again. Ondien kept rubbing the scar on her arm and smiling. She slipped out at one point and brought back some painkillers for Beauty. The evening did not stay still for a moment. One moment she was too close to Beauty, then too far away again. Nungi held out her greasy plate for more goose meat, then pulled it back, resentful that it was Ondien who was dishing it out. Her two companions drank so much wine that they fell asleep on the couches. From where Ondien was sitting on the rug, they looked like cadavers.

'My sisters,' she said out loud, and her voice was strange. The red wine had made her melancholy. She was alone in this morgue, and outside the Karoo sky was clear and merciless. She took the pain pills that Beauty had left on the coffee table.

*

'You're only the second white woman to stay in my guest house,' Mrs Nyathi says on the veranda after dinner. The dachshunds, it turns out, have bladder-control problems. The two lie leaking on the chairs, leaving behind damp spots that filter through to the buttocks of unsuspecting sitters. While nodding at Mrs Nyathi, Ondien suddenly feels the damp warmth below her. She glares at the two dogs on Mrs Nyathi's lap.

'The other woman was a nurse who studied here at the college,' Mrs Nyathi continues. She puffs on her cigar. 'Things aren't looking good for her. She lives near the lodge where you're playing after your Lesotho gig.'

Gig falls strangely on Mrs Nyathi's tongue, too youthful a word for her. Ondien cannot get her head around this woman. But she imagines the confusion is mutual.

'Who is my predecessor and why aren't things looking good for her?'

'She's gone back to Venterstad. She does things that white women don't normally do. She cares for the sick and for orphans. Near that lodge. But that's a different story.'

Mrs Nyathi lets the smoke hang between them. She says nothing more.

The dampness spreads across Ondien's backside. The isolation in Vloedspruit and Mrs Nyathi's hypnotic presence are making her want to stay. She is in no mood for the gig in Lesotho or the one following that. Somewhere in the godforsaken Eastern Cape, she told Mrs Nyathi last night, there is an extravagant private game reserve, Twilight Lodge, where VNLS has been invited to play in two weeks' time. The Lesotho gig is a minor distraction along the way. One of Ondien's former professors at the School of Oriental and African Studies was a middle-aged ex-South African who had, after years of exile, got stuck in London, but had long-standing, albeit fading, ANC connections. He had recommended her. A national soccer team staying at the lodge after the World Cup would apparently have to be entertained. And there would be plenty of VIPs, of that she was assured repeatedly and emphatically. Government people, industrialists, Black Economic Empowerment types, of course, and celebrities. The invitation impressed on her what an immense privilege it was to be performing at this historic occasion. A token white is required, she suspects, to put European soccer players at ease, but one picked by hand – someone with the right credentials, who embraces Africa with the appropriate conspicuousness. She smiles wryly. She does not think her hosts have the vaguest clue what is awaiting them.

Mrs Nyathi lifts Trixie, rubs her own nose back and forth over the dog's muzzle.

'Yes,' she says and screws up her face, 'you and Mixie are Mommy's toys, hey? Here for me to play with.'

Trixie wriggles. Mrs Nyathi lets her settle in next to Mixie on the knee blanket.

Beauty joins Ondien and Mrs Nyathi. She sits down painfully, aware of each joint. Mixie jumps off Mrs Nyathi's lap and stands up, paws against Beauty's leg. She picks up the little body, presses it to her stomach. From Mrs Nyathi's lap, Trixie licks the cigar balanced on the rim of the ashtray. She pulls her nose back sharply. Mrs Nyathi puckers her lips, lifts the dog so that it may lick her mouth.

Ondien leans over to Beauty in the half-dark and touches her hand. Beauty pulls back.

178

'Shall I get some pills?' Ondien whispers.

Beauty shakes her head.

Music becomes audible inside, spreading like light across the veranda. It is Nungi, playing one of Mrs Nyathi's records. Youssou N'Dour, the little prince from Dakar. Nungi appears in the door, belting it out with the music. She tries to get Ondien to dance with her. Ondien first resists, then surrenders. She sees how Mrs Nyathi's fingers and fat little toes start moving, sees how the older woman wishes it were she that Nungi was sweeping across the veranda like a lover.

At night, when she struggles to sleep, Ondien sits up in her bed for long periods. Tonight is such a night. The voice of Youssou N'Dour is still ringing in her head. She tries to bend it into something else, but it evades her attempts. Yet another storm is building up outside her bedroom window. She touches the satin draping. Their stay here feels so provisional – a trip that has failed to start properly, that cannot get going. On reflection, she realises it is in fact a trip that has lost momentum. There is almost nowhere left to go.

Ondien's suitcases are being packed by the maids. Mrs Nyathi insisted. They are swift and able, their movements between cupboard and four-poster stirring the drapings. ('A packing and unpacking service is part of what we offer,' said Mrs Nyathi. Nobody offered to pack for Beauty and Nungi.)

Ondien walks through the house with her kwela whistle, abstractedly testing tunes. She sinks into the low-slung sofa on the veranda. The whistle drops from her mouth. Bones, small soft bones, crunch below her. She jumps up, picking up the little dog (is it Trixie or Mixie?). The eyes are open, but there is no sound.

'Whimper, little dog, or at least move!'

Beauty is standing in the door, hand over her mouth. Ondien turns away. She holds the dog under its stomach, feeling the little bones one by one. An interrupted trickle of urine is dripping on the sofa. She gingerly puts the dachshund down on the floor. From the village the noise of soccer applause is rising. For a brief moment everything looks fine, but no – the hind body is dragging uselessly. Trixie whimpers softly once and then lies down.

Ondien wants to take Beauty inside, but Mrs Nyathi has appeared in the door. She looks at the little dog, lying in a puddle of urine.

'Mrs Nyathi, I'm so sorry, I didn't notice . . . '

Mrs Nyathi picks up the dachshund, looks it in the eye. 'Trixie?' she asks, as if the dog can answer.

Trixie is hanging limply, not reacting to anything. But there is still breath. A paw is quivering. Mrs Nyathi shrugs her shoulders. Ondien cannot gauge her expression.

'To sing for her won't help,' Mrs Nyathi says, as if Ondien had offered. 'I've seen death in that hospital where I used to work. This one won't make it.'

Beauty wants to hold Trixie, but Mrs Nyathi keeps the dog out of her reach. She climbs down the steps to the veranda and disappears around the corner of the house.

'Leave it, Beauty, there's nothing more we can do.'

The taxi is being loaded by the garden gate. Ondien is supervising Mrs Nyathi's maids, who are carrying their sound equipment from a storeroom in the backyard. What is left of Trixie is visible in the long grass. Next to it, the wooden plank with which the dog's skull was crushed is glinting.

From the veranda behind them Mrs Nyathi is waving. They watch her standing there until they have turned the corner. Only once they have crossed the border into Lesotho does Beauty take Mixie out from under a small blanket in her carry bag.

'Beauty! How could you? And the poor thing has almost suffocated.' Ondien takes the dog from her. 'Can't turn around now, we'll have to take her along and bring her back.'

She is suddenly feeling lighter, happy about the little dog's body in their midst. The three of them look at each other in turn, stroking the long spine. Nungi laughs brightly. Here, on the other side of the border, a greater sense of freedom is washing over them than they have felt since returning to the country. An old familiarity between them is returning.

The higher they drive into the mountains, the cooler the air becomes. Outside there are kraals with thatched huts, streams in which melted water rushes. They drive past a blind man. He prods the air with his walking stick as if wanting to feel them, his eyes like silver coins.

The large (and largely male) turn-out may have something to do with the printing error on the poster: *Victorian Naked Ladies' Society*, it reads on the lampposts along the main street, on the gate in front of the hall and above the hall's entrance. Ondien shrugs her shoulders.

'Go with the flow,' says Nungi.

'Hopefully that doesn't mean you're going to comply!' Ondien says. They laugh.

The venue is located in the only street with streetlights. The audience is a hodge-podge. Entertainment is a rarity here. Shiny young people from the town wearing two-tone shoes or Nikes. Men arrive from the hills with blankets around their shoulders, ponies tied to lamp posts. A few broad-bottomed women with children sleeping on their backs after a day tilling the fields.

The local promoter is nowhere to be found. There is only one ticket-seller and no one to help set up the equipment. Ondien tries in vain to reach the sound engineer on her phone. He arrives twenty minutes late. It is not clear that he understands Ondien's instructions.

Without collaborating musicians, the sound tonight is thin. Ondien is doing her best with the kwela whistle and the saxophone. Beauty and Nungi each have a harmonica. Otherwise the performance is vintage VNLS. Initially, Ondien experiences the familiar discomfort: she is the only white face. It is only when she decides that she is entitled to her white fears, that they are not unfounded, that she starts relaxing. She is assessing the audience, finely calibrating the performance. Nungi and Beauty are observing her carefully – without appearing to do so – and adjusting their actions cheerily. Ondien makes her concessions to the audience, allows them to recognise rhythms. The traditional South African elements are foregrounded this evening, the wide register of influences from North and West Africa are tempered. Then, when she has *got* them, when they start dancing unguardedly, she cannot help but pounce. She reacts with a left-field improvisation, lets confusion wash over the hall. Beauty and Nungi lose her for a few seconds, but then fall seamlessly into line. Ondien keeps Beauty in the corner of her eye. Her forearms are as thin as sticks – getting thinner with each performance since Paris.

Ondien's eye is caught by a man standing utterly still at the edge of the light. A white man. She looks at his shoulders, losing her rhythm and voice for a moment. The audience stops dancing. They wait; after half a minute, they start fidgeting. She cuts the performance short. The evening has been long enough. When she walks off the stage, the other two following her, the audience just stands there in silence. The microphone whistles.

He approaches her outside, behind the hall. In his khaki shorts, his legs brown in the white light that is emanating from the hall, he looks like a farmer from the Free State, one of those men who drive white pickup trucks beyond the northern border, where she also grew up. There is a vague smell of engine oil in the air.

'I don't understand much of what you, or you' – he looks at Nungi and then at Beauty, who is standing with Mixie in her arms – 'do. But you've entertained this bunch, that's for sure.'

'Do you have somewhere to stay?' he asks when they fail to respond.

Ondien looks at the other two. Beauty presses her cheek against the dog's. It was the presumed power in those upper legs, Ondien later thought, and the set of perfect teeth, that made her ignore Nungi's expression, and Beauty's hesitancy.

'Hendrik,' he says. Only Ondien takes the hand he holds out. The next morning in the shower her hand will still smell of oil.

*

Ondien's skull vibrates against the Land Rover's window. Heavy tools press against her feet.

'It's midnight, we have to sleep over somewhere,' she said to Beauty and Nungi, shrugging her shoulders, when Hendrik was out of earshot earlier. 'Do you really want to trek all the way back to Nyathi's place?'

Nungi was glowering. Beauty was counting Mixie's vertebrae. Before Ondien could confirm, Hendrik had already started to load the sound equipment into the Land Rover. She did not ask where or how far. Ondien let the taxi, which was waiting to take them back to Vloedspruit, go.

Nobody speaks. They are going higher and higher, Hendrik's forearm on the gear like an extension of the engine. Ondien is becoming lighter in the dark, and increasingly blind. When the road starts getting rough, memories shake loose. Before Lesotho there were the small South African towns. Before the towns there was Cape Town. And, before Cape Town, there was Paris. Before Paris, London. But it is in Paris where her mind now lingers. And with Thierry.

After she turned her back on the academic world of music in London (the loose threads of her unfinished PhD – *The Role of Dance and Ritual in the Polyphonic and Polyrhythmic Construction of Traditional Zulu Music* – she had decided, could not be tied together), Ondien arrived in Paris, penniless. She had met Beauty and Nungi during a previous research trip to KwaZulu-Natal. Their voices were already on a few recordings that she had added to the SOAS music library's collection. They accepted her invitation to Paris exuberantly. Thierry, a Parisian world music promoter, was a contact of a contact at SOAS.

A friend of Thierry's was in Mali for a year. The three of them could stay in the friend's flat in the eighteenth arrondissement. Over beers and falafels from a Turkish takeaway, the three South Africans conceived VNLS one evening. Later she would remember VNLS as her idea, Thierry would as his.

It was not long before she and Thierry were bathing in each other's sweat between his sheets in his Marais *appartement*. These were the days when, enveloped by a sheet and fog, she could still walk out onto his balcony above the roofs and catch a glimpse of new and promising seasons. Into which currents of her thoughts did Thierry tap so powerfully? she later wondered. Why did she plunge into things so mindlessly? She imagined it was something to do with the mystique surrounding things continental in her Free State childhood, with her mother's thwarted dream of a singing career in European opera houses. Interwoven with this was her obsession with music cultures. She was impressed by the years that Thierry had spent in the heart of the music scenes in Senegal and Algeria, by his experience in the Parisian world music scene. She was tired of her lonely attempts to write art music in an academic sphere, the marginal pseudo-radical performances with student musicians in university auditoriums. All with such deadpan sincerity. Thierry would help her make music rather than theorise about it. The real thing, *la vraie chose*. And she was, of course, moved by the fact that he, in his way, in his world, through associations that she could barely understand or suspect, was clearly moved by her.

*

Ondien looks around. In the back of the Land Rover she can make out Nungi's head on Beauty's shoulder. Beauty's eyes are shining.

Hendrik looks at Ondien. 'Almost there.'

She holds her watch right before her eyes. Two o'clock. Where on God's earth is he taking them? Hendrik's teeth are white in the dark. She can hear the little dog panting. She can smell its urine. She does not look around again.

VNLS's first performances were in tiny *clubs africains*. In these places, with their walls of velvet and names like *Zouzou* or *Boum-Boum* in neon above the entrances, it felt like 1971. They had to steer towards the little stages between women from further up north in Africa, women with choco-late skins, stretched limbs, platform shoes and Afros. The air was thick and rich, the bodies as smooth and fluid as oil. These nights of glowing cocktails were not the Africa that Ondien knew. It made her skin tingle. For the first time since her student performances for connoisseurs in auditoriums, she could *do* something again, rather than just write or think. And it *was* the real thing. Beauty and Nungi thrived. Their rhythms became slippery, their voices sweeter and stranger.

After a few weeks, Thierry moved their performances to mainstream places, in the sixth or eleventh arrondisse-ments, their audiences now predominantly white. *Musique et la danse Zouloues*, the posters and handbills announced. Beauty and Nungi's performances were suddenly muted. The intimacy and the intoxication of the *clubs africains* were lost. After the first performance, she objected to *et la danse*.

'We sing,' she said.

Thierry shrugged his shoulders, his mouth drooping – his most characteristic gesture, she soon realised.

'What is it that these two sexy girls do, then?' He pointed to Beauty and Nungi.

Midnight, on his balcony, after the second performance, she said: 'But it's not just *musique Zouloue*, it's more complex. You're putting us in a box.'

'Tone down the improvisations,' he said, 'and the digressions. You are losing the audience. Keep it simple.'

Several performances and similar conversations later, Thierry decided it was time to reconsider the image and the approach. He wanted to start with the name, but Ondien would not budge. VNLS it had to be. He wanted to elevate the *comédie*, and the *sensualité*.

'We're trying to entertain here,' he said. 'How to defuse the seriousness, bring some levity, that's the question. How to find the *lieu du désir* in your audience. Think of Josephine Baker. Think of the two girls – '

'They have names, Beauty and Nungi.'

'Think of Beauty and Nungi in Josephine Baker banana skirts – before you say anything, think of that iconic image, how powerful allusions to it are. In ironic fashion, of course. We have to think: what is our greatest asset, what lures people to VNLS shows?'

He took a photograph from his pocket, put it down on the table: Beauty and Nungi in full swing, hips and breasts swollen and glistening in the stage light.

'We've never wanted to be an ethnic curiosity; the girls are not the Saartjie Baartmans of the music world. Our stuff is meant to be subversive, an attack on the system.'

He shook his head. 'You South Africans are too caught up in the snares of your own little political tale. Too serious, too *pudibonde*. You don't get the La Baker phenomenon. She was more, much more, than a *petite danseuse sauvage*. What I'm proposing is in the spirit of the times; the audience will understand what we're playing with.'

'That's not what I want to do. Or Beauty and Nungi.'

He sat back, inhaled the last smoke from his cigarette. 'So, now you're speaking on their behalf?' He shot the cigarette through the window, across the roofs. 'What you want to do, Ondien, is not important. The question is: do you want to play or not?'

They changed course, developing the Josephine Baker act, just like Thierry wanted. He was in full control of the production. He sat there every day, in the second row of the empty theatre. Beauty and Nungi did what was expected of them, unperturbed. The ideas went beyond the La Baker imagery, became more layered. The stage set-up, the concept, was now that of a circus – Ondien as tamer, *la maîtresse de spectacle*. The other two women paraded as skittish, wild dancers with wide eyes, banana skirts and necklaces made of the fangs of wild dogs. A musical with black Betty Boop twins from the tropics. Ondien felt her aversion intensifying.

She was spending her nights in the flat in the eighteenth with Beauty and Nungi again. The evening before the première she arrived on Thierry's doorstep.

'Naked commerce is the driving force in your world, isn't it? That and your ego. Your cynicism is starting to make me *hate* the stage!'

'I must give them what they want.' Shoulders pulled

up, mouth drooping. 'The French want fun, their taste is sophisticated.'

'Sophisticated!?' she shouted. 'There are world music festivals in this city where unexpected things happen. There one gets glimpses of sophistication. In your little theatres I see nothing of it. Just humiliation. For me it's about irony, about delicate play, for you it's about idiotic *nostalgie de la boue!*'

'I haven't got state funding to promote obscure and childish experiments. I must make a living! The market is the market!' Palms turned upwards. His expression changed, his hands slipping around her buttocks. 'Come on, Ondien, stay here tonight. The girls may be yours, but you are mine.'

She pushed his hands away and walked down the five flights to the street. She did not look up at the light emanating from his balcony.

Tonight everything will change, she thought when she walked into the silvery limelight on the opening night. Now she could swim freely, she knew, like in an ocean. For a moment she considered sabotaging it all, but then looked at Beauty and Nungi. She held back, did what she had to. It was their evening, Beauty and Nungi's.

The Zulu women's skins shone, the audience responded. The opening scene is set in an unidentified landscape near the equator. Ondien has to crack the whip above the supposedly terrified native girls' heads. She chases the sexy, ululating little barbarians into a cage to be taken away across the ocean, to the frozen north, their eyes white and big. The second scene is set on the ship. A storm is raging, the girls are panic-stricken in their cage of rough-hewn wooden poles. In an effort to dispel their fears, they start singing and dancing. A young sailor hears them and is instantly enchanted by the vitality, the wild abandon. He attempts a stiff little dance of his own next to the cage, on the slippery, tilting deck. (The unoiled stage machinery grumbles when it makes the ship sway.) In Paris the two girls become wretched exhibitions in Ondien's cruel circus. The dancing sailor wins a lot of money in a drunken game of dice and becomes the owner of a Parisian entertainment hall. He attends a circus performance and takes pity on the girls. He wants to buy them, offers a good price, then doubles it, but the circus mistress refuses. ('Go to the Tropics and catch your own, monsieur! These two I tamed myself.')

To cut a long story short: with the help of a bunch of muscled fellow sailors – as queer as well-hung models in Jean Paul Gaultier outfits – the entertainment-hall owner frees the girls one night. Ondien's fuming character summons the gendarmes. By the time the two girls are found, they are singing and dancing proudly, bewitchingly, as Les Deux Sauvages in Parisian concert halls – darlings, now, of the French public, who can, at last, imagine natural rhythms throbbing through their own rigid bodies again. When the gendarmes interrupt a performance to capture the girls, the audience's noble, untamed instincts are revived. Rioting and violence threaten. The gendarmes and the sadistic circus mistress are forced to retreat. From the distant Tropics an ancient force has been channelled. The girls have been released from their bonds of slavery by their exotic talents. When the circus fails, Ondien's character falls into abject poverty. Humiliated and begging, she comes to seek mercy at the feet of the two chanteuses . . .

Afterwards they – or, rather, Thierry and Nungi –finished off several bottles of Algerian and Lebanese red wine in an over-lit restaurant.

Thierry was as pleased as Punch. 'Everyone thinks you're highly original,' he said, 'an act for our time. *Provoquant*. Tongue-in-cheek. Political correctness's nemesis.'

She and Beauty were absent though present. When the waiters started stacking chairs on tables around them, Thierry and Nungi still sat right up against each other, smoking. A bleary-eyed Nungi snorted some lines with Thierry, just there, off the table, in front of the waiters, his hand on her leg. Thierry's face showed no expression when Ondien got up and walked out.

At four in the morning, Ondien's phone rang. Beauty was in the intensive care unit in the Pitié-Salpêtrière hospital. The call was from the hospital. Thierry had left Ondien's number with the staff and disappeared without a trace.

'Motorbike,' the matron said when Ondien had at last found the right wing. 'Rue Jean-Macé. Almost every bone.' She shook her head, paging through the file notes. 'The nose, cheekbone, ribs, pelvis, femur, foot.' The matron was a fat woman, her own bones comfortably cushioned against shattering.

'A bunch of nasty fractures. Bones penetrating through skin, dislocations. They're putting her back together with steel.' The woman gestured as if she was hitting a chisel with a hammer. 'She will be in the operating theatre for quite some time.'

While Beauty was in surgery, Ondien waited. The matron sat with her for a while in the bright corridor, legs spread apart, spongy little hands folded across her stomach. She was wearing white stockings and white men's shoes with rubber soles. She told Ondien how, before the revolution, the hospital had served as a prison for Paris's prostitutes. The women were locked up, then coerced to pair off with convicts and sent to French-colonial North America. Until, that is, the masses from the pest-ridden sewer of Faubourg Saint-Marcel came to forcefully liberate them.

'If I had lived then,' the matron said while getting up and walking away, 'I would probably have been one of the liberating masses. Or, perhaps,' she said gigglingly over her shoulder, 'one of the prostitutes.'

When she arrived back at her flat in the eighteenth, Beauty having been transferred from the operating theatre to intensive care, Nungi was packing.

'If you're heading to the Marais, you're making a big mistake, Nungi.'

'Always the madam, hey? Always wants to keep the best for herself!'

Ondien was speechless. She could not even ask what exactly had happened to Beauty. Nungi stormed out, cracked suitcase in hand, and then, after a few seconds, returned for her Zulu costume on the drying rack before slamming the door behind her.

For three weeks, Beauty was in the Pitié-Salpêtrière. Apart from the broken bones, there were internal injuries, bruised organs. She was reluctant initially, but then came out with the story: the three of them outside the restaurant, Thierry wanting to take both of them home with him, Beauty refusing, and not wanting to leave Nungi alone with Thierry either; Nungi brusquely pushing Beauty aside, Thierry pushing Beauty against a backyard wall, tearing off her underwear. Nungi looking on impassively. Beauty running blindly into the street.

It was the beginning of winter. Nungi was now living with Thierry. When Beauty was discharged from hospital three weeks after the accident, Thierry locked Ondien and Beauty out in the cold. Literally and figuratively. The lock to the flat in the eighteenth was replaced, with most of their possessions still inside. The incestuous little world of ethnic music in Paris shut them out overnight. No one booked VNLS any more. Perhaps they would still be able to play at one of the annual festivals, or maybe Ondien could get in touch with her contacts in London again, but Nungi was gone and she and Beauty had nowhere to live, and little money left. *Le Cap de Bonne-Espérance* it was to be, on the cheapest flight they could find.

Shortly before their plane departed, a sullen Nungi arrived at Charles de Gaulle. It was Beauty who had told her that they were leaving. Nungi and Ondien had not exchanged a word in weeks. They embraced Nungi. First Beauty, but in her new, timid manner, as if she was scared the bones would break again in the same places. Then Ondien, her hands cupping Nungi's cheeks, their foreheads touching for a moment. Ondien took the cracked suitcase and carried it for her.

In Cape Town it is summer, Ondien thought when she sank back in the aeroplane seat, the other two to her right and left, their forearms against hers.

The Land Rover comes to a halt. She must have dozed off. The little dog has crawled onto her lap. Half-past two. In the darkness and cold, holding a small torch, Hendrik leads them to a building. Inside he lights a candle. Above them is a low corrugated-iron roof. It is colder inside than outside. Between the stone walls, sleeping bags have been rolled out onto three iron beds, as if specially prepared for them. Hendrik disappears in the dark, returns after a while with a paraffin heater. Beauty and Nungi sit upright next to each other on a bed. Hendrik smells of engines and red grass. It puts Ondien at ease: smells from her childhood days on the Free State farm.

She is blind here in Hendrik's place after the sharp morning light outside. His house is half a kilometre down the slope from the outbuilding where they are sleeping, and surrounded by a plateau of blonde grass, dotted with sandstone rocks. It is similar to their building – sandstone and corrugated iron – but it's much larger, having clearly been expanded in a piecemeal fashion. She walks in behind Hendrik, and straight into his back.

Her eyes have now adjusted. She is still half-frozen after her cold morning shower. She has in fact not warmed up since their arrival the previous night, the lacklustre little paraffin heater notwithstanding. A shaft of light falls in from a back room.

Tools and parts hang from every inch of the walls and ceilings. She sits down on a camping chair, the smell of oil and grease surrounding them.

'What is all of this? What do you *do* here?'

His face opens up, he smiles with perfect teeth. 'Live,' he says, 'and work. Fix things, build machines.'

It is not clear where his living space ends and the workshop begins. To her side, by the front door, there is a single bed and a hearth, a little cupboard. On the other side, there are workbenches with vice clamps, iron tools hanging everywhere.

'Come and see,' he says.

They walk further in, past the workbenches, through the beam of light, through various dim rooms. He steers her by the elbow, past rotors and tubes, oil filters and engines. A collection of iron and rubber and screws and tins are stacked on shelves.

'How do you know where to find things?'

'Everything is where I put it. I'm here alone.'

'So, what are you building?'

'Different things. I buy appliances that are thrown out in South Africa – washing machines, radios, televisions. Sometimes cars. Then I fix them up and sell them here. It's my business. Rest of the stuff's just a hobby.'

She loses track of the number of rooms. A few doors remain closed. They walk out into a backyard with a lean-to supported by poles. Underneath it is a row of rusty vehicles on flat tyres or wooden blocks.

'So, you're carrying the torch of technology. Seems to me you're a kind of modern missionary here among the Basothos.'

He smiles. When he turns around, she notices sweat starting to soak through the back of his khaki shirt, despite the cold.

She turns around and starts. The barrel of a cannon stares her in the face. A row of old tanks on caterpillar wheels stand under a second lean-to.

'They date from the 1940s. All running again now. And see this?' He walks past the tanks, pointing to a rusty

Volkswagen Beetle with a split back window. 'One of the very first ones. A few were built in the 1930s for top brass in the German army. Who knows who might have driven this one –'

'I must go now –'

'Wait, the tour isn't finished.'

He walks out the back. She hesitates, then follows.

There is no grass here. On this side of the house/workshop, a large hole has been excavated into the slope. A stone quarry. From where she and the other two spent the night, it is invisible. Half-cut blocks of stone are dotted around. It is quiet; nothing is moving. The place is pale and dim.

'Come for dinner tonight. Bring the two black girls.'

'Their names are Beauty and Nungi,' she says.

'Bring them with you,' he says. 'I live here with these people, it's not a problem.'

Ondien digs out her cellphone from underneath the clothes in her bag. She has missed eleven calls since they left the previous day. She holds the phone above her head. No signal. Somewhere along the road, the missed calls must have registered last night. She switches off the phone. The gig in the Eastern Cape is only a few days away. Nothing's rushing them. The cold here has started entering her core, convincing her to stay a while.

'Beauty and Nungi didn't want to come.' The two Zulu women silently shook their heads, remaining seated on the beds, when Ondien left for Hendrik's place.

'Then they'll have to go without food.'

She looks at him.

He smiles. 'A joke. I'll give you something to take back for them.'

On the way here, small falcons circled above her in the dusk, sweeping down from time to time to snatch prey off rocks.

'Snow rats,' Hendrik says when she asks. 'The herdboys roast them on spits.'

He turns a lump of meat in the hearth. (Is it goat?)

'So, tell me more about your music. It was like a carnival.'

'Yes,' she says coolly, 'like a church fête, I guess, or a circus.'

'How does one come up with such music?'

'You mean music with such disruptions and abrupt transitions, such dissonances and syncopations?'

He says nothing, just keeps looking into the fire.

'I think,' she continues, 'it's like building a machine. The different elements first appear as shreds moving around in my mind. Then they start to find a centre of gravity. Gradually, the shreds revolve more closely to the centre. I wait for them to gain mass. I weigh the cloud, waiting for the right moment to write it down. But then, when I walk on to the stage, I rip it all apart again.' She smiles. 'Do you ever dismantle your machines?'

He says nothing, turns the meat again, looks into a pot. In the glow of the fire, she is warming up for the first time since their arrival. But, as usual, she has not taken proper account of her audience. He has closed up, become sullen.

There is too much meat on her plate and it is tough. Hendrik dishes up floury potatoes from the pot. They eat in silence.

'That is not how one builds a machine,' he says after a while. 'I will have to show you.'

'Why are you here?' he wants to know after a further silence.

She is darting too swiftly and too cleverly over his questions. She can feel it. Something is building up. But she continues: 'Perhaps I'm grasping towards a core,' she says, 'an origin.' She breaks open a potato with her fingers. 'Perhaps I want to escape the centrifugal forces, the *éléments exotiques*. I'm but a simple Free State girl, you know.' He looks at her, seeing whether she's mocking. And whether it is self-mockery or aimed at him.

She walks up the slope, towards where Beauty and Nungi are waiting behind thick walls. She looks around in the dark. He is standing in the doorway. There seems to be anger in his shoulders. He keeps standing there. She walks back to him, even though she knows she should not.

In Hendrik's bed everything is silent and urgent, his body against her like stone. She becomes aware of the membranes between her fingers. She thinks of fish ejecting strings of phosphorous eggs in the mountain streams.

Early afternoon, the following day. Deep grass stretches in all directions, as far as the eye can see. Ondien is on her own. The blond grass is pulling her in, trapping her. She sits down. Down here one is aware of nothing but scurrying rats and the blue sky above. Inside her skull it is quiet; the music is waiting, she hopes, behind floodgates. She decides she will ask Hendrik to sing a few songs from the *FAK*, the book of Afrikaans folk songs. She will record him in the stone quarry, where there is a little acoustic texture, at least an echo. Yes, she will make him do it and then use samples of it.

When she was a PhD student, she had an idea for a piece of music that would incorporate such fragments. The structure of the first movement came to her when she was at a London conference, listening to a paper by an exiled South African ethnomusicologist. 'Numbing the Ear: The Afrikaans Folk Music Project (1948–1994) and the Construction of an Aural Past' was the title. The only other Afrikaans person in her field of study that she had ever met while she was outside the country. Jakkie, if she remembers correctly, Jakkie de Wet. From some Canadian university or other. Afterwards, during the lunch break, and for the rest of the conference, she took care to avoid him.

'We want to leave,' Beauty says. She is on her knees, pushing a bowl of water towards Mixie. 'I think she's missing her little sister.' She gets up with difficulty.

'Where the fuck are we anyway?' Nungi wants to know. 'Are we hostages?'

'I promise you,' Ondien says. 'Tomorrow we'll leave.' She looks at Nungi and Beauty. In three days' time they have to be at Twilight Lodge for their performance. She regrets bringing them here, and making them stay a second night.

They haven't touched the cold goat's meat and potatoes that Ondien brought back the previous evening. They are listening to the silence.

The third morning. They wake up in strange light. There is deep, soft snow outside, their first snow since Paris. The cold in the hut is bitter, the little paraffin heater's flame glowing blue like glacier ice. They venture outside. They sink into the snow, their socks getting soaked. Mixie is wrapped in a pullover. She is clambering higher up against Beauty's chest, escaping the whiteness. There are scratchmarks on Beauty's neck.

They sit in a circle with their feet against the heater. Hendrik brings more blankets and three new pairs of boots, as if bought specially for them.

'Tell me if you want to move to my place. There's a fire there.'

'We're fine here,' Ondien says through clenched jaws.

'The phone's dead,' he says. 'We're cut off.'

The blankets smell of iron, of rust. Late morning it starts again: small snowflakes on the corrugated-iron roof.

When the sun emerges, Ondien goes for a walk in the snow. She gives Hendrik's house a wide berth, looping round and down to the stone quarry. She pricks her ears, waiting for the music, for fragments. It has been a while since she has heard anything. Against the white page of this landscape it has to come. She looks around at her tracks. How present one becomes in snow.

Where she reaches a narrow valley at the bottom, the snow has been driven in so deep, and piled so high, that telephone wires are virtually touching the fresh powder. Her legs disappear up to the knees. She bends over, her ear against the wire. Voices. She smiles. She wants to intercept them, use them to make something. She waits. A few notes, nothing more. It is the American minimalists of her student days that are unexpectedly back in her cold ears. Riley or Reich, she cannot be sure, and the droning of more obscure composers – Morton Feldman, La Monte Young.

She recalls Hendrik's announcement that the phone is dead. She holds her ear against the wire again. Unmistake-able, the voices. Her breath melts away a small hollow. She lies back. Flakes settle on her cheeks. If the snow were to bury her, the search parties would come and walk back and forth over her face, calling and calling. She would not be able to respond, but would change their voices to music in her head . . . Her heart is knocking against her chest; something wants to break through. She sharpens all her senses: it is something new, but it is not music. She has never written a poem, but she knows: it is a line of poetry.

She hears her name. Nungi. The line disappears instantly. When she sits up, both Nungi and Beauty are standing there, knee-deep: Beauty with a frowning Mixie, Nungi with a black stick in her hand. Beauty is humming to the dog in her arms.

'We want to go,' Nungi says. 'We want to leave now.'

'How can we, Nungi? Look around you – '

'Why did you bring us to this place? Did we ask to come here?' Nungi clicks with her tongue, looking across the plateau. 'We always do everything for you, everything you want to do.'

'We're trapped, Nungi, surely that's obvious . . . '

Nungi is not listening. She is drawing a line in the snow with her stick. She and Beauty are on one side of the line, Ondien on the other.

'You're there, we're here. So it's always been,' Nungi says.

The wind dies down. For a while they stand in silence. Then Beauty drags one leg out of the snow. It clumps down on Ondien's side of the line. Nungi walks away. Beauty follows, then Ondien. They walk with exaggerated movements, their shadows stretching and shrinking absurdly. Beauty's shadow wobbles most. Ondien tries to feel Beauty's pain in her own body, the chill of steel against bone.

The rest of the day takes shape around the cavity of the lost line of poetry, Ondien's thoughts arranged around the edges. Perhaps, she thinks, it is time, once she has returned to civilisation, to disband VNLS and take up her research again. She can see the title of her last – incomplete – chapter, as if written in snow: *Where does music end and speech begin?* There were so many questions. In which ancient mouths did music and speech part? How does one synchronise them again? Fieldwork was required. She would search for her answers in the singing-speaking throats of the world, in enclaves where something has survived from the time of the bone flute. She had wanted to invoke proto-noises, to use them to create something new. Not poetry, but something in the *region* of poetry . . .

She smiles. The centrifugal forces are taking hold again. Could such detours perhaps lead one back to the shard of poetry?

Beauty is sprinkling breadcrumbs in the snow.

'For the birds,' she says. 'The snow is hiding the food. And their throats are frozen, they can't sing. They won't find each other to mate. They'll all become extinct.'

When she enters Hendrik's place at dusk, he is sitting motionlessly in front of the hearth with dark glasses. High flames reflect in the black lenses.

'Hendrik?'

He takes a long time to answer. She can feel the cold emanating from the rooms beyond this one. It looks as if he has become blind.

'The phone,' she says behind his back. 'I thought you said it's out of order.'

'It is.'

He takes off the glasses – old-fashioned ones, with leather patches on the sides. He opens a door, switches on a light. It is a room in which she has not been before. There are no windows. He is clearly building something big here. On a workbench there is a large structure with oil-smeared parts around it. Chains are hanging over pulleys from a rafter. She approaches the bench, as if recognising something, as if the smell of grease and rubber is jogging her memory. He waits, but she fails to ask any questions.

'I'm not building Frankenstein's monster, you know.'

His teeth are showing in the electric light. He moves behind her, comes right up to her.

'What is it?'

He lowers his voice. 'Perhaps a machine for chopping up women.'

She laughs, a little too loudly. He is now standing next to her. He tests one of the chains, pulling it taut.

'Would be perfect, hey? Everything just right: the isolation, the forces of nature, the silence. The three of you not having a bloody clue where you are.' He turns, looks her in the eye. 'One flees slowly in deep snow, you know.'

He lets go of the chain. It swings. Like snow rats in falcons' shadows, she thinks.

Then he smiles, his teeth shiny. 'Jokes,' he says. 'You like to mock me, don't you? All that clever talk.' He nods at the thing on the bench. 'It's a stone crusher. For the quarry.'

He lifts his head, comes even closer. 'A question for you. What's the story with your two girls?'

'Nungi and Beauty. What do you mean?'

'Why can one only get to them through you? Can't they speak for themselves?'

She lifts her chin, says nothing. An oily thing is dangling from the ceiling, a piece of one of his machines. It looks like a bat.

He wants her to stay. 'Please,' he says, his eyes cast down again.

The thing comes loose. It *is* a bat; it flits over her head, outwards. She looks at Hendrik, at his forearms and thick hands. She walks quickly through the rooms to the front door.

'You have to know where she is, Nungi, you're responsible too!'

'She's not a child. I'm not her keeper.'

Mixie is lying on Beauty's sleeping bag. Beauty has disappeared at some point during Ondien's afternoon nap, which she took after a sleepless night. Ondien stands outside the front door, calling Beauty's name. The snow has almost melted; only patches are left between tufts of grass. She starts running down the hill. There Beauty is now, walking up the hill, with a wide curve around Hendrik's place.

'What's wrong, Beauty?'

Her eyes are glassy. Her cheek has been grazed. She is not saying anything.

'You ask her, she won't say a word to me,' Ondien says to Nungi inside. Nungi asks something in Zulu. A short conversation follows. Ondien only picks up a word here and there.

'*Nkontshane,*' Nungi says, 'a wild dog.'

'What? It makes no sense.'

'A wild dog attacked her,' Nungi says and sits down on the bed furthest away from them.

Ondien catches Beauty's eye. Beauty takes off her head-scarf. There is dust in her hair, sandstone dust.

'Please, Beauty. Tell me. Tell me what happened in the quarry?'

Beauty gets up, clearly aware of each bone, each screw of surgical steel. She sits down next to Nungi, right up against her.

Ondien considers things for a moment. Then she gets up. With long strides, she starts walking down the hill towards Hendrik's place. Nungi and Beauty rush after her.

'I know it's him,' Ondien says, 'Hendrik, he's the *nkontshane.*'

'Leave it,' Nungi calls after her. 'You're just going to make it worse. Nothing can help us here.'

Beauty is a few steps behind Nungi, struggling to keep up. Hendrik is waiting in his front door, leaning against the frame with folded arms.

Then: the drone of an engine. A white double-cab pickup truck appears. It is floating like a ship through the long grass, over the invisible road, stopping by Hendrik's front door. The women arrive at the moment that two police-men get out of the vehicle. One is wiry, the other has sad shoulders.

She points at Hendrik. 'It's him,' she says. She points at Beauty. 'She's the victim.' She gets her breath back, then starts wondering how the police managed to get here so quickly, and who had called them. Something is amiss. The two policemen are frowning. Hendrik is looking bemused.

'Don't know what you're talking about, madam. We're here to investigate the theft of a dog.'

She frowns. 'Are you kidding me?'

'We take the theft of animals seriously, madam. We have major problems with cattle theft.'

'We're not talking about cattle.'

'Big or small, crime is crime. What would become of the world if we started measuring stolen goods?'

The policeman looks up the hill. Here and there, where the grass has been flattened by snow, Mixie pops into sight. She is running down to them.

'We've had a complaint from beyond the border. And a hint that the suspects had fled to a remote place.'

'You're not serious.'

Ondien looks from one policeman to the other in disbelief, to Hendrik and back again. Hendrik is not saying a word.

'A crime has been committed here, yes, but it has nothing to do with a dog.'

'No?' The wiry man lifts an eyebrow. 'Why, then, do we seem to have the evidence right here?'

He steps forward, intercepts Mixie when she enters the clearing between them. A trickle of urine runs down his forearm, dripping off his elbow. The policeman with the sad shoulders makes a note in a dirty pad.

Ondien shakes her head. 'A misunderstanding, an absurd misunderstanding. One phone call will clear it all up.'

'No phone,' says Hendrik.

'No need to take statements,' the wiry policeman says, as if someone had offered. He nods his head slowly, authoritatively. 'We can see what's going on here.' He turns to Ondien. 'You're the responsible one?'

She is too dumbfounded to respond. She is waiting for something to happen, for Hendrik to come and chase them off with one of his tanks, or with his Nazi Beetle. He is, after all, one of her own. The only one here of her kind. Between him and the Zulu women, only Ondien and the police vehicle stand. Neither Nungi nor Beauty says a word.

Ondien is rocking back and forth in the back seat. She should probably be grateful that they have not handcuffed her. Occasionally she turns around. Mixie is standing up against the back window and whining soundlessly. The policemen did not want her to keep the dog with her. As they reach the foothills, her phone finds a signal. She makes a call.

'Mrs Nyathi! I'm so relieved to hear your voice. There's a big misunderstanding. I've been arrested. About your dog! You have to clear it all up, right now –'

'Ooh, it's all out of my hands now, dear, I can't meddle in police affairs –'

'You don't understand. You brought the charge, after all. We're bringing the dog back, Mrs Nyathi! I have to go and fetch the girls, Beauty and Nungi. They're not safe. Tomorrow we have to be at Twilight Lodge –'

'Listen, that place has burnt down. The party's been cancelled. Rumour is that my former lodger set the place alight. Shortly before she died – '

'Enough,' says the one policeman, 'stop talking.'

'We'll take your phone,' says the other. The signal is lost.

The road is rough. Ondien rubs the scar on her upper arm. They drive over passes, they become trapped behind lowing cattle. It is further than Ondien remembers. She looks at the dull rocks outside, hears Mixie's nails as she tries to gain a grip against the steel. She suddenly thinks of her sister Vera who now probably lives in a Middle Eastern desert, finally and mercifully stripped of all context. She thinks of her brother Cornelius, sitting in a conference room at a glass table – it could be any city, any time zone – hands calmly folded, eyes focused, but always on two points: here *and* in the distance. She thinks of her younger sister Zelda, not of her exhaustion or her Satan's child, but of a time when they were children. The two of them on their bicycles, side by side on a two-track road, hair streaming backwards. The landscape is empty, as if there is no one else on earth. The sun is shining brightly, their feet hanging free beside the pedals. To one side of the road, neatly dug, is her mother's bed of nasturtiums.

She sits forward. She looks at the wiry policeman, then at the one with the sad shoulders.

'Could you sing something for me?' she asks. 'Something from here.'

They don't answer.

'Could I sing something for you, then?'

*

208

Mrs Nyathi lifts Mixie in front of her, inspecting her from different angles, as if confirming that she got back exactly what she lost. Once she is sure, she loses interest. She bends down, lets Mixie go, as if setting a wild animal free. Mixie disappears around the corner of the house.

The two Lesotho policemen looked disappointed when they arrived at the police station and it became clear that Mrs Nyathi had withdrawn the charge. They were reluctant to let go of their prize catch. Ondien's urgent pleas to go and pick up the other two women in the mountains fell on deaf ears. She was deported without ceremony.

Ondien calls the Lesotho police's Maseru headquarters from Bella Gardens. She reports Beauty and Nungi as missing.

'How do you know they want to be found? Who are you? What is your relationship to the missing women?'

She hesitates before answering the last question. 'They are like sisters to me,' she says.

She wants to explain how they are the fuel for her metamorphoses, that they enable her to slip through boundaries. And through herself.

'Without them, I am stuck in my own skull, like in a cage.'

'Huh?'

She tells of her own arrest, but just manages to confuse the man further. She describes Hendrik, as well as the two policemen. They would know where Beauty and Nungi are.

'What are the policemen's names?'

'I don't know,' she says. 'The one is wiry, the other has sad shoulders.'

'Who are you? Who put you in a cage? Are you a relative of the abducted women?' He is at the end of his tether.

'They've not been abducted —'

'So, why are you wasting our time? Talk to the South African police. You're not even a citizen of Lesotho.'

The boat leaves shore. This a party without guests. Or without the desired guests. After Twilight Lodge had been destroyed in the fire, the soccer teams' visit was cancelled. So too was the visit of the VIPs, the political and industrial elite, who are now seeking out the centre of events elsewhere. This party is the only one still going ahead, a remnant of thwarted big plans. A boat ride on the Gariep dam, a subdued affair. The guests consist of a small circle of local important types. Municipal officials: a mayor, a heavy woman who is apparently a director of health. A provincial MEC or two. A few white farmers who just about manage to remain in favour with the local black hierarchies are tolerated on the margins. Tables are loaded with food for absent guests. Flies are circling the buffet.

The boat is luxurious and heavy, as if carved from ebony. In the cabin, the carpets are dark, with a medieval heraldic design. The furniture is shiny and varnished. Chandeliers are swaying slowly from the ceiling. Ondien escapes the stuffy cabin, walking out onto the deck. Dead heat hangs above the grey water. The smell of minerals rises from the surface. At the top end of the lake, a concrete wall reaches up like a cliff. The landscape around the lake is barren, as if nothing could live there.

Ondien has to face the heat inside to sing. The list-lessness penetrates to the core of her sweaty, uncertain performance. Her voice is thin.

Like an insect drunk with light and sun, she fluctuates, hovering just below or just above the note. The excessive courage, the sense that anything is possible, that she could appropriate anything – that has gone.

The last note is still in the air when her phone starts ringing. It is Mrs Nyathi.

'I have news of your girls,' she says. 'The police have notified me. Both gone back to KwaZulu. Days ago already. To their families.'

'To their families,' Ondien repeats.

'Yes, to their own people. *Now* they'll be able to sing properly, I tell you!'

There is silence for a while.

'Any message for me?'

'No, but a package arrived for you from Lesotho. I've opened it. A Zulu outfit it is. Not all too clean, either. I'm having it dry-cleaned for you, ok?'

'Hope I'll be seeing you some time,' Mrs Nyathi continues when Ondien does not answer. 'It's pretty lonely for a widow all on her own in the mountains, you know. And without any music too.'

MOTHER'S QUARTET

For more than a year Ondien has neither sung, nor written, any music. She does not, in fact, ever listen to a single note. That is, if she can help it. In Johannesburg's shopping malls, as in shopping malls everywhere, silence is hidden behind a curtain of muzak. And it is the shopping malls she is seeking out. She finds delight, now, in everything that is new and smooth. She has had enough of the old world's gently weathered façades, of the artful curves of cobbled lanes. It is better here, the continental elements reimagined and embedded in fantastical monuments: shops transforming into courtyards and carparks, concrete additions accreting like flotsam. In here, in the bright light, it is possible to be emptied out, like in a monastery or a Buddhist retreat.

It is in one of these places, while she is having a cup of coffee, without a book or music, that she receives a call from her older brother, Cornelius, who lives in London.

'Last I heard you had moved from London to Paris to make music,' he says.

'Where did you get my number, Cornelius?'

'Zelda.'

Zelda is her younger sister who lives in Phoenix. They speak almost as infrequently as she and Cornelius.

'Last month I was in South Africa for meetings. If I had known you were in Johannesburg, we could have met up.'

Before, when Ondien was a postgraduate student in London, she managed to see Cornelius once. A few times afterwards she tried to establish contact again, but his banker's life was too busy, his travel schedule too full.

'I wouldn't have been able to meet. I'm not seeing anyone, I'm waiting.'

'Waiting?'

'For the music to return.'

'Music? In Johannesburg?' He snorts. 'A suggestion,' he says. 'Come and visit me in London. For as long as you want. Perhaps here you'll find your music again.'

As if, she thinks, Cornelius's ear would comprehend anything other than the droning of things electrical in the shafts of office buildings.

'Why now, suddenly, Cornelius? What about all the other things that are so demanding of your time?'

'Something has changed,' he says, 'or everything.'

For a while she is silent. She looks at the people around her, Sandton's pedestrian traffic. None of the delicate play of the European street here – no swift glances stretching erotic vectors back and forth like silk thread. People look at her bluntly, people who carry their bodies differently than in the North, lacking all concept of the relativity between their own and other flesh. They occupy space contemptuously, as if infinite distance were possible between bodies. A dour and spoilt lot, the people of Johannesburg. Defensive and full of bravado.

'I can't just pack up and leave in order to satisfy your whim, Cornelius. I'm settled here.'

She does not work. She lives on what remains of her inheritance in a garden flat that has been burgled four times in the past three months. Most of the small inheritance has been absorbed by living expenses in Paris or on loss-making tours in South Africa with her band, the Victorian Native Ladies' Society, or VNLS. Until recently she was doing volunteer work in Johannesburg, in a rehabilitation centre for children with brain injuries, but was asked to leave. She now spends her days squatting in these muffled coffee shops, as if it were the Rive Gauche sixty years earlier. She is emptying herself of all that remains: this is how she thinks of her days in the shopping malls.

She does not have a single friend left in this country. The sum of her human interactions, since returning to Johannesburg, has been with Mrs Zuckermann (her land-lady, a frail widow who has now been taken into a geriatric home), the director and children in the child rehabilita-tion centre and the editor of a fading local musicology journal. The latter entailed a few phone conversations about a proposed (now abandoned) article. She has seen a few old acquaintances: a former (now married) lover, a university friend who is a disillusioned academic at Wits university ('It's all so racialised now, one cannot function any longer.' 'What do you mean "now"?' Ondien wanted to know.) She did not seek out their company again. Her old friends have either left the country, or she has lost touch with them. Perhaps, she considers, she has outgrown friendship. And family ties. Or perhaps such relationships – any relationships – in unpolluted form are impossible in this country. She does have a cat. Flame is his name. A lean blue Burmese.

'I thought you said you were just waiting. For music, for some kind of intervention.'

She frowns. How many years since Cornelius left the country? Nine, ten? Apart from briefly at her father's funeral, they have not spoken since their single meeting in London.

She can hear him breathe.

'Do you know that Vera and Frank left for Dubai a few months ago?' he asks. 'Did you see them before they left?'

'No and no.'

She had no desire to look up her sister Vera (older than her, younger than Cornelius) or her husband Frank, the über-important CEO, in their Italian villa in Bryanston.

'What do you know about Zelda? Heard that she had to get another court order against that psychopath of an ex of hers?'

Ondien bumps lightly against the little table. Coffee spills. There are a few moments' silence.

He continues. 'I know it's unexpected to hear from me, Ondien . . . '

'Completely unexpected.'

'Do you remember blood, how it's supposed to be thicker than – ?'

Her voice rises. 'Cornelius, spare me the aphorisms. A weak spot in your armour would surprise me. But if you need support or something, just say so.'

His voice changes too. 'I no longer sleep at night, Ondien. I'm standing here in an empty office, above a street full of black cabs. This entire building is made of glass, even the lifts. One is visible from every every goddamn angle . . . '

ZELDA

When Ondien enters through the gates, Zelda is waiting in Phoenix Airport's arrivals hall. She is holding the child's hand and it is straining. Ondien addresses the child first, holds out the gift. 'I brought you something, Stanley.'

The child looks at her from under his eyebrows. She waits for him to grab it or knock it from her hands, but he takes the parcel and slowly turns it round and round without opening it.

Zelda has lost weight. She addresses Ondien in English. Ondien responds in Afrikaans, partially to exclude the child. Zelda struggles with the car keys, half blind in the dim parking garage. They get into a white car. She begs Stanley to fasten his seat belt. She refuses to drive unless he obeys. The child sits with folded arms, shouting huskily and vehemently until his mother closes her eyes and leans back against the headrest. The voice echoes hard against concrete. It envelops Ondien like ice. Zelda relents. She closes her window and starts driving. The noise ceases.

'It was Cornelius's idea, the trip,' says Ondien. 'There's a flavour of personal crisis in London. Of fragility, if you can believe that of our brother. But I can't really figure out what's going on.'

It was Ondien's suggestion to Cornelius that she fly here first, to Zelda, for a weekend. Then to him in London. And from there to Dubai, to Vera, a round of sibling visits. Cornelius is funding it all.

The highway on which they are driving passes underneath the runway. A plane thunders over them, over a thick concrete bridge. Stanley hangs his head upside down out of the car window.

Zelda points out the headquarters of the pharmaceutical company where she is employed as a regional sales manager. Low-slung office buildings right next to the highway, as brown as the barren hills behind them. Like barracks. Rows of flags in the sun: the Stars and Stripes alternating with the company logo.

The house is in a newly built suburb, slapped down here during the property bubble. One of those toy neighbourhoods with neat lawns, white postboxes and paved driveways. At least half the houses are standing empty. Computer-controlled sprinklers are spraying in the desert heat. Inside the house air conditioning is humming.

'Tea?'

Zelda looks lost in her kitchen. She searches in one cupboard, then another.

'Only herbal tea, I'm afraid. Oh, and coffee.'

'How about something stronger?'

Zelda frowns. 'Have you forgotten? It's morning here. I'm heading to work.'

We can't all indulge in bohemian slacking, she might have wanted to add, Ondien imagines – some of us have responsibilities.

Stanley has to be taken to a preschool and day-care centre, far from the house and far from Zelda's workplace. Zelda half drags, half carries the child outside. He holds on to the door frame with both hands. He would probably want to stay behind in order to do away with her, Ondien thinks. The child grabs Zelda by the hair, by her mousy brown bob.

It strikes Ondien that he is unnaturally strong, stronger than Zelda. After a brief struggle, Zelda and Stanley drive away in the white car.

Ondien does not unpack. She wanders through the grey light suffusing the house. Through net curtains the slope of a bare, dry mountain is visible. She opens the fridge, stands in the glow. It is almost empty, bar a few packets of processed cheese and meat. Half a carton of long-life milk. The carpets smell of glue, as if they have just been laid. In the child's room there is a pine bed with a duvet (a 'comforter', her Americanised sister would call it), a bare desk and a chair. The comforter strikes her as the only soft thing in the room. There are no magazines anywhere in the house, no mail waiting to be read. The walls are bare and white. It is as if the place has been rented for the day, a set with props, hastily prepared for a film shoot.

When Ondien awakes from a jet-lag nap, blue light is shining through her bedroom door. She walks into the empty living room. Early evening. The enormous television set is on. A silent American football match. The front door opens. It is Zelda. Ondien notices Stanley in a corner behind her, where he has been sitting all along. Her scalp tightens at the thought of her sleeping self alone with the child in the house. Zelda is grey with tiredness. A hot wind enters the house behind her. She puts Chinese takeaways on the table.

Initially they eat in silence. The child pushes bits of vegetables from his plate. They collect in puddles of soy on the table. Zelda stares at him without saying anything.

Stanley's gaze meets hers and he makes an unearthly sound. His speech is not normal, Ondien has noticed. When she saw the child before in South Africa, she did not realise; she kept her distance, observing his cruel spells from afar.

'Does he have a speech impediment, or is he just his father's child?'

'Oh, please, Ondien. He is sitting right next to us.' She is now speaking Afrikaans too.

'But he doesn't understand a word!'

Stanley has stopped eating. He is looking intently at Ondien, a restless fork in his hand.

'I know he's impossible, Ondien, but he is six years old. And he has a hearing problem.'

'Sorry, I didn't know that.'

'When he hears a strange language, it's as if he's being teased. It provokes him. That's why he was so upset at Dad's funeral.'

That is Ondien's clearest memory of that grim visit to South Africa. Stanley moaning loudly, straining towards the open grave and kicking in soil while the elderly Basotho farm labourers were trying to sing something. The child seen from behind, a convulsive little figure kicking up dust, his mother trying to hold him back. On the other side of the hole, the handful of singing people, hunched together in an attempt to occupy as little space as possible.

'At first I spoke Afrikaans to him, and his father English, to make him bilingual. A speech therapist and child psychologist said it was increasing his frustration and behavioural problems. When Cayle finally left, I spoke only English.'

'Tell me,' Zelda switches back to American, the Afrikaans and South African English just under the surface, 'what's happened to your music, to your life in London and Paris? How did you end up amongst the mine dumps?'

Ondien shrugs her shoulders. 'I think the music has left me.' She came, she thinks, to a certain point where she couldn't hear anything any longer. For so long, it was such an obsession, so deep in her skull, and then it was suddenly gone. She snaps her fingers. 'Just like that.'

Zelda nods wearily. 'It's called "giving up". Believe me, I know it when I see it.'

Ondien says nothing.

'So, what are you doing over there in Johannesburg?'

'At first I did some dry academic work. I thought: if you can no longer feel the music, then you may as well listen to it from a distance. For a while I was a volunteer in a rehabilitation centre for children with neurological injuries. Wanted to write an article about the musical abilities of children with aphasia.'

'Aphasia?'

'Loss of language capacity. Upsetting to observe, at the beginning. Some of the children can only sing and no longer speak. Some keep repeating ossified words or phrases, a kind of ghost language. Some make up their own stuff, create incredibly complex sentences, swap letters and syllables, talk gibberish . . . Some understand what they are saying, others don't. Some hear their own mistakes, but can't help them. Once they realise they're not understood, they become immensely frustrated. Others are completely unaware. The happiest ones are those who don't know what they've lost or forgotten. The one who could only sing couldn't understand a word of her own songs.' Ondien looks down, shakes her head thoughtfully. 'But she was the most blissful human I've ever encountered.'

'So, why did you leave?'

'I started helping with the therapy. "Melodic intonation therapy", it's called.'

'What is that?'

Zelda's questions are automatic, for the sake of politeness. Her sister has, after all, come from afar. Her head droops towards the table, her eyes bleary.

'Basic exercises to change speech into music. The idea is to elicit language from damaged parts of the brain through linking speech to rhythm and melody.'

'And what happened?'

Zelda looks as if she could fall asleep at any moment.

'I didn't follow the rules. My compositions – my tunes for the phrases and sentences – were apparently too meandering, too unstable.' Like a muezzin's calls to prayer from a minaret, she thinks. 'Or something like that. I tried new methods, experiments. According to the director of the centre I was worsening some children's conditions. "It's not an avant-garde music lesson," she said when she was monitoring me, "it's a delicate and responsible task."' She imitates the director's voice: 'You lack sympathy, your banal curiosity is driving you to use vulnerable children for irresponsible experiments.'

Zelda notices the way Ondien looks at Stanley while speaking. Zelda shakes her head slowly, as if the movement is demanding more than she has left in her.

'Nothing wrong with his brain.' She is speaking Afrikaans again.

Just the inherited mental pathology, Ondien thinks.

'I try to see and hear things from his perspective,' Zelda says, 'through his eyes, his ears . . . Bedtime,' Zelda says to Stanley.

The child makes a sulking noise. He slinks off his chair and runs to the television. He lies down on the couch, flicking through the channels frenetically.

Zelda sighs. 'The same story every night. I'll find the energy to deal with him later.' She gets up, draws the curtains on the street side, ensures every window is locked.

'South African habits?'

Zelda looks over to the child, back to Ondien. Afrikaans, again. 'It's about Cayle. I'm scared he'll find us. We just got this house. After the last court order.' She shrinks her shoulders. 'He always finds us.'

'What was the threat this time?'

Zelda looks Ondien in the eye. 'To cut out Stanley's intestines and feed them to me before I'm forced to eat my own.'

Upon her saying the word 'intestines', the television halts on a channel. Stanley's head turns slightly.

Ondien looks away. 'I shouldn't have asked.'

'There's been worse. Once, elsewhere, before the protection programme, before we had a secret address, he tried to break down the front door with a spade. Stanley and I waited inside for the police, or for the door to break.' Zelda looks smaller and smaller as she is speaking. Her hair is dull. 'A few months ago' – Her sister looks as if she has to concentrate hard to unearth the story – 'I had to travel for work. I tried everything, but I could find no one to look after my child. Nothing was working out. The after-school centre is just for day visits; others who had looked after him before didn't want to do it again. I had no choice; he had to go with me. On the plane he grabbed my laptop and smashed it on the floor. Ran around like a crazy person. A stewardess threatened that he would become a safety risk if I didn't control him.'

She tells Ondien how the hotel in Florida arranged a minder so that she could attend her meetings. A Mexican woman arrived. Zelda was explicit: they were not to leave the hotel room. When she returned at dusk, they were gone. For weeks she had barely slept. Her psychological defences were down and the shock hit her like a fist in the throat. She phoned the concierge, who phoned the police. She took the lift down. Outside, in the street, there was a limousine with dark windows. She suddenly became convinced that Stanley was inside, that someone was abducting him. She ran after the car, hitting against the opaque windows until her hands ached. It drove away. She just kept standing there, in the street, amongst the traffic. Heavy American cars, Ondien thinks. He was gone, Zelda continues. Across from the hotel, behind a wall, was a funfair. Zelda could see the coloured lights flickering, could hear the merry-go-round.

The concierge came and led her away by the arm. Inside, next to the lift, she slid her palm over the concrete wall. Someone had told her once, she remembered, that, when the core of a large building is poured, a labourer sometimes falls in, occasionally even more than one. Because the process cannot be stopped, every building apparently has one or two mushy spots somewhere deep inside. With her fingers she searched for a suture in the concrete, imagining the grey silence of a cement grave. A congealed nest. A cool mother's womb. Filled with peace.

Back in the hotel room, she looked out the window. There, on a path at the funfair, in the light of merry-go-rounds, they were. Stanley and the Mexican woman. Stanley looked up, and it felt as if Cayle himself was looking at her. She realised that she did not want the child back.

Stanley jumps from the couch, runs to the front door and slips out into the dark. Zelda's shoulders are drooping, her eyes are shot through with blood. For a moment Ondien thinks Zelda is going to faint. The conversations – Ondien's exegesis on brain-damaged children and Zelda's own hotel story – have only exhausted Zelda further, Ondien realises.

'I'll fetch him,' Ondien says. She walks out the open front door. A last remnant of light creates a pale fringe over the mountain peak. The mountain looks higher than in daylight, and closer. She hears Stanley's footsteps in the backyard. She walks around the house. There he is. She cannot make out whether he is looking towards or away from her. She feels a chill in her stomach: a piercing sound, as of steel on steel, emanates from the child's throat. It stops as suddenly as it began. He moves nimbly, disappears through the wooden fence. She follows, just able to scrape through the hole herself. The fence smells as if it has been freshly sawn. Behind the fence the landscape starts rising. She calls after him, but the little figure keeps running. She follows. When she stops for a rest and looks up, he is standing right in front of her.

She is out of breath.

'Something is seriously wrong with you, Stanley,' she says to the child, in Afrikaans.

He comes up with a string of swear words and sexual vulgarities which take her breath away. 'You fuck your dad,' he says in conclusion. 'You tear your cunt and rip out your heart.'

She winces, shocked. Another noise comes from his throat, more muffled now.

'Relentless little fucker,' she mumbles in Afrikaans, breathlessly, '*duiwelsgebroed*'.

The child instantly ceases its screeching.

'Devil,' he says brightly in the silence. Her mouth opens. There is no longer anger in his voice, rather the satisfaction of a pupil who has answered a question correctly. She catches her breath, takes in the landscape, her eyes now used to the dark. The desert air is cool. Small stones are shining, shards of mica are shimmering in moonlight. Stanley burrows in his ear, takes something out. He offers it to her. She hesitates, then takes it. His hearing aid. It feels waxy. He is as quiet as a mouse, points to her ear. She inserts it. Nothing but a hissing sound. She smiles slightly, for the first time in months.

'I can hear it,' she says and nods. 'Yes, I'm hearing it.'

He turns and runs, homewards. When she comes back and enters his room to return the device, he is lying with shiny eyes in the dark, under his comforter. On his bedside table, bottles of psycho-medicine are arranged in a row. On the desk is the gift that Ondien brought with her. He has unwrapped it. Opperman's *Kleuterverseboek*, an anthology of Afrikaans poems for children. All the way from South Africa (and even there no longer so easily obtainable).

*

Breakfast.

'Give the child up, let his father have him. Come back to South Africa.'

Ondien does not know why she is saying this. Perhaps just to bring hope. She does not want to return to South Africa herself. But here she wouldn't want to stay either, in this godforsaken, bloodless landscape. She looks at her sister. She is grey. Ondien suddenly feels guilty about what she has said. She thinks of the child in his bed last night when, for a moment, he was almost vulnerable, like a puppy in a bag with a rock just before it is hurled into a river. But it was a brief pause. Before breakfast, when Ondien approached him again, trying to build on the moment they'd shared last night by reading Stanley a poem from the *Kleuterverseboek*, his face twisted again. Someone else, the little brute that lives deep under his skin, had gained the upper hand again, overnight.

The child was still in his bed, warm with sleep. She leaned over him, opened the *Verseboek* between them, and read in a soft voice:

> '*Engeltjie, engeltjie, vlieg dadelik voort!*
> *Jou vader is dood, jou moeder is dood*
> *En jou kindertjies eet droë brood.*'

'Mom, the bitch is telling me stuff in that language!' he screeched, and let out a grating moan.

'What so amazed me about Cayle,' Zelda says over dry toast, 'was how such an incredibly beautiful man could be so incredibly cruel.'

Her hair hangs in slightly oily strings around her ears. She continues in monotone.

'You know, sometimes I consider simply surrendering myself to him, just letting him do what he wants. Getting it all over with.'

Zelda looks as if she cannot carry her own head, as if she is on the verge of falling forward and splitting open her chin on the table. Here she is sitting, in the artificial air, wasting away, Ondien thinks, the sister who once was my friend, with no one but this berserk child for company. Nothing here indicates her presence. Not a picture or a photo that reveals a thing. Her husband or the child will come and kill her in her bed and, once someone has thrown out her clothes and vacuumed a few loose hairs from the carpets, no one will know who lived here.

'This is not a house,' Ondien says. She looks around them. 'It is a sketch, an estate agent's hasty mock-up of how someone might live in such a place.'

CORNELIUS

Cornelius arrives from the airport, just back from Luxembourg. He looks smaller and tougher than she remembers him. His suit, once no doubt meticulously cut to size on Savile Row or in Hong Kong, is now somewhat loose-fitting. There is a new wiriness about him, his muscles small and dense from working out in the hotel gymnasiums of the world.

Her plane had landed earlier in the morning. The concierge let her into Cornelius's flat in Kensington, where the Romanian cleaning woman showed her to her room. She took the key to the private gardens in the Georgian square and sat there on an iron bench, in the pale light and silence. Except for a squirrel and a woman pushing a designer pram in the opposite corner, nothing moved.

Cornelius looks bashful. Perhaps the unexpected intimacy of their phone conversation a week or two earlier, perhaps the fact that they hardly recognise each other.

'You look different,' he says, and looks her fleetingly in the eye.

He does not elaborate, but she can imagine: bony, colourless, rhythmless. No longer the bright-eyed and bushy-tailed white girl obsessed with things ethnic.

'I can cook us a pasta,' she says.

He smiles. 'You will find nada in my cupboards, I can hardly find my own kitchen.'

They dine in Mayfair, in a grandiose eighteenth-century townhouse with art installations and a DJ spinning lounge music with electronic improvisations. Cornelius announces himself at the door in his traceless London accent. They order immediately.

Cornelius works his way through the delicate portions of an eight-course tasting menu: cool complex soups in fine glasses, shards of monkfish on vegetable flowers, medallions of lamb, lightly scorched scallops, cylindrical stacks of crab meat, dabs, mousses and foams.

They talk about Zelda. Ondien shakes her head, looks at the video installation projected on one of the restaurant walls: the image of a man going up in flames. There is an expression of bliss on the man's face.

'There is almost nothing left of our sister,' she says.

'Yes, I phoned her recently. Difficult to talk to her, she's lost much of her Afrikaans.'

Conversation, she thinks: at the best of times a joint game by the speaker and listener against the forces of confusion. He shifts the conversation away. They talk about Johannesburg, the recession, the economic cataclysm in Britain. On the wall next to them, the man keeps burning. Gradually the man disappears; only flames remain.

Ondien looks at the smooth Londoner in front of her, an ideal specimen of the borderless world's financial elite. She has difficulty matching this image with that of the semi-incoherent man to whom she spoke on the phone a week or two ago. But here he is. With his aura of a life beyond national identity. It is all about art, she thinks, in his world. The art, obviously, of financial alchemy. The art of conversations with neutral, smooth surfaces and deeply embedded codes. The art of consumption in the luxury markets of the most sophisticated metropoles. Contemporary art as investment market, edible art in the most sought-after restaurants, the art of charm and seduction. The art of power.

Another video installation is playing silently on the wall behind Cornelius. Snow falls from the ceiling and morphs into leaves. The leaves gather and change into a young woman on a penny farthing. The penny farthing changes into a spinning wheel, the young woman becomes as old as time in front of one's eyes and makes the wheel spin. A strong wind blows backwards and the woman gradually dissolves in the wind. She changes into leaves again, which change back into snow and disappear towards the ceiling. A few notes rise up inside Ondien, like in her student composer days. A short phrase. Strings, a texture. She holds her breath, waits. Cornelius quickly looks around them. To gauge the effect on the other guests of her presumably odd facial expression, she imagines. But she does not care. She closes her eyes, tries to develop the motif, or at least hold on to it, but it disappears.

'What is wrong?'

'Nothing,' she says.

Paper-thin sheets of caramelised sugar are balancing on Cornelius's basil ice cream. He orders coffee. His skin looks cool and dry. There is a fleetingness about him, a swift alertness. She cannot place it; it is new. The world is still his oyster, but keeping his balance, preventing his feet from slipping from under him, apparently now requires more artful magic than ever before.

She realises a blunt approach is required to free him up, to hear what is really going on. The manner of Free State farm kids shooting the breeze on a riverbank, getting something off their chest.

She sits back. 'So, what's biting you, Cornelius?'

He looks straight at her and she takes fright. A shocking, fiery vulnerability. He signals for the waiter. They will take their coffee in another room.

The waiter, white linen napkin over the forearm, leads them up the stairs to the top floor. *The Library*, it says in flickering neon on the wooden panelling. They sink into deep purple couches in a room filled with psychedelic props from the 1970s juxtaposed with elements from the original library. Against the walls on two sides are rows of lava lamps; a third wall carries shelves with eighteenth-century manuscripts.

'They're going to let me go,' he says.

She nods slowly. 'I'm not too surprised,' she says. 'The economic realities . . .'

'That's not it . . .'

'An opportunity, perhaps, Cornelius, to break out? Perhaps you can now escape the anaemia, do something quite new . . . ?'

'What else can I do, Ondien? I spend my days in confer-ence rooms, between glass sheets. Calculations, negotiations. Finely calibrated conversations, the painful formulation of sentences that shift money around invisibly. The more abstract, the better. That is my life. Just that. And don't think I can retire. The recession has taken its toll. My investments are buggered.'

There are chocolates in a little wooden bowl between them, handmade with cocoa from Borneo and flavoured with truffle oil, lavender and saffron. Cornelius stirs cream into his coffee. He puts down the teaspoon and his mood changes abruptly. He softens; something floating but intense comes over him.

'It's a liberation of sorts, I guess, or ought to be. I should tell you. Something has changed over the last few months. First it started reporting itself quietly, like a child tugging at the sleeve. You know in my heyday I had more girlfriends – affairs, shags, whatever – than I could count. Pretty girls, Chelsea or Kensington girls from private schools, an asset on a banker's arm. A kind of transaction in itself, of course; they take their pound of flesh, such girls. But then, for a long time, I had zero need for relationships. Dedicated myself with monomania – or, perhaps,' he smiles, 'monogamy – to my job. But something kept gnawing at the edges. Something was building up. One evening in a hotel, I can't recall, Los Angeles or Tokyo or somewhere, after a day of aggressive, gruelling meetings, I started reading a little book. Someone left it behind in the room. Thomas de Quincey's *Confessions of an English Opium Eater*. A floodwave hit me from those pages. Something like a swarm of bats. All the things that I had never allowed to break through. Desire, yearning, loss. I was facing myself. De Quincey wrote about his "constitutional determination to reverie". In a flash it occurred to me, that's what I'm staring in the eye: the neglect of my own urge to swoon, the refusal to acknowledge how deeply dream-fucked I am. I suddenly experienced the most intense regret – no, grief – over the years of self-denial, the methods of my obsessive escape from rural South Africa. The years of dreamlessness.'

He takes a sip of coffee. She too. It is scalding, as if being heated by something in the air.

Cornelius goes on. How would a project look, he considered, whereby repressed dreams are brought to light? In what kind of workshop could one have the Self welded to the Unknown? It had to be a fearless project, he decided, a hard, impersonal scheme. The polar opposite of the psychotherapist's couch, that subdued little laboratory where the core structures of bourgeois life get tattooed into the deeper tissue.

Communion with Infinity – that was his urge, that was the ultimate purpose. He had to strip off his skin, layer by layer, had to feel the feculent air on raw flesh. He wanted to see the city like an insect, from below. He would become a disciple of the terrae incognitae, he would learn to carve out the subterranean city map, the networks of sewage tunnels and cellars, on the Soul. And, if he were to discover that the Soul does not exist, then on the Intestines.

He felt his way in the dark. The methods were banal, the means were those available to the novice. One realised there were levels here, he explains; one had to be patient.

Level I were the nightclubs, the hollows that lie like catacombs under Victorian rail aqueducts in South London. Halls like caverns where men were dancing shirtless, slick with sweat that would rise in steamy vapours and hover in front of their faces.

'You smell it, those places, the fragrance of mud or fungus or roots. The smell of fresh blood. The first hint of Escape. Somewhere behind it, beyond consciousness, you suspect the strong fresh aroma of Freedom. And beyond that, further yet, Oblivion.'

He shows level II with both index fingers.

There, in shadows behind a torch, at a tunnel entrance, the guide was beckoning: Infinity's pharmacist. You held out your hand and allowed yourself to be led. The route, with its multiple stations, had been prepared for you. The pharmacist-guide pointed out the entrance. But the trip was yours alone. Cornelius tried out the mind-altering things. All right, it was no longer De Quincey's 1820s, and laudanum wasn't available in every corner shop. But alternatives were plentiful. All the usual, those that stimulated the dopamine levels especially – the short, powerful kicks. Whatever he could lay his hands on he took. MDMA, GHB, crystal meth, ketamine, the lot. The music was tight as a drum and hard as rock. Boundaries, whether cellar walls or human skin, became permeable.

With his finger, he writes a III on the table.

Sex was now exclusively with men, as frequently as possible and with as many as possible at a time. Palms against cold walls, electricity shocking through the spine . . .

Ondien lifts an eyebrow, her voice an octave higher than earlier. 'All those women who answered your phone in your days of tight collars . . . Who'd have guessed?'

He places a chocolate on his tongue, continues.

He understood the role of chance, and risk, where it concerned capital. But he wanted to know about randomness: random meetings, random losses. He found himself in flats, rooms and places that astounded him, emerged from waking dreams not knowing where he was or how he had ended up there. Whether it was high above or deep below the city, he could not tell. A factory, a power station. Burnt-out gasworks. Places smelling of rust, of vinyl, where concrete rubs you raw, where dripping water causes limestone stalactites to hang, where the sweat and saliva of a little crowd would drip onto you.

'I took stuff that would wake up every fibre, that would keep you awake for twenty hours on the torture rack. After the tenth hour you gaze at the men who are waiting with hard hands. You decide you can flay yourself with your own muscle power, can tear open the carcass and give it up for slaughter . . . '

Cornelius's eyes glow coldly.

He never knew, he goes on, from which direction – and whether – the morning light would come. It took a long time before it appeared, the light, from behind all the bodies, from behind the weight of boots.

'Every morning I saw the morning sun rise over a new city.'

For a while he remains silent.

'Level IV?' she wants to know.

His eyes change. One night he locked himself out of his flat; the concierge was already off duty. The rest of the night he walked in the rain, arms stretched out, face upwards, probably thirty or forty kilometres. Round and round, in wide circles. A spiral outwards and a spiral inwards. The entire time a certain paragraph from De Quincey was circling around in his head.

'Wait, I'll find it for you.' He fiddles with his iPhone, finds the passage on the internet. He reads with a clear voice:

'The sense of space, and in the end the sense of time, were both powerfully affected. Buildings, landscapes, et cetera, were exhibited in proportions so vast as the bodily eye is not fitted to receive. Space swelled, and was amplified to an extent of unutterable infinity. This, however, did not disturb me so much as the vast expansion of time; I sometimes seemed to have lived for seventy or 100 years in one night – nay, sometimes had feelings representative of a millennium passed in that time, or, however, of a duration far beyond the limits of any human experience . . . '

He puts the phone in his pocket and looks at her, the glow of the lava lamps against his cheek.

'While I was walking through the city, I looked up, and the rain was metallic, like quicksilver on the skin. And then it filled my nose, unmistakeably: the smell of Freedom. I had graduated to the next level. I was almost there, just short of Oblivion.'

He sits further forward.

'There were moments when I hesitated, in the dark amongst bodies, in the scorching light of a stranger's flat.

When I thought: this is the furthest I can ever venture from our childhood places on that farm.'

He looks up. He is speaking with a boy's voice now.

'Yes, it was the greatest distance I could put between me and that Free State garden with its nasturtiums. But, wherever I found myself, with all those things in the blood creating images inside the skull, I only needed to think of that garden to cause nasturtiums to grow all around me: over the walls, ceilings and floors of the strange room I was in. Over rust marks and water stains. Over graffiti and soot. And, when our mother's singing voice swept through like wind, the flowers would tremble lightly . . . '

He coughs drily, finds his grown-up voice again.

One evening he was in a club, he continues. He bought weightless crystals from a blond man in the toilets and deposited them on his tongue amidst chrome taps and steel urinals. The dance floor was cool and bright, air was being pumped in through tubes against the ceiling. The music was as brittle as glass. The floor like a mirror, the ceiling like a mirror. He froze. He saw her approach across smooth muscled shoulders: a floating goddess. She introduced herself: Mater Lacrimarum.

'She stopped right above me and addressed me: "Cornelius!" "How do you know my name?" I asked. "You must praise the worm," she said, "and pray to the wormy grave."'

The following morning he awoke next to a beautiful young Saudi, Cornelius recounts. On his other side on the bare mattress was a young man from Berlin with tattoos on his forearms and the eyes of a stag.

'Coffee?' he asked the swarthy Saudi.

The man shook his head. 'It's Ramadan.'

'Do you know Mater Lacrimarum?' Cornelius wanted to know from him.

The man shook his head. He poured a glass of water from the fridge and gulped it down.

'Do you know Mater Lacrimarum?' he wanted to know urgently from the Berliner, but there was no answer.

Ondien waits for Cornelius to continue, but he is done.

'The dreamlessness,' she asks, 'has it passed? And the messengers of Infinity – do they now visit you freely?'

He smiles wryly.

'There was unexpectedly another level, level V. The Pharmacist, now a skeleton, is waiting with a bottle in his hand marked X. For effect I can probably thrust a scythe in his hand too . . . No, it's all over, Ondien, the project. I'm struggling. Mood swings, depression, paranoia. Everything black. Our Calvinism teaches us, of course, that joy never comes without pain. Or ecstasy without major pain. My bank's going to fire me. I'm simply not functioning any longer, I'm fucking up my transactions, one after the other.'

They remain silent for a long time. The lava lamps bubble imperturbably, hypnotically.

She looks at him. 'Tell me, were you at our mother's funeral?'

He quickly looks down, shakes his head.

'Me neither,' she says, and looks down too.

After a while: 'Why me, Cornelius? Why did you make me come here?'

'I was scared,' he says, and his eyes startle her again. 'So scared. Of everyone, you're most like her. Like our mother.'

He leans towards her, as if he is going to rest his head on her lap. She lifts her hand towards his temple.

Notes in her head, more insistent than before, right under the skull. Flutes, then silence. Something waiting, fingers stirring behind a sheet. It bursts through. Tone clusters as black as coal.

A funeral march, *that* is what is building up.

Upon returning late the next evening, after a day's meetings in Stockholm, he sits down next to her on the sofa. He leans his head back, eyes closed.

'What are you reading?' he asks.

She closes the book to show him. He does not open his eyes.

'Louis Wolfson,' she says, *'Le Schizo et les langues.'*

'Yes? Who's Wolfson?'

An automatic response, just to keep the conversation going. 'An American who wrote in French in the seventies about his schizophrenia, and his dogged project to forget his mother tongue.'

'Yes?'

He is close to sleep now, so it seems, or fainting.

She explains how English was the language in which Wolfson's hated mother used to bombard him daily with a stream of meanness and invective. His strategy was, immediately upon hearing the English words, to substitute it in his head with words or fragments from other languages of which the English sounds reminded him. He wanted to decapitate and disempower the language. The problem, she explains, was that the more he tried to forget, the more he forced himself to remember. The wounds that the mother tongue had carved on him were reopened by every attempt to displace them. And yet, and yet. His project, she explains, also opened a glimmer of possibility that, one day, he would be able to forge a new relationship with the mother tongue. That he would be able to return to it, as if to a lost land.

She looks at Cornelius. He is asleep, as pale as ash.

VERA

'One evening there was barking at the gate. When we came out of the house, our dog was on fire. A streak of light through the garden. Back and forth. It was terrible. Frank had to shoot the dog through the head with his pistol.'

Vera sinks back into the couch.

'The security guard had vanished. Somewhere in the dark, we knew, the gang was waiting. But the pistol must have frightened them off. Nothing further happened. But, yes, that was the last straw. A month later we left Joburg.'

Contrary to plans, it is not in Frank and Vera's villa in a desert ghetto where she gets to see her sister for the first time since their father's funeral. Over the phone, beforehand, Vera had gone on about their desert house. A spacious place, brand new, a lawn and pool amidst all the sand. Very quiet. As safe as can be. The international school right there in the complex, inside the walls. Ondien was prepared for a visit to a sandy compound.

Instead, they are sitting here, across from each other, on the sixty-first floor of one of the highest buildings in Dubai. Ondien does not even know whose apartment it is. A cryptic SMS message from Vera was waiting on her cellphone when her plane landed: *Change of plan. Meet me at HHHR Towers, Sheikh Zayed Road, apartment 6101.*

'No, I'm not asking why you're here in Dubai; I mean why are you *here*? In this apartment?'

As she is speaking, Ondien gestures towards the living room, the soft furnishings, the tassels and shiny artefacts. Over Vera's shoulder, she looks through the exterior glass wall. Vanishing points and horizons of the desert landscape multiply blindly in the mirrored façades of other buildings. In here the light is softened by dark brocade, deep pile carpets and chestnut wood. Arabic calligraphy on handmade paper is displayed on the walls.

Vera looks away, towards the desert reflections, and the desert itself, disappearing in the distant sunlight.

The last time Ondien saw Vera, she was elegant and upright on their covered patio, with the stiff neck and stacked hair of a Bryanston wife. Her forehead was unnaturally smooth, just a few fine lines around the mouth. Gold decorating the ears and hands. Over her shoulder the gardener was visible in his blue overalls, out of focus. When Frank joined them, Vera's voice became louder, switching to whiny nasal English, the hypocrite-speak of corporate Northern Johannesburg.

Now Vera is disorientated, restless. She looks around as if she is searching for something, as if she has forgotten what it is that makes one important.

'Things didn't work out as expected,' she says. 'Dubai isn't all it's made out to be. Frank and I aren't what we used to be.' Ondien nods. Vera continues. 'Frank's company is teetering on the edge. A month ago the board asked him to resign.'

'Surely he'll get rewarded handsomely – doesn't his contract provide? Isn't that how things work in that world?'

Vera looks away.

'There are investigations,' she says. 'It's been going on for months.'

She explains that the South African and British tax authorities are auditing Frank. That the company is alleging that he has enriched himself, there will probably be fraud charges. The company won't pay him a cent pending completion of all this.

'And our investments . . . ' She shakes her head. 'There is little left. Falling markets. Huge legal fees in different countries. There is talk that the Brits or South Africans may issue a warrant for his arrest, that they're going to freeze accounts. Issues here in Dubai around extradition . . . My own life' – she spreads out her fingers, looks at her own hand – 'has taken a different turn.'

She tells of the Arab, owner of a Dubai construction company, of the romance which has flourished so unexpectedly.

'I just knew,' she says vehemently, 'there was life in me yet.' She taps with perfect nails against her sternum. 'I couldn't just roll over with Frank. How many sacrifices haven't I had to make already? My own happiness has to count for something too.' She bursts into tears. While weeping, she gestures towards the apartment's interior. 'I'm living here now, with Shahin. How could I resist? He's awoken something in me again.'

She blows her nose, finds her strength again.

'But I'm also scared. After all the wining and dining, he suddenly became very possessive.'

She recounts how she was still living with Frank and the children, but Shahin wanted her here. He started exerting pressure, at first subtly, but then he warned that he would have her charged with adultery, that she would be stoned to death on a public square, unless she agreed to marry him.

'You have to understand,' she says, 'I don't know if it's true, whether such things can happen. Surely they're not all that barbaric here, it's not Iran or Afghanistan after all, but I don't have a choice. I'm scared. And, if Frank goes to jail, somebody has to look after the children financially. Shahin wants a proper Muslim wedding . . . '

'The jet lag is catching up with me,' Ondien says, and holds her head. 'Can you show me where I'll be sleeping?'

Vera sits forward, speaks urgently. 'Please, you can't sleep here. An unmarried woman under the same roof won't do. He has strict rules. We've booked a hotel for you.' She looks at the door. 'He'll be back any minute.'

She has hardly finished speaking when they hear the lift, which enters the apartment directly, opening. Vera jumps up; her heels click down the corridor, on the marble floor. Ondien heads for the guest toilet.

She splashes water from the gilt taps over her face, looks at herself in the mirror. She is not wearing any make-up. She will be relieved to get out of here. The new Vera, the messy emotions, are too much for her. The tantrum style rearing its head, the hysterical register that one associates with a face contorted with weeping, loose strands of hair, smudged make-up. God, no, she would rather have the stiff corporate wife from Bryanston with her anointed Botoxed forehead.

Ondien breathes deeply and opens the toilet door. Vera introduces her to Shahin. He is swarthy with fine features, his eyes piercing. She half expected a traditional head covering, like a wise man in a passion play from her and Vera's Free State school days, but he is wearing a suit. In Shahin's presence, Vera often lowers her eyes.

'We've booked you a hotel,' says Shahin, 'the Kempinski at the Mall of the Emirates. I'll take you.'

In the underground carpark they get into his four-wheel-drive vehicle. The alarm gives a shrill whistle when he unlocks it. The car is canary yellow and stands high on its wheels. *HUMMER*, Ondien reads in chrome on the bonnet. Thick streams of icy air blow into the cabin.

At the hotel, Shahin checks her in. She waits. When they get to the room, someone in white gloves is there for them.

'Your personal butler,' says Shahin. 'We thought you'd be comfortable here.'

Inside the spacious suite Ondien walks up to the glass that occupies an entire wall. It overlooks an indoor ski slope, a vast freezer in which figures in bright clothing are zigzagging across snow.

The butler presses a remote-control button. A cosy fire flickers on in the fireplace next to her. In front of the flames lies a bear skin with a stuffed head still attached to it.

Shahin waves away the butler.

'Before I go, let me provide you with some guidance,' he says. She turns around. He continues. 'Don't even think of taking Vera away from here, from me. The force of the law will deal with her. And with you. You're now in my country. And she's an adulterer.'

This is so out of the blue that Ondien is speechless for a moment. Then something surges in her, like vomit. In a flash she is the self-conscious young gender studies and music student again, the militant SOAS ethnomusicologist. She feels more reckless than she has in ages.

'Islamic law is a load of shit,' she says. 'You Arabic men and your little homosocial world – all it's designed for is to allow you to freely fuck each other, and little boys and girls to boot, out in the desert.'

He does not react in the way she hoped he would. He utters a cool, dry little laugh, looks at his bulky golden watch.

'You are full of Western misapprehensions. I believe you've been confused by those CNN and BBC images of the Taliban. That is not how things are here. But, yes, we do have our ways.'

He takes his time rearranging the cuffs of his silk-and-wool suit, one side, then the other, until they are perfect. He smiles neatly and then departs.

She is left alone with the blueish snow out there (or out there but in there). Machines are spewing clouds of fine flakes over the slope. She regrets her outburst. Her frustration and resentment towards Vera are boiling over. She has little appetite for helping to sort out this mess.

Ondien wanders aimlessly through the vast shopping complex that merges with the hotel and skiing centre. She walks into a store with an exhibition of life-sized toy animals in artificial snow: polar bears, white lions, Siberian tigers, snow leopards, white sabre-toothed tigers, a white dinosaur. A sales clerk approaches her. She has a sweet smile, a transparent hijab draped over charcoal-black hair.

'Many of these animals don't even occur in nature,' Ondien says.

The woman's smile does not change.

'Feel how soft,' she says. She takes Ondien's hand gently and lets it rest on the sabre-toothed tiger's neck. The silky fur against Ondien's palm causes an unexpected sob to rise in her chest. And there she has it: her funeral march. Instruments are tuned. A short silence and then it starts to play in her skull, from the very first note.

Vera calls. She is upset. 'What did you say to Shahin? He was silent with anger when he returned.'

'What are you scared of?'

'That he'd send someone to do something to my children.'

'Has he threatened to?'

'Not this time, no, but previously, when I wanted to end the relationship.'

Ondien and Vera meet at the hotel, amongst Westerners in the coffee shop. Vera takes off her hijab, but keeps on her Jackie Onassis sunglasses. The dark glass covers half her face.

'You look like Grace Kelly,' Ondien says drily, but Vera is not amused. Her mouth is tense.

'It is important that you don't spoil things for me here, Ondien. I don't know why I agreed to your visit. I just wanted to see you, see someone . . . perhaps it was a mistake. You've always been a troublemaker.'

Ondien breathes deeply, grits her teeth.

'Vera, why don't you go back to Frank and the kids? Face the crisis, support your children, your husband.'

Vera shakes her head, looks away, astonished that Ondien cannot take in the complexity of her situation.

'You don't understand. There will be nothing left of the assets. Frank may go to jail. Perhaps he'll be extradited to South Africa. Just about the entire board and most shareholders are black and from the political inner circle. Frank's the scapegoat. It was humiliating enough to have to grovel and fawn to be tolerated on the edges of the new South African hierarchies. And, now? To go and stand in front of a judge as an accused? The wife of a white white-collar criminal in a South African jail? That I will never endure.'

What about possibilities for you and your children somewhere else, a completely new beginning? she wants to ask, but she says nothing, just sniffs her hand: it still smells of the sabre-toothed tiger's nylon fur. The music swells, fills her skull, lifts her heart, the darkness of it notwithstanding.

She looks Vera straight in the eye. 'Vera, were you at our mother's funeral, back then?'

Vera looks at her with a raw expression. She shakes her head, starts weeping so unexpectedly that people at other tables turn their heads.

'I am so lost,' she says. 'Everything has collapsed, I am worthless to my children, I am so ashamed, I mean nothing to anyone, I am a useless woman.'

Vera is crying disconsolately, her face ugly. She drops onto her knees next to the little table, her cheek against Ondien's hand. 'I want my mother,' she says. 'I just want my mother.'

Ondien scarcely hears Vera. The music in her head is so beautiful, it moves her so terribly. Ondien gently pulls back her hand.

'I'll go to Frank and the children, Vera, and make sure everything's fine there. Do you have a message for them?'

She shakes her head in between sobs, slumps flatly onto the floor. Face down, high heels next to her buttocks. She looks snottily down at the floor.

'Just let me know the children are ok.'

ONDIEN

On the plane back to Johannesburg the funeral march is playing in her head. In massive, surging chunks. It is moving at the pace of a storm. She tries to keep up, jots down ideas and sequences and motifs: on pieces of paper, in the margins of magazine pages, on the stub of her plane ticket. On a napkin.

When she arrives in the city from the airport, the door to her flat is open. The security gate is hanging askew from its hinges. The flat is virtually empty. The furniture is gone, the sink ripped out of the bathroom. Her collection of musical instruments from North and West Africa has been stolen; the same goes for her LPs and old-fashioned turntable. Her clothes, the kaftans and costumes in which she used to perform in the VNLS days. The whole lot. Someone must have stripped the place repeatedly. In the bedroom the bowl of cat food has been left behind, largely uneaten.

'Flame!' she calls for the cat.

Nothing. All that has been left behind, in the bedroom cupboard: her Casio synthesiser from the 1980s. She feels light. This is all she owns now: one suitcase and a dinky keyboard.

She gets in her car and drives to the Free State. To the farm where she grew up. She drives without stopping, until the sharp winter light makes her eyes burn. In town she stops at the co-op. She no longer knows anyone behind the counter or amongst the shelves. She buys nasturtium seeds, a little fork and garden gloves.

The homestead is somewhat neglected, but unchanged. The garden is dry and flowerless.

'This was my mother's garden,' she says when a woman comes out, without first greeting her. 'I'd like to replant a corner of it. One small bed of flowers. Do you mind?'

The woman's hands are in the pockets of a stretched cardigan. She looks stupefied, or perhaps just bored. She looks at the little fork in Ondien's hands.

'An overloaded gesture, I know, sentimental. Still, grant me this. I have the seeds with me. And a small garden fork. If I may only borrow a little water . . . '

'Do what you like,' the woman says. She turns around and enters the house.

Ondien drops onto her knees, in the garden where her mother once walked and sang. Clichéd arias, always. Puccini or Verdi. 'Sì, mi chiamano Mimì' from *La Bohème*, 'Ah, fors'è lui' from *La Traviata*. The sun burns her back, the tears come.

When she is done, she rinses her hands at an outside tap. She leaves without speaking to the dull woman again.

When she is too tired to drive any further, she stops and sleeps in a motel. All night trucks brake and depart in front of her window.

Someone's grimy sleeping bag on the kitchen floor. The pane of the kitchen window has been removed. A stranger has spent the night in her flat. When dusk falls, she awaits the guest. She waits until late. No one comes. She goes outside in the dark to see if someone is hiding there. The garden has become neglected in the weeks since Mrs Zuckermann – Mrs Z, as she calls her – moved out. Mrs Z's children are in New York and Toronto. It has been a decade since they last visited. Mrs Z writes them letters that go unanswered. Her friends are either dead or have emigrated to Israel or the US. Not a soul to look after things in her absence, no one to administer anything. Two months have passed since Ondien last paid rent.

The grass is long around Ondien's feet, the leaves of shrubs dry between her fingers. In a corner of the garden sparks are flying. She approaches. Something is hanging from the electric fence, but she cannot see what it is. She fetches the key to the main house. In Mr Zuckermann's little library with shelves full of books on Zionism, she finds a small ladder. She carries it out and climbs onto it, stretches a hand towards the thing hanging there. It's rubbery to the touch. Flame the cat.

In the kitchen light she studies the pink carcass, the skin stripped off completely. It smells of death. It looks too small to be her cat – its neck like a twig that one could snap between two fingers – but it is. The stomach has been cut open, it has been gutted. (Was someone planning to eat it?)

She cannot immediately decide what to do with the carcass. There is music in her head that first needs to be purged. For now, she will put it in a plastic bag and leave it outside, behind the flat.

For the remainder of the evening she composes as if in a fever. The march is finished, she is working on a new movement to precede it: on the horizon clouds are approaching. There is the roll of percussion, then the wind instruments take over, stately and skirling, pushing against the dark. Then death, the abrupt entrance of the quarter chords. It is the sound of a swarm of locusts: hatching in the underworld, expanding like gas. The air around their wings stirs the Styx's water when they cross. The swarm has been sent to fetch the dead. They arrive and devour the body where it is cooling down. Then they alight for the flight back. They carry the body away in ten thousand pieces, diluting it like a cloud. All these unusual things she hears. The Casio is next to her. With one hand she is tinkling – the tinkling is standing in for a sweeping, surging orchestra. The funeral march is now but one movement of her piece; it is becoming a requiem.

By four in the morning her fingers are stiff and cold. She lies down in the sleeping bag for some warmth, too tired to be bothered by the rancidness. When she gets up, her body is sore from the hard floor. She is itching. Perhaps there are bedbugs in the bag. Not really a liveable place any longer, this flat. But, yes, it is free accommodation. To be a white homeless woman in Johannesburg, to be sleeping under bridges, cannot be a joke. She suddenly realises she has not eaten since getting off a plane two days ago.

The gardener no longer comes, no one has been paying him. The pool has been emptied, probably the last thing he did before absconding. The concrete sides are baking in the winter sun. Scratchy with tiredness and thirst she walks out on the sun-bleached diving board. She tests its bounce, jumping up and down a little, as if she is on the verge of diving. It creaks as it moves. A tuft of grass has already grown through a crack in the bottom. Ondien goes into the house, finds a few tins of cheap meatballs, things that Mrs Z used to feed her domestics. Then she fetches a little spade and a flowerpot from Mrs Z's garage. In it she plants the leftover nasturtium seeds.

Early evening. A Highveld storm is building. There is a flash between cloud and wire: the electric fence has been struck. Late evening, when she is lying in the rancid sleeping bag, she hears someone breaking out the burglar bars in front of Mrs Z's windows. She is lying there like a mummy, waiting for the intruders to come and do her harm. She can hear footsteps back and forth through the garden as they carry things off. But the footsteps pass, they do not come to her. Either they do not know she is there, or an unspoken understanding is developing: she does not bother them and they do not bother her.

The next morning she enters the house. Wires are hanging where the television has been ripped out. Across the carpets lie the muddy marks of feet, there is a broken plate on the kitchen floor. She takes what she needs. What is left in the pantry she packs in a box. She takes pots and pans, plates and cutlery. Sheets. She cannot find any blankets:

probably all stolen. She carries two chairs and a mattress through the garden, to her flat.

She visits Mrs Z in the care home. She is lying with her chin on a white sheet.

'Be sure to pay your rent into my account,' she says.

'Of course, Mrs Zuckermann. Promptly, every month.'

'You are like a daughter to me.'

Mrs Z knows as well as she that there is no truth in this. Their relationship was purely commercial. And now it is in a vague no-man's-land: the strongest ties she has with Mrs Z are the things she steals from her house in order to survive. And the fact that she is a squatter in her back garden. She does not even know why she is standing here with the ungerminated flowers in her hands. Guilt, probably. If she were ever to bring flowers again, they would have to be bought with the proceeds from what she is stealing from Mrs Z's home. There is no money left.

'And please look after the house, there's no one else to do it. When I pass on, it all goes to my children. Remember that.'

'Of course, Mrs Zuckermann.' (And who exactly, does the woman imagine, ought to be paying all the bills?)

'Everything in order at home? The garden still neat?'

'Winter hasn't touched your garden, Mrs Zuckermann. It's as lush as if it were midsummer.' (Is she expecting Ondien to pay the gardener too?)

'How about Arthur? Still his happy self? Not missing me?'

Ondien has to think for a moment. Her husband's name was Samuel. Then she recalls the photograph of a dog in Mrs Z's bedroom. A spaniel that has been dead for years.

'Fit as a fiddle, Mrs Zuckermann, more boisterous than ever. Welcomes me every time with a swing of the tail.' Her voice becomes quieter. 'He does miss you a little, though.'

For the first time Mrs Z smiles wanly.

'I have to go now, Mrs Zuckermann. I'm leaving you this container I've planted with flowers; they should come up soon.'

While Ondien is walking away, she hears Mrs Z tell a nurse to go and throw out 'this pot of soil'.

When she comes home after the visit, half of the things she took from the house have been stolen from her flat again. A thief amongst thieves, that is what she is becoming. You steal from someone weaker, the stronger ones steal from you. You return to your weaker victim. Things circulate. A life cycle, an ecosystem. She is becoming part of natural life in this country, the instinctive processes sustaining themselves behind shiny surfaces. She is learning, she is approaching the real nature of things. Music and theft are the paths leading her to the light.

She is now penniless; she cannot even afford a cup of coffee in the shopping malls. She survives on what she is able to carry out of Mrs Z's house. Over the next day or two she takes everything she can fit into her car to a pawnshop in Braamfontein. Before the thieves can lay their hands on it and before her fuel runs out and she is stranded.

At night the activities in Mrs Z's house continue unabated. One night the footsteps come close to the flat. Ondien holds her breath. There is breathing at the kitchen's paneless window. From the bedroom, peeking out of the rancid sleeping bag, she is unable to see a face, but she can see little rhythmic clouds of vapour pushing inwards. It glows against light filtering in from outside. Her visitor is sniffing the flat's smells. A torch clicks on, a beam slips around. She holds her breath. Then voices, outside by the pool. The vapour pulls back, the footsteps move away. Then she hears them scale the wall, out towards the street.

She remembers Flame, somewhere in a plastic bag. She finds a spade in Mrs Z's storeroom. She is surprised it has not been stolen yet. In the main house, there is almost nothing left. The kitchen cupboards have been ripped out. Doors have been lifted from their hinges. Wall-to-wall carpets have been torn from the floor.

She buries the cat. It is the first time in days that she is able to stop writing down music for a while. The soil is hard. It is a shallow grave. Afterwards she sits on a kitchen stool on the unmown lawn. There, in the sun, she performs the funeral march movement of her requiem on the Casio. She is trying it out.

The next evening she is composing again. A siren screams past and breaks her concentration. Silence reigns in her head once more. She can now only think of the electric wires gleaming above the garden wall. But she has to continue, she has to intercept the thick surges of sound in the air. She has to play it inwardly, mutilate herself with it.

Her cellphone rings. She is surprised it has not been cut off; she has not paid a bill for some time. It is Mrs Z.

'Mrs Zuckermann, what a surprise!'

She is sitting with her feet on one of Mrs Z's dining-room chairs.

'Are you my daughter?'

She is wrong-footed.

'Mrs Zuckermann, your daughter is in America. I'm your lodger.'

'You've never responded to any of my letters. Not even one. And my grandchildren? Do you know what grief it is for me not to know them?' Her voice cracks. 'Do you have any idea of my sorrow, dying here alone? In this cruel, dishonest place, this country full of goyim with bloody hands?'

'You are not alone, Mrs Zuckermann.'

Mrs Z starts to cry softly. The phone goes dead.

She returns to her music sheets and the Casio. To the requiem. She toys with the idea of voices, a choir, and at least fragments of the traditional mass liturgy. But the piece is too amorphous, too unconventional. It is changing shape like a cloud. She cannot get a grip on it. She can only follow where the skull musicians lead. A few voices do ultimately appear; it is becoming a twenty-first-century oratorio. There are monks, chanting atonally, layer upon layer. A soprano voice, briefly, somewhere in the fogginess – a young boy, as pure and clear as the fiercest physical pain: *'libera animas omnium fidelium defunctorum de poenis inferni et de profundo lacu.'*

Then everything bordering the lyrical, the tonal and the melodic drains away. The music bends, doubles, starts to devour itself. The instruments are now played in all conceivable ways. Strings are ignored, the edges of violins are scratched, flutes are obstructed breathily, the piano is being played with bricks dampening the strings, like a sickly harpsichord. The piano wants to destroy itself, the monks' throats are constricted, each note an ugly little cry of fear. The devoured body has arrived with the locusts in the underworld. The swarm descends into the swamp. Shards of bone dissolve in locust bellies. This she imagines with one hand on the Casio's keys – a child's tinkling is all that emerges.

She stops the tinkling. At the window a face has appeared. She did not hear footsteps. Yet she is not startled. He – the face – neither. They look at each other. For a while neither of them moves. Behind the chirping of crickets and the highway traffic, she hears silence. Highveld silence. Like a dove's feather against the wrist.

Small and black and shiny, the face. Prominent cheek-bones, hollow cheeks. A cruel face, so it seems, but she would not want to judge hastily. She should give him a chance, leave his options open.

'Come in,' she says, 'I've been expecting you. The boundaries here are now porous, after all, everyone's welcome, anyone can come and get. Take what you want. Even my Casio, if you wish. And here' – she waves the sheaf of music paper in his direction – 'take the music too if you choose. Perhaps you could perform it somewhere. I'm sure there are many funerals where you come from. Or, even better, burn it on a cold winter's evening, for a hint of warmth.'

He says nothing. His eyes scan the room, take it all in, settle on her again. She nods comprehendingly at his silence.

'If it is me you want, I won't stop you either. As I said, take what you want.'

There is still no sign that he understands her. He pulls himself up by the window frame, hops in with a smooth movement. He is as small as a pygmy. She can smell him. She looks at his hands, considers whether they are skilled enough to skin a cat in a single movement.

She gets up, he stiffens. She moves slowly, turns her back on him, opens the cupboard door to take out two teacups (from Mrs Z's kitchen, of course).

'You must forgive me, the kettle's been stolen. I only have a pan from Mrs Zuckermann's house in which to boil water. See,' she smiles and looks around. He is watching her closely. 'I'm also a looter . . . Perhaps,' she says into the cupboard, 'we can try to be friends. What do you think?' She continues making tea, looks at him from the corner of her eye. He opens the cupboard behind him, throws things on the floor. He gets hold of a box of salty biscuits, takes what is left, throws the empty packet on the floor. The crumbs fall from his mouth as he is eating.

She sits down slowly on Mrs Z's dining-room chair. 'I'm just a looter myself,' she repeats. 'I'm also only squatting here. You and I, we're in the same boat.'

She clears her throat, shifts in the chair.

'I know I understand little of your thoughts, your degree of need and all that, but let's experiment. Let's each share something. As an icebreaker,' she says, 'let me tell you about my mother. Of her neat flower beds, how she used to sing in the garden. How her voice disappeared in the high Free State sky.'

The pan of tea water gives off slow steam. There is silence. She continues.

'Let's give friendship a try,' she says. 'As my friend you would probably want to ask (wouldn't you?): "what else? Is that all that's left of your mother, Ondien? The little flowers, a few notes in the afternoon?"'

She pours the tea, the heat against her face. In the skull music there appears, amidst atonal chanting, a graceful shred of melody which vanishes before it can be caught. Chords, just two or three, sweet and high, like snowy peaks above clouds. The suggestion, over a bass line, of glass bells. The melody slips, major into minor, shadows drift over thoughts. Thus one remembers, she thinks. And thus one forgets, *is* forgotten. Even by your own music.

She continues in the silence. She can feel the power draining from her muscles. 'Another question you would want to ask is: "can one grieve alone? Grief," you would frown and shake your head, "as private language, Ondien? Here in your little room, in a barren garden, hands flitting over a stunted organ?"'

She breathes deeply. His hands keep moving, his eyes are quick, his scalp is breaking out in shiny sweat.

'And,' she coughs, her voice sounding thin and flat, 'you would have asked: "could it yield anything, Ondien, your search for someone in a cloud of sound, in the chambers of bone behind the ear?" "Probably not," I'd have to answer. And yet,' she says, 'come and listen, come and stand here next to the organ.' She swallows, keeping an eye on his movements, avoiding sudden movements herself. 'As if I'm the accompanist and you the soloist. Let me play.' She swallows again, steadies her hands. 'I'll play the bit near the end of the final movement where the locusts, the underworld's devouring undertakers, gather to land. Listen closely: there is an instant, just the briefest of moments, when the swarm takes on the shape of the deceased . . . '

Between the mattress and table he blocks her way, takes her hard by the upper arm.

'You've talked enough,' he says, 'talking is over.'

LOOSE

In rasic theatre, the partakers empathize with the experience of the performers playing. This empathy with the performer rather than with the plot is what permits Indian theatre to 'wander', to explore detours and hidden pathways, unexpected turns in the performance. [...] The partakers' interest is not tied to the story but to the enactment of the story; the partakers do not want to 'see what happens next' but to 'experience how the performer performs whatever is happening'.

Richard Schechner,
Performance Theory

He dreams he is doing ballet with a Japanese man at the Voortrekker monument. The man is half sitting, half standing against a low granite wall. He walks to the man, turns around and presses his back against his chest. The man puts his arms around him and they move across the expansive paving. Besides firmness, there is empathy in the man's grip, in the manner in which he is steering them. It is simultaneously without doubt and without insistence. Gently the Japanese man is initiating him, as if wanting to say: everything is ok, we can do it. (He utters no word in the dream, the Japanese man.) The trust grows swiftly and, as they become more synchronised, all his restlessness and grief dissolve. It is as if there is a transfer of skill to him directly from the man's body. And it consoles him, this flow. Like a blood transfusion: a biological consolation. He knows – they know together now – the exact direction they should go, what the next movement will be. His chest heats up, becomes warm like a bird's nest. Around them the hills are barren and beautiful. The highways astonish him with their sweeping width. He is light and gracious.

When he wakes up in the early morning hours with a lingering feeling of fondness for his nurturing dance partner, he walks out onto the balcony. In front of him lie the amphitheatre of the city and Table Bay. One loose cloudlet is hanging above the city, motionless. He stretches his hand out towards it. It looks so close. Where did it come from, all that grief that had to be danced away in the dream?

He leans forward against the balustrade. It must be the conversation of the previous evening that gave the dream its shape – or movement. Sam called from the north and excitedly explained how he was using Butoh as inspiration for his latest choreography. Sam is a young man, a contemporary dance student.

'Butoh?' he enquired.

'Difficult to explain,' Sam said. 'It's a Japanese style – I'll have to show you. It works for my body, that's all I know. I feel it just like that.' He could hear Sam snapping his fingers.

Sam's forte is dance – movement – rather than description.

Like all his previous encounters of this kind – perhaps it goes for most encounters that cause unexpected joy to burgeon between two people – his meeting with Sam was unlikely. After years of absence, he had been trapped for some time in Pretoria, the despised city of his youth, occupied with gruelling family matters.

Yes, trapped: in this place that has become so dusty and messy, the seat of successive governments, all ultimately of the same hue (or at least flavour). He had shaken the dust of this place from his feet a long time ago, he thought. He feels tricked. There is hardly any diversion here. No cultural activity to speak of, little to lift him from his torpor, from being extinguished.

As a last resort, he attends a student drama festival at Pretoria's university. Without much expectation or hope. And his lack of hope was not unfounded. The performances are incoherent, sometimes embarrassing. Musicals, improvised dramas with adolescent themes. No, wait, he is too merciless in his judgement; it is, after all, the work of kids, loose-limbed kids still finding their form. And what could they know of the world beyond the boundaries of this dull city?

Even so, there is one performance that makes an impression. Dance theatre, physical theatre. The stage represents a claustrophobic flat in Cape Town in the 1980s. A soldier has returned from the border war to his wife and child after being seriously wounded. He has been irreparably traumatised and numbed. He is like a creature in a cage. The child's escape into a fantasy world provokes his ire. At some point, in order to demonstrate the principle of unreality, he stabs the child's imaginary friend to death with a knife. The actor-dancer's sequences of movements, in between his deadly silences, are a tour de force. He has a gun in his hand throughout the movements. He is shirtless, his muscles like rock under skin the colour of strong tea. Long black hair tied back tightly. Loose-fitting linen trousers. He is engaged in a bitter battle with the floor and walls.

He strains against gravity; then, suddenly the earth lets go and he tumbles weightlessly upwards, towards the ceiling.

What could these students understand of the era in which the piece is set? he thinks. Nevertheless, it is quite engaging. A slightly watered-down version of what Pina Bausch might have done with such material. The kind of movement piece that does not create abstract shapes, but is built around the temperament of individual dancers. The risk of injury, of damage, provides the main source of energy. Bones just short of shattering point, cartilage and sinews under high pressure. Dancers throwing their bodies frenziedly against the floor, the escaping breaths sounding like something between a sigh and a hiccup. Sweat bespattering the front row. The audience shrinking away, tingling, imagining their own bodies into the dancers' . . .

As he walks to his car after the performance, someone calls from behind. 'Excuse me?'

He stops, turns around, observes him. It is he, the soldier, hair now loose over his shoulders. Shirted. Sandals on his feet. Surrounded by light. Everything about him now in fact different. Around twenty-one, he would guess. Instantly, there is a quivering, unsteady kind of dynamic between them.

'Yes?'

He loses his nerve, the young man, clearly unsure how to proceed. 'I saw you,' is all he says. 'In the second row.'

He smiles at the actor. He can come to his aid, can compliment him honestly, albeit stiffly.

'Congratulations, it was good. Such a closed character, so many internal shifts. The choreography gave you a potent vehicle.'

'I'm Sam.' His hair is shiny and black. A mane like Samson's.

He introduces himself, invites Sam for coffee. The young man ponders the invitation for a moment, his eyes full of light and obstinacy. 'How about the Botanical Gardens?' Sam says.

He shrugs his shoulders, smiles slightly. 'Why not?'

'Come, get on,' Sam says. He is pointing at a motorised scooter.

He raises his hand. 'My car is here – '

'Come on,' says Sam. He smiles with white teeth. 'Come and feel the wind.'

Sam takes out two helmets from the Vespa's luggage box. Old-fashioned ones. Silver. Leather straps fastening under the chin, like war helmets. They get on.

'Ready?' asks Sam, and pulls away without waiting for an answer. Sam is a good twenty years younger than he is, he thinks. He has to laugh at himself. Just yesterday, so it feels, he was still young too. And where is he now, after a minute's conversation with a young stranger? (Well, plus an hour-long prelude in the auditorium.) Like a dirty old(er) man against Sam's warm back, behind him on the Vespa. Sam with his perfectly round little buttocks on the saddle. The two of them elated in the exhaust fumes. The scooter is not that fast, but the warm currents blow Sam's hair in all directions from under the helmet. It flicks like a feather duster across his own face.

They stop at a petrol station, buy things to eat and drink. They continue. Through Sam's hair, which is blowing onto his face, he observes the dismal suburbs, the walls and barbed wire. It feels as if he has never been in this city before. They walk deep into the Botanical Gardens, to a shadowy spot, a waterfall. When they sit down, he again becomes aware of his age, of the difference between them. He mentions it, playfully.

'Age,' Sam says, his hair in full sunlight, 'what's age?', and shrugs his shoulders.

He is starting to like Sam.

It is a weekday afternoon. There is no one else here. The sun is falling in at an angle through the leaves. The waterfall's spray is floating lazily in the shafts of light. Falling seeds nestle in the folds of their clothes. They are lying on the grass, elbows behind their heads.

'It's a joke,' Sam says, 'to work in the university's theatres.'

Sam tells him about the piles of dusty old stage props lying around behind the stage, thigh-deep.

'Every time you go on stage, you have to scramble over the piles of stuff. Pretty risky. In this show I had to wait on all fours on Jesus before coming on. The spaghetti Jesus, we call it. Just lying there, life-size, on a plastic cross, woven from rattan. Like a big empty basket.'

He looks at the falling water, water that will never again flow over the same rocks. Later on, they walk further up the hill. The whirring of an engine becomes audible. The water, he realises, is being circulated; it flows up the mountain and then down again, in a closed cycle. Sam hops across the rocks like a mountain goat. He is not far behind. He wonders whether all the rocks are real, knocks on a few of them.

A week later, Sam invites him to see another performance he is in and that he also choreographed. It is better than the previous one. Sam goes through surprising transformations. His hair hangs in wild curls over his shoulders. He is animal-like, with a Tarzan cloth around his loins. Stripes of warpaint adorn his cheeks and torso. Sometimes he flattens himself and creeps like a cat. At one point his arms become as long as the tentacles of an octopus. Joined together with a group of dancers, he forms an anemone that bursts open in a tangle of hands and elbows. He lies on his back and propels himself with his feet, spins and throws himself down so that one can hear (or thinks that one hears) bones cracking. He hangs from a rope by his feet, swaying, dipping his hair in paint and painting patterns across the stage. For a while, his tracks look like Sanskrit letters, but, as he continues swinging, they become denser, like ancient marks: the alphabet of a heavy-footed species. One of the dancers dips himself in the paint and, as they rub up against each other, colour spreads from body to body. Skin to skin. While he is watching, he thinks of his own mute, non-writing body.

'Like wood,' he described it to Sam in the Botanical Gardens, making him laugh. What he did not add, what Sam would find out for himself, was: my body does have its moments. Physical love shocks me into suppleness, administers a tiny current of electricity. In a flash, it teaches me new tricks, makes me adept. A Pinocchio I may be, but sometimes, for a few minutes, I enter the world of humans.

'So, where does it come from, the ways you writhe and wriggle: what would you say is the source?'

The performance over, they are sitting in a coffee shop. Sam is visibly exhausted.

'You search around, I guess.' Sam shrugs his shoulders; a fist against his chest indicates where he tends to search. 'You remember stuff.'

'Such as?'

Without a moment's hesitation, Sam tells him in detail about his family background. He has never known his father. The latter, so he has pieced together from various accounts, has been in and out of mental institutions his entire life. In the performance in which he was a soldier, he kept his (imagined) father in his mind to propel his movements. He continues. In the seventies, before he was born, his mother had a relationship with a married white man. In the account he had heard, she moved in with him, worked as a maid and bore him two children, living with the man and his wife as a kind of family. Each time she became pregnant, she had to be admitted to a mental institution. Both times she intended to either abort the child or give it up for adoption, only changing her mind at the last moment.

'With such parents, I have to wonder about my own genes,' Sam says with a smile. 'But maybe, if my body keeps moving, then I could avoid going on their kind of bad trips.'

He is curious, but is hesitant to ask about the racial issue, the fact that Sam grew up as an Indian boy with two whiter children. He still carries in him the ossified sensitivities of the South Africa of his youth. He does not trust that he will get the tone right, even though Sam is a post-apartheid child. He would also want to ask Sam how it feels to attend this university, which still hosts mostly spoilt white students.

'One shouldn't be too full of stuff, though; you must become a vessel, a basket into which audiences can load everything they want to. You sacrifice yourself when you perform. There has to be enough space.'

Sam takes him on the scooter to his home at the edge of the city, in a walled residential complex that has recently been developed on a pale stretch of veld. Houses are dotted around, with open patches of grass and building sites in between. Some of the open plots are black and velvety, the grass having been burnt off. They stop in front of a small townhouse.

Sam makes tea in mugs. They go out into a little walled garden. A warm, quiet winter's afternoon. A square of faded wintry grass rustling beneath their feet, a square of blue sky above them. They sit down on a cotton cloth that Sam has spread out. Behind the walls there is the droning of a highway.

He tells Sam of a dance performance he once saw in a European city. A Dutch choreographer. A piece for two dancers and a cameraman. The dancers dance, the cameraman moving around them. The image is transmitted to a large screen at the back of the stage: a doubling, the video image delayed by half a second. While they are dancing, the dancers can see themselves, can observe their own movements of a moment ago. The cameraman's movements become increasingly complicated. He gets down on his back beneath the dancers, they bend around him, become trapped on each side of him. Then the dancers leave the stage, dancing down the aisle, the cameraman following them, to the foyer, where they continue. All that is left for the audience in the auditorium is the video image. The male dancer suddenly disappears through a side door. The woman stops moving, standing still for a moment while looking right into the camera (the image on the back wall of the stage is one of desolation, bewilderment). Then she turns around and walks out the auditorium's main entrance, leaving behind the cameraman and the audience. The last image is of her – a lonely figure – walking down the street, where a row of cherry trees is in full bloom, becoming smaller until she disappears.

'What about her ballet shoes on the tar?!' Sam wants to know. He is smiling.

Sam clearly likes the story. His arms are moving with excitement.

'Let's move a little,' Sam says. 'Let's loosen up.' He gets up, shakes the fingers of both hands, hopping, crunching the grass beneath his soles.

He shakes his head. 'No, I think my joints have grown stiff over the years, or perhaps the rigidity is genetic.'

Sam pulls him up by the hand. 'Just let go,' he says, 'there's no body that can't loosen itself. Nobody's genetically stiff. You have strong muscles on your skeleton – just let them move. Just work out your body's patterns. You should leave behind all the gym nonsense; the weight of weights settles into your muscles after a while.'

He stands there sheepishly, self-conscious in Sam's sphere of movement. Sam shakes and flaps his own body. He makes a half-hearted attempt himself, like an injured bird.

Sam stops. 'Ok, let's start with the hands,' he says.

They take their positions opposite each other, hands between them. They are looking each other in the eye. The hands start moving. First slowly, tentatively. Then faster, more naturally. The hands evade, search, play, lead each other, grab at each other, push and pull and bend and weave the air, turn around, flit and slip around each other, towards each other, mimicking each other. The knuckles click against each other, the nerves in the fingertips tingle, sending swift messages, the fingers become claws, projecting shadows onto each other, following and chasing each other, nails flash, smaller and smaller movements, faster and faster, a tiny gale is being stirred up, a cloudlet of electricity, until the hands simultaneously come to a halt and hold on to each other crossing each other. The frequencies of their vibrations are now close. Their palms are burning, as if a chemical reaction has been catalysed. The entropy is high, their hands are about to sublimate to gas. A bird with toxic green wings appears, hovering right by their faces, whirring frantically to keep still, a sugarbird perhaps, sensing that nectar is to be found in the air between them.

Still looking him in the eye, he asks Sam: 'What are we loosening ourselves for, what are we preparing for? What is the main performance? What,' he continues, Sam's eyes soft as a doe's and his skin like quicksand, 'if you let the muscles go and then never regain a grip on them? What if they then have their own existence?' A life of staggering, he thinks, of non-coordination and dissolution.

Sam says nothing for a while. He withdraws his hands and sits down, resting his chin on his knees, rustling with his fingers in the dry grass.

'Last year,' Sam says, 'I was sitting just like this on a beach in the Transkei. Camped out there with friends. Just slept on the beach, ate stuff from the sea. Became a nature boy. We ate shrooms almost every day . . . '

'Shrooms?'

'Magic mushrooms. For days on end I sat there, just like this, hands in the sand, speaking to God. Many of my moves still come from those conversations.' He looks up. 'Nothing wrong with dissolution.'

After a brief silence, he smiles and adds: 'Later we realised there were worms in the shrooms.'

In between Sam's classes at the university, they spend time together. They drink tea, see films. He is here on sabbatical, has interrupted his professional life in New York for a while. Before meeting Sam, he was often at a loose end, searching for meaningful ways to spend his time. Every now and then he had to flee to his flat in Cape Town to escape the emotional intensity of the renewed involvement with his family.

He cannot help but observe himself, by Sam's side, from an ironic distance, with an amused half-smile. He is approaching middle age, Sam is not much more than a child. But then: there is wisdom beyond age in Sam's body. He has startling knowledge in the blood.

They go to a hairdresser. He watches as Sam gets his hair cut. The hairdresser has draped a black cloak around him, pulled it in around his neck. It billows, as if filled with wind. Locks fall on the floor. On impulse he bends over and surreptitiously slips one into his palm. When he looks up, his eye catches Sam's in the mirror. Sam's staring eye, unseeing. Sam's body stiffens and he falls off the chair, shuddering a few times. His legs are jerking, hair clings to his trousers. He kneels down by Sam's side. He immediately grasps it is a fit, but does not know what to do. He holds his hand under Sam's head to stop it from banging against the floor. When Sam surfaces, the hairdresser is standing over him with scissors in his hand. Sam's eyes are filled with terror.

It is not the only time that Sam is overcome by a seizure. One night, when they are sharing his bed in a guest house, Sam's pumping knees wake him up. He holds him tight: a thrashing animal. When Sam comes to, the light now on, he tells of the dream he was having when the attack came. In the dream he was walking with a dog, somewhere on a gloomy farm. The dog disappeared behind a woodpile and started barking. He called to the dog, but it would not return. When he went looking, he found his father's half-decomposed body behind the pile.

'How did you know it was your father?' he asks after a while.

'Just knew it. Could feel it in my bones. He was a bum in rags, a hobo.'

He withdraws to his flat in Cape Town. He did not want to leave Sam behind in Pretoria, but Sam could not accompany him; he is fully dedicated to his dancing life. He cannot sacrifice even a weekend because of auditions and rehearsals. The family crises in Pretoria make his throat constrict. Nothing is moving in him now; he is a stagnant pool. For half a lifetime he was geographically removed from the dynamics in his overly happy, overly intimate family, and then with cosmic inequity, death and divorce and other forms of heartache strike the family while he is here. There is a tearing of the family tissue, right at the core. For a variety of reasons he is the one whose intervention is indicated, who must attempt to mend it. For a long time he had been planning to break away from his sapping professional life in Manhattan. He did not, however, imagine it happening like this.

He tries to get some rest in the Cape Town flat after a period of exceptional psychic demands. The attempts to become looser together with Sam were, it seems, unsuccessful. In fact, it probably made matters worse, challenging the stiffness when he was not prepared for it. He becomes agoraphobic, only ventures out every few days to buy what is essential. Sam's messages pop up on his cellphone. He does not respond, lets his phone die. He stops reading emails, cuts off all communication. He spends his days motionless on the bed: rigor mortis on white sheets in sunlight. He stops eating, extends an arm slowly to open the window, lives on water and sunlight and air. For twelve days he descends to hell. Or, in fact, ascends to the blinding heavens. He holes himself up on the seventh floor, with an unimpeded view over the city and the bay. He stops going out at all, no longer washes himself. Makes friends, from a distance, with the pigeons as well as the homeless. He gets to know the latter's routines. There is a man who comes at dusk, every day, to fetch his possessions from a manhole. He opens the lid in the pavement and takes out plastic bags, a sleeping bag, pieces of clothing, neatly closes the lid, his own sliver of private space. He pushes his shopping trolley up to the mountain, then down into the city in the morning, like an old woman going shopping. He becomes one with these people, if not in their lack of material things, then at least in the crumbling of the soul. (How presumptuous, he thinks later. What does he know of such suffering?) He collects small narratives that one can construct from a fixed observation point, studies the city in its shades of grey. His only conversation partners are the flocks of pigeons that descend onto corrugated-iron roofs. He calls out to them, whispers intimately to them when his limbs become heavy with hunger. The pigeons avoid his balcony – perhaps they instinctively sense his immobility, that he is earthbound. When it rains, the city appears and disappears. He observes the world through a silver sheet of water tumbling from the roof. Water and pigeons mingle with buildings and streets. His limbs let go of their weight; he is becoming light, losing substance. It is a precondition for his return to the land of the living: he must dissolve.

After a few days he gets up. It is late afternoon. He opens the balcony doors. On the small balcony he does a few exercises. He is trying to find grace. He improvises his own clumsy pieces of choreography. There is sorrow in his bones. Slowly he starts displacing it through his movements on the balcony. Where the sorrow originates does not matter, he decides, just how one gets rid of it. But he knows he will keep gravitating towards the source. One cannot deny origins. Muscles, after all, start moving from the bone. He switches his phone on again, and an hour later Sam calls him to tell him about Butoh, about how it has taken over his body.

The next day he unlocks the door and walks out without hesitation, breathing salty air into his lungs, the aromas of sea and fynbos. His strength has returned. He is hungry.

He is back in Pretoria. Sam is so dedicated to his stage art that they hardly see each other. He gives Sam up to his movements, to the stage. Even though he is a student, Sam's talents are such that he is in high demand in the trickle of stage productions that parade as public cultural life here. On the one occasion that he does see Sam, there are new stories. Sam tells of a period when he and his mother lived in a Hare Krishna temple, how he was molested there, how his mother was incapable of preventing it, how he then gained weight terribly as a young schoolboy, becoming almost immobile. During his teenage years there was a bulimic period, followed by a fanatical regime of fitness and diet. The narrative of all these manias is offered soberly, without self-pity. At some point, nevertheless, it all becomes too much. He has gained a new simplicity of physique and clarity of mind. He feels scorched clean, at odds with these difficult things of the body and the past. They become loosened from one another, he and Sam.

Then he meets another young man, an accountant. Bert. He does not know where all this youthfulness surrounding him is coming from. He is not seeking it out. One might perhaps say that Bert is a little lacking in imagination, yes, but is that necessarily a disadvantage? Imagination, after all, requires so much energy. The accountant has a good sense of humour. He is steady. Their bodies fit, his and Bert's. The man has a staggering erotic repertoire which does not accord with his image of Afrikaans decency. Outside the erotic sphere they are like marionettes. Neither of them challenge the puppet master, they are satisfied with the clumsy manner in which their bodies cut the air. They do not ask questions of the muscles, do not bend their bodies into question marks.

He no longer sees Sam. At night, in the guest house, he circles endlessly around the bed in which the accountant is sleeping as if in a coma. Past the foot of the bed to the other bedside table and back. He has to touch his pillow each time before the next about-turn. A dumb zoo animal. He forces himself to stop, looks out of the window. The profiles of tropical plants are visible against the night sky. Now he knows. That's what he is waiting for: for the body on the bed to start rattling so that he may hold it and contain the convulsions. But the sleeping one keeps snoring without stirring.

In the midst of all his thoughts about bodily movements, his sister, who is going through a traumatic divorce, says, 'It has become an integral part of me, the stress; it's in my blood. I am constantly trembling and my fingers have become crooked and stiff.'

On an impulse he says, 'Come.'

He and his sister get up from where they are having coffee in the guest house. While they walk, he calls Sam. Sam is not surprised to hear from him again, chatters as if nothing has happened. Full of light and goodwill.

'I need your help,' he says.

'Of course,' Sam says.

They arrange to meet in a theatre on the dull campus. His sister, he tells Sam, was a ballerina in her young days. She started dancing on her toes too early, without their parents' knowledge, when her feet were still soft and not fully formed. Then little bones in her feet shifted and ruined her ballet dreams. She had to stop dancing and even today, thirty years on, it hurts when she walks.

That was perhaps the beginning of his sister's withering, he thinks, when her feet were ruined. Long before her husband accelerated the shrivelling. Perhaps she reached the height of her joy and freedom when, as a child, she stretched upwards on her toes, in a heavenwards curve, like an unknown letter. He looks at her. She is slightly hunched, as if straining to get enough oxygen in her body. As if the bones have started to bend and shift everywhere.

'So, here's a substitute for you, someone with better instincts than mine.' That is how he introduces his sister when they meet in front of the theatre. Everyone is smiling.

Sam is standing behind her. They are on the stage. They do a few exercises to refresh her memory and to start forcing her skeleton back into position. He is sitting in the empty theatre, towards the back. Sam runs up the aisle to the technical control console, switches on the lights. Spotlights in pastel colours surround his sister. Sam switches on the music. For the first time in years, she starts to dance. Tentatively. Shadows of old movements starting to unwind the body's memory. Then she stops.

'I'm a bit lost,' she says, 'it's too bare.' She looks tiny on the stage.

His sister, he thinks in the dark, has the kind of temperament that makes her vulnerable to the core. Love simply flows from her – without hindrance, dangerously. The man in whose web she has become trapped, whose claws have left such indelible marks, sensed it instantly. He sucked her dry and then started torturing her for the emptiness that remained.

'We need a centre point,' Sam says, 'to make it less wild and empty.'

Sam disappears behind the stage, brings out the spaghetti Jesus. Smoke also starts bubbling out, floating towards her. Sam emerges with a flamboyant jump.

'Smoke to dance with!' Sam says, and lifts her in his arms.

They start dancing a pas de deux, their bare feet in the smoke. The choreography is being improvised. It centres around a delicate entanglement of arms and a rubbing of heads – her blondeness against Sam's long hair, which has the colour and gloss of crude oil. Initially she is stiff, but gradually she relaxes (from the dark he looks at her ribs, on the verge of cutting through the skin). They sink to the floor with their buttocks and backs propped against each other. He starts recognising something of his sister in her movements again.

At one point his sister performs a sequence that so upsets him he has to look away. She detaches herself from Sam. She keeps her feet in one place, and, straining and stretching, bends herself into such distorted self-embracing twists that she almost tears apart. She is trying to erase herself.

Sam is behind his sister. He knows Sam cannot see him, the light is too bright for that, but Sam has enough experience to make his audience feel as if he is looking straight at them.

When the music stops, her chest is heaving. For the first time in years, it looks as if something healing is flowing through her, as if she is starting to regain her original shape. She smiles at Sam for a while and he at her. She nods her head slowly, he nods his head slowly. Neither says anything.

Through his sister's resurrection, Sam touches his own heart again. It is a biological process, as in the dream: something is physically flowing through the dark, like a warm snake, settling like a dark and soft thing in his intestines.

Now he is feeling torn between Sam and Bert. He tells each about the other, decides it is the decent thing to do.

Sam shrugs his shoulders. 'It's cool.'

No! he thinks. It is not cool. He wishes Sam were less of a hippy, were possessive and suffocating. Perhaps then he would be able to fall in love with him more swiftly. But perhaps the love would dissolve more swiftly too, then.

He cannot let Sam go, he realises, he can only be in this place if it is with Sam. Sam who has nothing to do with his past here. He can only bear being in this city for so long as the strangeness that Sam is enabling him to feel endures. Sam makes it a different place, a nowhere place. While he is at Sam's side (Sam with his restless limbs!), he can remove himself in his mind. He is both here and not here.

He and Sam are sitting in a coffee shop, in the kind of artificial shopping-centre environment that passes for public space in this country. He takes Sam's hand, forgetting for a moment where they are. It takes a while before he notices that people are staring. An echo of his militant younger self returns, when he would have snapped at the starers, but he just smirks, restrains himself. He just puts his other hand on Sam's as well, shifting closer and hooking his ankles around Sam's as if this could segue into a dance movement.

When he takes his eyes off Sam's, Bert is standing there, not far from their table, where he has perhaps been for some time. They look at each other, he and Bert. Bert looks at Sam. Bert turns around and walks away.

It is Sam's final performance, for the purposes of his studies. His exam. Sam has arranged a complimentary ticket for him. The audience consists largely of family members of the dance students. The performances last far too long, there are more amateurish efforts than one's concentration can endure. During intermission, he sits alone in the cool air outside.

Sam's performance follows the intermission. It frightens him. It is the Butoh piece. When the stage lights are switched on, Sam is sitting in a chalk circle. There is nothing else on stage. Like something from modernist photography – an Edward Weston study of the body as abstraction. Sam's head is bent forward, arms around the knees. Only his rounded back is facing the audience. A solid block. It fragments into a mosaic of muscles. He is moving from his core, minimally, only the individual muscles shifting and twisting. He moves very slowly, with utter control.

He is naked, painted reddish-brown from head to toe. He writhes, wrenches himself away from the stage. A creature from the primordial slime. Caliban from *The Tempest*. He keeps low against the stage. As he struggles, the paint comes off; he is leaving behind a trail. His mouth is wide open, white teeth bared against the darkness.

After the performance, Sam joins him on a little bench between the theatre and the carpark.

'Notions of shame and the vulnerability of ideas about the self. That's what I read into it,' he tells Sam. 'But I now realise: no, it's about the more difficult stuff behind emotions.'

Things that precede emotions, he thinks, for which there are no words. The body as a rock, making marks against a cave wall.

Sam is inscrutable. He looks like an angel of dark glass.

'It made me feel things that I didn't know one was allowed to feel,' is all that Sam has to say. And: 'It's the opposite of narrative.'

He weaves his fingers through Sam's curls, still damp after a shower (for rinsing off the paint). He does not know whether this thing with Sam is moving forward. It seems to be edging loosely sideways, crab-like. From one dance performance to the next. How does one push it into a direction? Perhaps the absence of direction is the idea. Loose shards, infinite performance. The carpark behind them empties out; they are left alone in the fumes. He leans over and kisses Sam on the lips. In silence, on the concrete bench.

The crack of dawn. Near the guesthouse where he is staying, there is a fitness park where Sam wants to stretch, to jog, to engage his core muscles. They go there on the scooter. When they enter it, they are the only ones there, that is, other than the rough sleepers peering from underneath shrubs. Fog hovers in the lower parts. He knows this place from his youth, but now it is different. He feels uncomfortable, unsafe. Sam is not bothered, walking past the eyes in his loose-limbed way. They start jogging. Next to the running paths, there is apparatus for various kinds of exercise, screwed together with creosote poles and steel, now rusting and rotting. He just watches Sam when he stops for his stretching exercises, shakes his head when Sam tries to get him to join in.

They run further. He looks at Sam. So dapper and compact. So full of goodwill, muscle power and New Age clarity. His teeth whiter than ever. When they turn a corner, they are forced to a halt by the scene in front of them. Two bloody feet at eye height. They look up. One can hear the jacaranda branch, from which the body is hanging, creak. Lightly, as the figure is swaying. A rope around the neck. Sam is speechless, starts trembling. He puts his hands around Sam's shoulders. It is the man from his dream hanging there, he thinks, the Japanese dancer. He averts his eyes. When he looks up again, he sees his eyes have deceived him. It is a vagrant. The face is in the shadows. The grimy raincoat is hanging open, the body naked beneath it. How long he has been dead, he could not say. Did he hang himself? It does not look that way. And yet: perhaps he climbed the tree, put the noose around his neck and jumped. He is aware of Sam's hair against his cheek. He holds his breath, waiting for the fit, but it does not come. He guides Sam away, his hand still around him. He does not look back. Does one still report a death here? Would the police be interested? Especially if it is a homeless person?

For the first time in many years a memory from his youth returns. A day when he and a childhood friend came to jog and clamber over things in this place. Summer, late afternoon. A carefree place, then, where (white) children could run around barefoot and without fear at dusk. Once, after a run, they came out the gate, and found a man sitting there in his running outfit. On the bench to which they had locked their bicycles. Asleep. Oldish, about sixty. When unlocking his bike, he brushed against the man and felt that he was cold. He looked at the man's lips, and then at his friend. The friend had already realised. Before he did. They kept looking at each other, got on their bicycles and sped away.

He gets on the Vespa in front, Sam at the back. They drive slowly through the streets. They do not go to the police. Sam still has not said a word. Sam's arms are tight around him, Sam's cheek against his neck. Over his shoulder he looks back at the overgrown jogging park. He thinks Sam has read his father into the dark space, where the hanged man's face should have been. Swallows dive through air over their heads, sweep along with them. The silver helmets click against each other when the scooter hits dips.

It is strange, he thinks with the droning in his ears, to travel through this country. Full of impenetrable impressions. Sam is the only element of it he understands. But can he really read Sam? Whether he can or not, as they are driving, he starts loving Sam. With each pothole and bump it strengthens, the love, the intensity of it becoming almost unbearable.

He drives them to Sam's home (he has no idea how he will manage to get back). When they take off their helmets, he notices Sam is still distraught. He is trembling less, though. Sam takes a plastic tub from the fridge. He offers it. Blueish mushrooms. Shrooms. He takes one, then another. Sam takes three or four. They chew on the slightly rotten mushrooms in silence next to the humming fridge.

They go out into the little garden, step onto the dead grass. They wait another twenty minutes until everything looks and sounds different: the colours deeper, the noise of the highway like a vast swarm of bees.

'Hungry,' says Sam.

They go to a nearby place to eat. Sam is sitting behind him, giving instructions. The scooter ride feels like a trip through the clouds on a silver rocket. The wheels lift a few centimetres above the tar. He looks over his shoulder to see whether a red flame is spewing from the back. Like the rocket rides from his childhood. He remembers how he would grab hold of the steering wheel as if he could truly control the craft. His father would insert a coin. For a few seconds nothing happened. Then the machine started flickering and vibrating. The trip (or lack thereof) was always a disappointment, and over before you could blink an eye.

The restaurant is in a shopping centre, right at the edge of the city, on an otherwise empty plain. Cars are gleaming in the sun on a tarred carpark surrounded by fields of grass and pylons.

They are sitting in the cool restaurant against the back wall. Tiles on the floor, stainless-steel tables. Bright light. Sam is wearing a downy white jersey (angora? mohair?). It forms a kind of halo around him so that his body has no clear boundaries but frays at the edges. Behind Sam, there is surprising wallpaper. A paradisiacal landscape. In soft shades of yellow, orange and rusty brown, here and there some sky-blue mist. Everything flooded with celestial light emanating from an indeterminate source. As if the landscape is glowing from inside. Snowy peaks, cliffs, dizzying waterfalls.

The waiter takes their order. He keeps looking at the wallpaper behind Sam: knotty trees growing from crevasses in the steep cliffs, hanging gardens, ferns disappearing into the spray, birds like bright flakes against the rushing water. On a rocky outcrop above the waterfall: an angel on his toes, wings stretched wide.

He is feeling clear, filled with insights and the urgency to sharpen these insights.

He focuses on Sam, forgets the landscape for a moment.

'So, where is all this heading?' It sounds blunt, the question, when he hears himself asking it.

Sam stiffens, acts as if nothing has been said. It seems as if the landscape behind him darkens. Is there a tiny figure hanging above the watery turbulence? He focuses on it. The figure is actually moving, yes, swaying ever so slightly. He now also notices a ruin on the soft green grass above the abyss, bathed in the omnipresent light.

The food arrives, but they instantly forget about it. Behind Sam, the water keeps falling and falling. Sam pours a glass of mineral water, then slowly empties it without putting it down.

He repeats the question. Their knives and forks remain on the table. Blindingly clean.

'I don't know,' Sam says. 'Nowhere?'

He looks out of the restaurant window. Some distance away, in the haze, the profile of the Voortrekker monument is vaguely discernible.

He opens his mouth once or twice, closing it without saying anything. Then: 'Nowhere? Over? Just like that, without warning? As suddenly as it started?'

Sam smiles, teeth as white as snow. 'No, that's not what I meant. Not over. Nowhere, everywhere. All the same. Everything is what it is, no? Or what it is becoming. Why must things have a fixed shape? You should prise the shapes open.'

Sam's wrist makes a shadow movement, as if he is practising a piece of choreography.

He gets up. 'That's not enough.' He wants to add: I need proper beginnings and endings, structure. 'I'm going now.'

He leaves two R100 notes on the table for the untouched food, gets up and walks out without looking at Sam or the waterfall. Only when he gets outside does he realise that there is no way for him to get back to the city. Had it not been for the mushroom juice in his blood, he might have stopped himself, but now he starts walking on the hard shoulder, along the busy road. He is ready for the long trek. In the distance, he can see the outlines of the Voortrekker monument. He is walking towards it. He takes off his shoes so as to feel the tar under his feet. The further he goes – cars speeding past, the engine heat against his skin – the looser he becomes.

He takes his shirt off too. He is sweating. The silver helmet appears next to him, and the Vespa. Sam is driving along slowly, has to put his foot down every now and then to balance himself.

'Your feet,' Sam says, 'they're bleeding.'

He looks at Sam and then down at his feet. 'I find it beautiful,' he says, 'the blood.'

He keeps walking. Sam stops on by the side of the road, kicks out the scooter's stand. Sam walks after him, takes him by the shoulder, holding out the helmet.

'Come on,' Sam says, 'don't sulk.'

Behind Sam cars are speeding like spaceships in orbit. He stops, but does not take the helmet from him. Sam takes off his own helmet. His hair is strewn out like a black sun.

'We can talk about it if you want.'

Sam embraces him tightly, silently, a helmet dangling in each hand. Just as swiftly, he disengages himself again. Sam puts the helmet on for him, tying the buckle under his chin in a fatherly manner. A few long strands of hair still cling to the inside of the helmet. Sam tests whether it fits snugly, then knocks on it three times with his knuckle.

'It is not enough,' he says to Sam and shakes his head, 'to look at you when you're dancing. Not enough to ride around with our bodies pressed against each other. We are on a false track. I need more. Substance, direction. I don't want to hear some sort of cliché like "the only constant is movement". Or nonsense about amorphous shapes –'

Sam puts a finger to his lips, silencing him.

'On second thoughts,' says Sam. 'Let's not talk. You should learn to do without words. There are better things.'

They walk back to the scooter. He gets on the back and they go: his arms around Sam, his helmet knocking against Sam's. Like when they met for the first time. Would this, after all, have to do: endless journeys on the back of a silver rocket, wind and movement and looseness? Far-off sightings of Sam on a stage? Milling about in idyllic or overgrown gardens? He empties his mind. Sam's hair is blowing against his cheeks. Neither says anything. It is just them and the cars and the warm wind. The smell of melting tar.

Sam turns his head, says something that gets blown away.

'What?'

'I want to show you something.'

They drive into the city centre. He tightens his arms around Sam. He has not been here for years. It looks pretty gloomy. They drive past a church. In his childhood, he recalls, he sang in a school-choir competition here. A Dutch Reformed church it was back then: a piece of architectural brutalism, the overwhelming weight of concrete miraculously suspended at precarious angles. Small shards of coloured glass in the concrete. Now it has a high fence. A sign above the entrance indicates that it is a haven for street children and refugees.

They stop in one of the shoddiest streets in the city centre. A paper bag blows down the street. Weightless and pale, half-translucent. The street is empty, the cars' windows blind in the afternoon sun. He wonders who is sitting in the cars, watching them. He hears a hyena laughing, or perhaps a wild dog. (He no longer knows the animals.)

On the pavement someone is waiting for them. Sam must have contacted him earlier. The man is standing in front of a seventies office building, in shades of blue and grey, with lots of broken panes. Sam introduces him to the man. Somewhere behind them, the barking sounds again.

He looks queryingly at Sam and the friend. The latter cocks his head too, listens for a moment.

'The zoo,' he says. 'Just a block away. Hyenas.'

There is nothing where the front door used to be. They enter. The lift shaft is empty. Just a piece of cardboard up to hip-height instead of a lift door. They walk up the stairs. People are living here. Dishwater (or perhaps sewage) is trickling down the stairs. When you peer through open doors, there are children's faces in the dim light. Buckets and food smells. The smoke of a coal fire. Half-naked bodies, West-African French on radios. On the top floor they encounter the only door, made of steel. Sam's friend unlocks it with difficulty.

'Come and have a look at his exhibition,' Sam says.

A kind of improvised art gallery. The internal walls have been removed across the entire floor to form a long, low space interspersed with pillars. There is a small group of people in the opposite corner. The carpets have been ripped out. Carpet glue still clings to the concrete floor and sticks to your soles. There are photos hanging on the walls. *Suburb* is the title of the exhibition. The photos are big, two by three metres each. There are three series: 'Ghost Pools' is the first. A photo of a carpark in front of a suburban house which now houses a swimming-pool business. If you look carefully, you can see the outlines in the concrete of a former swimming pool. Another photo is of an empty municipal swimming pool in which concrete is growing through the cracks. Another one of a children's pool in a small park. Leaves float on the surface. A woman is standing in the water, bent over, washing foaming laundry. Her dress is tucked into her underwear. 'Burn, baby, burn' is the title of the second series. Photos of burnt-out suburban homes. Then comes 'Gardens of Eden'. Urban gardens: wintry gardens snapped through barbed wire, forgotten little rock gardens in public parks, lilies on a traffic island, a shattered greenhouse on a plot which is now a taxi rank – a single orchid surviving amidst shards of glass. Ever smaller, the gardens.

'You're just in time,' says Sam's friend the photographer when they walk past the photographs. 'Night's on its way, there's no electricity here.'

By the time they get to the 'Gardens of Eden', dusk has deepened; he can only vaguely make out the images.

'How does one get people to attend an exhibition here?' he asks the photographer.

'Lure them with cheap wine. Stuff to smoke. Friends and vagrants. Half the wine at the opening was filched by local meth addicts and glue sniffers. I took some shots of it. Am still planning to hang it with the rest of the stuff. I think I'll call it "Bums who OD on art". Maybe I should add some photos of this bunch as well.' He gestures towards the little group in the corner. White kids in their twenties, barefoot. Someone has switched on some music, wine is being swigged by candlelight. Everyone is speaking Afrikaans.

It is warm here at the top, as if the heat of the coal fires on lower storeys is rising and gathering under the ceiling. The photographer takes off his shirt. *BOER* is tattooed on his muscular chest. His joint is shedding tiny flakes of ash. He absent-mindedly touches his nipple and pecs with a fingertip. The flakes smudge – two grey lines, flickering like phosphorus in the pale light, are drawn across his chest.

The group in the corner offer him something to smoke and sniff. Strong stuff, he is told. He declines. He is no longer a youngster with the urge to experiment. He is in any event still enjoying the unnatural clarity of the mushrooms.

'Show us your Butoh again,' someone urges Sam.

While Sam takes off his clothes and gets in position on the floor, he takes a cigarette that is offered him. He retreats, opens a window. From the zoo: the sound of monkeys. Not a thing stirring in the street. Someone places a circle of candles around Sam.

The performance is far slower than the one on the stage before. As it progresses, it slows down even further, to virtual non-movement. The air solidifies around Sam. He stretches his mouth open in an ancient grin. In the half-dark his teeth are whiter than ever. Sam holds the grin until it seems as if his mouth might never close again. The grin disturbs him; he has to look away. On either side of him the space disappears in the dark. Some of the ceiling tiles are missing; candlelight gleams against wires hanging from the holes. A screeching from the zoo. Peacocks? One starts, then others join in. It sounds like fear.

He walks to Sam when the performance is over. Sam is standing in the candlelight. He is still naked.

'Returning isn't possible,' he tells Sam.

Sam's eyes are glazed over. He is still in the process of returning from his body-world, from his pre-emotional state. 'What are you talking about? Returning to where?'

When he doesn't say anything, Sam says, 'Don't, then. Whatever it is, just leave it. Just leave it behind.'

He returns to the window. Sam keeps watching him, he notices from the corner of his eye. He wants Sam to follow, but he does not, just turns to the BOER, who has something to say about the Butoh. He turns towards the window, opens it wider. The silence of the city settles like an irreversible stiffness in his muscles.

Sam is not *with* him, he thinks, and he is, similarly, not with any of the people in this fatherless little crowd, none of whom he will ever see again after this evening. He is no more with *them* than he is with any of the squatters beneath them (beneath them? Perhaps they have already crawled up through the air ducts, perhaps they are waiting at the edges of the light to pounce and tear every last shred of clothing from these kids' bodies). Loose. They are all loose – loosened from each other. He turns around, observing the scene. He withdraws from the light, inching his way backwards. His hands search the wall behind him for the exit.

Only a single street light is working. Pieces of cardboard move across the pavement. Plastic bags are blowing down the street like flowers. A vagrant is pulling his possessions on a trolley with a broken wheel. It is making an unearthly noise. The waste is piling up in this city, he thinks, the place is filled with relics. Simultaneously recognisable and unrecognisable. One big performance space. Something smells new, fresh. It starts raining. He takes off his shoes. He starts walking. It will take him a long time, but he does not care: he will not stop until he has left the city behind completely, until he can no longer see a single light.

One of the first jacaranda blossoms falls on his face, slides down his cheek. He takes it in his hand, looks at it in the half-light. It contains an entire garden, he thinks, this flower.

ACKNOWLEDGEMENTS

The Afrikaans versions of most of these stories were written as part of a master's degree in creative writing at the University of Stellenbosch.

I'm grateful to Marlene van Niekerk and Willem Anker, my supervisors in the MA. Thanks to the following people who commented on (some of) the stories: Stevan Alcock, Pierre Brugman, Wynand Coetzer, Stephanus Muller, Sansia Naudé, Bibi Slippers, Richard Uschold and James Whyle. Thank you to my father, in whose home a few of these stories were written. Thanks also to Frederik de Jager and Fourie Botha, my original publisher and editor at Umuzi, and to Stefan Tobler, Sophie Lewis and Ana Fletcher at And Other Stories. I am also indebted to Rebecca Carter, my agent at Janklow & Nesbitt in London.

And thank you to Damon Galgut for writing an introduction to the collection.

Some sources that I found useful:

Auster, Paul, 1975. 'One-Man Language', *The New York Review of Books*. Volume 22, number 1.

De Quincey, Thomas, 1886. *Confessions of an English Opium Eater*. W Scott Publishing Company.

Heller-Roazen, Daniel, 2005. *Echolalias: On the Forgetting of Language*. Zone Books.

Morrison, Robert, 2010. *The English Opium Eater: A Biography of Thomas de Quincey*. Pegasus.

Ross, Alex, 2007. *The Rest is Noise: Listening to the Twentieth Century*. Farrar, Straus & Giroux.

Vollmann, William T, 2010. *Kissing the Mask: Beauty, Understatement and Femininity in Japanese Noh Theater, with Some Thoughts on Muses (Especially Helga Testorf), Transgender Women, Kabuki Goddesses, Porn Queens, Poets, Housewives, Makeup Artists, Geishas, Valkyries and Venus Figurines*. Ecco Press.

Wolfson, Louis, 1975. *Le Schizo et les langues*. Gallimard.

Dear readers,

We rely on subscriptions from people like you to tell these other stories – the types of stories most publishers consider too risky to take on.

Our subscribers don't just make the books physically happen. They also help us approach booksellers, because we can demonstrate that our books already have readers and fans. And they give us the security to publish in line with our values, which are collaborative, imaginative and 'shamelessly literary'.

All of our subscribers:

- receive a first-edition copy of each of the books they subscribe to
- are thanked by name at the end of these books
- are warmly invited to contribute to our plans and choice of future books

BECOME A SUBSCRIBER, OR GIVE A SUBSCRIPTION TO A FRIEND

Visit andotherstories.org/subscribe to become part of an alternative approach to publishing.

Subscriptions are:
£20 for two books per year
£35 for four books per year
£50 for six books per year

OTHER WAYS TO GET INVOLVED

If you'd like to know about upcoming events and reading groups (our foreign-language reading groups help us choose books to publish, for example) you can:

- join the mailing list at: andotherstories.org/join-us
- follow us on Twitter: @andothertweets
- join us on Facebook: facebook.com/AndOtherStoriesBooks
- follow our blog: Ampersand

This book was made possible thanks to the support of:

AG Hughes
Abigail Miller
Adam Butler
Adam Lenson
Adriana Maldonado
Aidan Cottrell-Boyce
Ajay Sharma
Alan Ramsey
Alastair Gillespie
Alec Begley
Alex Martin
Alex Ramsey
Alex Robertson
Alex Sutcliffe
Alexandra Buchler
Ali Smith
Alisa Brookes
Alison Hughes
Allison Graham
Alyse Ceirante
Amanda Anderson
Amanda Dalton
Amanda Jane Stratton
Amy Capelin
Amy Rushton
Andrea Reinacher
Andrew Marston
Andrew Nairn
Andy Burfield
Andy Paterson
Angharad Eyre
Angus MacDonald
Angus Walker
Ann Van Dyck
Anna Demming
Anna Holmwood
Anna Milsom
Anna Vinegrad
Anna-Karin Palm

Annabel Hagg
Anne Carus
Anne Claydon-Wallace
Anne Marie Jackson
Anne Maguire
Anne Meadows
Anne Waugh
Anonymous
Anthony Quinn
Antonio de Swift
Antony Pearce
Aoife Boyd
Archie Davies
Asher Norris

Barbara Adair
Barbara Mellor
Barbara Thanni
Barry Hall
Barry Norton
Bartolomiej Tyszka
Belinda Farrell
Ben Paynter
Ben Schofield
Ben Smith
Ben Thornton
Benjamin Judge
Benjamin Morris
Bettina Debon
Bianca Jackson
Blanka Stoltz
Bob Hill
Bob Richmond-Watson
Brenda Scott
Briallen Hopper
Brian Rogers
Bruce Ackers
Bruce & Maggie
    Holmes

C Baker
C Mieville
Candy Says Juju
    Sophie
Cara & Bali Haque
Carole JS Russo
Caroline Adie
Caroline Mildenhall
Caroline Rigby
Carolyn A Schroeder
Cath Drummond
Catherine Mansfield
Catherine Meek
Catherine Taylor
Cecilia Rossi
Cecily Maude
Charles Beckett
Charles Lambert
Charles Rowley
Charlotte Baines
Charlotte Holtam
Chris Day
Chris Elcock
Chris Gribble
Chris Hancox
Chris Stevenson
Chris Wood
Christina Baum
Christina Scholz
Christine Luker
Christopher Allen
Christopher Marlow
Ciara Ní Riain
Claire Fuller
Claire Mitchell
Clare Fisher
Clare Keates
Clare Lucas
Clarissa Botsford

Clemence Sebag
Clifford Posner
Clive Bellingham
Colin Burrow
Collette Eales
Courtney Lilly
Craig Barney

Damien Tuffnell
Dan Pope
Daniel Carpenter
Daniel Gillespie
Daniel Hahn
Daniel Hugill
Daniel Lipscombe
Daniela Steierberg
Dave Lander
David Archer
David Breuer
David Eales
David Gould
David Hedges
David Johnson-
    Davies
David Jones
David Smith
David Wardrop
Dawn Mazarakis
Debbie Pinfold
Deborah Jacob
Deborah Smith
Delia Cowley
Denis Stillewagt &
    Anca Fronescu
Denise Muir
Diana Fox Carney
Dimitris Melicertes
Dominique Brocard

E Jarnes
EJ Baker

Ed Tallent
Edward Baggs
Eileen Buttle
Elaine Rassaby
Eleanor Maier
Elena Traina
Eliza O'Toole
Elizabeth Draper
Ellen Wright
Emily Diamand
Emily Jeremiah
Emily Rhodes
Emily Taylor
Emily Yaewon Lee &
    Gregory Limpens
Emma Kenneally
Eric Langley
Eva Tobler-
    Zumstein
Evgenia Loginova
Ewan Tant

Federay Holmes
Fi McMillan
Fiona Doepel
Fiona Graham
Fiona Powlett Smith
Fran Carter
Fran Sanderson
Frances Chapman
Francesca Bray
Francis Taylor
Friederike Knabe

G Thrower
Gale Pryor
Garry Wilson
Gawain Espley
Gemma Tipton
Genevra Richardson
Geoffrey Fletcher

George Sandison &
    Daniela Laterza
George Wilkinson
Gill Boag-Munroe
Gillian Doherty
Gillian Spencer
Gillian Stern
Giselle Maynard
Gloria Sully
Glyn Ridgley
Gordon Cameron
Gordon Campbell
Grace Dyrness
Graham R Foster
Graham & Steph
    Parslow
Guy Haslam
Gwyn Wallace

Harriet Mossop
Harriet Sayer
Harriet Spencer
Helen Brady
Helen Buck
Helen Wormald
Helena Taylor
Helene Walters
Henrike Laehnemann
Holly Johnson &
    Pat Merloe
Howdy Reisdorf

Íde Corley
Ian Barnett
Ian Kirkwood
Ian McMillan
Inna Carson
Isabella Garment

J Collins
JA Calleja

JC Sutcliffe
Jack Brown
Jacky Oughton
Jacqueline Haskell
Jacqueline Lademann
Jacqueline Taylor
Jacquie Goacher
Jade Maitre
James & Mapi
James Cubbon
James Huddie
James Portlock
James Scudamore
James Tierney
Jane Whiteley
Jane Woollard
Janet Bolam
Janette Ryan
Jasmine
    Dee Cooper
Jason Spencer
Jeff Collins
Jen Grainger
Jenifer Logie
Jennifer Higgins
Jennifer Hurstfield
Jennifer O'Brien
Jennifer Watson
Jenny Diski
Jenny Newton
Jeremy Wood
Jess Wood
Jethro Soutar
Jillian Jones
Jo Elvery
Jo Harding
Jo Hope
Joan Clinch
Joanna Ellis
Joanne Hart
Jocelyn English

Jodie Free
Joel Love
Johan Forsell
John Allison
John Conway
John William
    Fallowfield
John Fisher
John Gent
John Stephen
    Grainger
John Hodgson
John Kelly
John McGill
John Nicholson
Jon Gower
Jon Iglesias
Jon Riches
Jonathan Ruppin
Jonathan Watkiss
Joseph Cooney
Joshua Davis
Judith Norton
Judy Kendall
Julian Duplain
Julian Lomas
Juliane Jarke
Julie Van Pelt
Julie Gibson
Juliet Swann
Juraj Janik

KL Ee
Kaarina Hollo
Kaitlin Olson
Kalbinder Dayal
Karan Deep Singh
Kari Dickson
Karla Fonesca
Kate Pullinger
Kate Rhind

Kate Wild
Katharine Freeman
Katharine Robbins
Kathryn Lewis
Katie Martin
Katie Prescott
Katie Smith
Kay Elmy
Keith Dunnett
Ken Walsh
Kevin Brockmeier
Kevin Pino
Kinga Burger
Koen Van Bockstal
Krystalli
    Glyniadakis

Lana Selby
Lander Hawes
Laura Clarke
Laura Solon
Lauren Cerand
Lauren Ellemore
Leanne Bass
Leonie Schwab
Lesley Lawn
Lesley Watters
Leslie Rose
Linda Harte
Lindsay Brammer
Lindsey Ford
Liz Ketch
Loretta Platts
Louise Bongiovanni
Louise Rogers
Louise S Smith
Lu
Lucie Donahue
Lucy Luke
Lynda Graham
Lynn Martin

M Manfre
Maeve Lambe
Maggie Peel
Maisie & Nick Carter
Mandy Boles
Marella Oppenheim
Mareta & Conor Doyle
Marina Castledine
Marina Galanti
Marina Lomunno
Marion England
Marion Tricoire
Mark Ainsbury
Mark Blacklock
Mark Lumley
Mark Richards
Mark Waters
Marta Muntasell
Martha Gifford
Martha Nicholson
Martin Conneely
Martin Cromie
Martin Hollywood
Martin Whelton
Mary Hall
Mary Nash
Mary Wang
Mason Billings
Mathias Enard
Matthew Francis
Matthew Todd
Maxime Dargaud-Fons
Michael Harrison
Michael Johnston
Michael Kitto
Michael & Christine
   Thompson
Michelle Roberts
Monika Olsen
Moshi Moshi Records

Nadine El-Hadi
Nan Haberman
Nan Craig
Naomi Frisby
Natalie Smith
Natalie Wardle
Nathaniel Barber
Neil Pretty
Nick Chapman
Nick James
Nick Nelson & Rachel
   Eley
Nick Sidwell
Nick Williams
Nicola Balkind
Nicola Hart
Nicola Hughes
Nina Alexandersen
Nina Power

Olga Alexandru
Olga Zilberbourg

Pat Crowe
Patricia Appleyard
Patrick Owen
Paul Bailey
Paul Brand
Paul M Cray
Paul C Daw
Paul Dettman
Paul Gamble
Paul Hollands
Paul Jones
Paul Miller
Paul Munday
Paulo Santos Pinto
Penelope Price
Peter Armstrong
Peter Burns
Peter Lawton

Peter Murray
Peter Rowland
Peter Vos
Philip Warren
Philippe Royer
Phillip Canning
Phyllis Reeve
Piet Van Bockstal
Pipa Clements

Rachel Kennedy
Rachel Lasserson
Rachel Van Riel
Rachel Watkins
Rachael Williams
Read MAW Books
Rebecca Atkinson
Rebecca Braun
Rebecca Carter
Rebecca Moss
Rebecca Rosenthal
Réjane Collard
Renata Larkin
Rhodri Jones
Richard Ellis
Richard Martin
Richard Smith
Robert Gillett
Robert Saunders
Robin Patterson
Rodolfo Barradas
Ronan Cormacain
Rory Sullivan
Ros Schwartz
Rose Cole
Rosemary Terry
Ross Macpherson
Roz Simpson
Russell Logan
Ruth Stokes

SE Guine
SJ Naudé
Sabine Griffiths
Sally Baker
Sam Gallivan
Sam Gordon
Sam Ruddock
Samantha
    Sabbarton-Wright
Samantha Schnee
Sandra Hall
Sandy Derbyshire
Sarah Benson
Sarah Bourne
Sarah Butler
Sarah Fakray
Sascha Feuchert
Sarah Pybus
Sarah Salmon
Sarah Salway
Saskia Restorick
Scott Morris
Sean Malone
Sean McGivern
Seini O'Connor
Sharon Evans
Sheridan Marshall
Sherine El-Sayed
Shirley Harwood
Sigrun Hodne
Simon Armstrong
Simon John Harvey
Simon Martin
Simon Okotie
Simon Pare
Simon Pennington
Simona Constantin
Simone O'Donovan
Sinead Rippington
Siobhan Higgins
Sioned Puw Rowlands

Sophia Wickham
Sophie Eustace
Sophie Hampton
Sophie Johnstone
Sophie North
Stefano D'Orilia
Stephen Abbott
Stephen Bass
Stephen H Oakey
Stephen Pearsall
Stephen Walker
Steven Williams
Stewart McAbney
Sue & Ed Aldred
Susan Ferguson
Susan Murray
Susan Tomaselli
Susanna Jones
Susie Roberson
Suzanne White
Sylvie Zannier-Betts

Tammy Watchorn
Tania Hershman
The Mighty Douche
    Softball Team
Thees Spreckelsen
Thomas Bell
Thomas Fritz
Thomas JD Gray
Tim Gray
Tim Jackson
Tim Robins
Tim Theroux
Timothy Harris
Tina Rotherham-
    Winqvist
Tom Bowden
Tom Darby
Tom Franklin
Tony Messenger

Tony & Joy Molyneaux
Tony Roa
Tracy Bauld
Trevor Lewis
Trilby Humphryes
Tristan Burke

Val Challen
Vanessa Jackson
Vanessa Nolan
Victoria Adams
Victoria Sye
Visaly Muthusamy
Vivien
    Doornekamp-Glass

Walter Prando
Wendy Irvine
Wendy Langridge
Wenna Price
William G Dennehy

Yukiko Hiranuma

Zara Todd
Zoe Brasier

other stories

Current & Upcoming Books

Title: *The Alphabet of Birds*
Author & translator: SJ Naudé
Editor: Stefan Tobler
Copy-editor: Ana Fletcher
Proofreader: Sarah Terry
Typesetter: Tetragon, London
Cover Design: Hannah Naughton
Format: Trade paperback with French flaps
Paper: Munken LP Opaque 70/15 FSC
Printer: TJ International Ltd, Padstow, Cornwall, UK